IN THE SHADOW OF THE MOUNTAIN

By CHRISTOFFER PETERSEN

Published by Aarluuk Press

ISBN: 978-1-521968-02-4

www.christoffer-petersen.com

Far off, where I lie low,
ICE-GLARES envelop me,
Memories hound me,
— them I must tend,

Author's translation from
ISBLINK
by
LUDVIG MYLIUS-ERICHSEN (1872-1907)

Fjernt, hvor jeg dølger mig,
ISBLINK ombølger mig,
Minder forfølger mig,
— dem maa jeg dyrk,

AUTHOR'S NOTE

As our climate changes and the sea ice around the North Pole diminishes, the question of who owns the North Pole becomes increasingly relevant. While no country can claim the North Pole, coastal states surrounding it have the sovereign right to exploit the natural resources of the continental shelf connected to their territory to a distance of 200 nautical miles*. Claims beyond that distance - a so-called *extended continental shelf* - must be filed with the Commission on the Limits of the Continental Shelf (CLCS), in accordance with the United Nations Convention on the Law of the Sea (UNCLOS), *article 76. Claims must be supported with data "describing the depth, shape, and geophysical characteristics of the seabed and sub-sea floor" (The Arctic Institute, 2017).

In the Shadow of the Mountain has been inspired by the 2012 LOMROG III Expedition to collect data in support of the Danish claim to the Lomonosov Ridge - the extended continental shelf that reaches beneath the North Pole. While the expedition was real, the characters and events in the following story are all fictitious, and are not to be construed as real in any way.

The fictional actions and adventures of Konstabel Fenna Brongaard are intended to encourage the reader to think about the Arctic, to consider its future, and to draw a little more attention to an area of the world that is often forgotten, and yet is becoming increasingly important in light of the changing climate on Earth. The North Pole may seem awfully far away for the average reader, but its reach is global.

In the Shadow of the Mountain is written in British English and makes use of several Danish and Greenlandic words.

The Desert

ARIZONA, USA

Chapter 1

YUMA PROVING GROUNDS, ARIZONA, USA
Fenna ignored the soft needle feet of the insect trespassing across her skin and pressed her forehead to the rubber lip of the Schmidt & Bender high magnification scope attached to the rail of her PGM 338 rifle. The dust in the bed of the canyon swirled behind the battered Jeep Cherokee. Her instructions were to look out for a 1999 model off-roader and the Cherokee matched for age, custom outfitting, and colour. Fenna made a note with a light brush of the pencil on the pad she had wedged into the dirt beside the PGM's trigger guard. She had placed it, as instructed, in the exact position her hand would fall when she let go of the trigger. Everything about her position was exact, precise, calculated, only her camouflage net was random, like a blanket it offered her a greater sense of security than a ghillie suit.

She had moved into position two nights earlier, using water from her hydration pack and dirt from the desert floor to disguise the netting that would cover her observation position.

The Jeep slowed to a stop, dust billowing in its wake and two men got out of the rear of the vehicle and peed by the side of the road. The driver stepped out for a smoke. Fenna watched the tip of his cigarette glow in the evening gloom and calculated the distance as if she was going to take the shot. Comments from the briefing rolled through her mind as the man smoked long after his companions had returned to the vehicle. He blew out another lungful and Fenna felt her own lungs swell with a rush of something, a charge of energy. A stream of sweat wet her armpits, her breasts, and slicked her short blonde hair to her forehead. Any stray thoughts of pasting and teasing hair dye into her hair in the bathroom of the summer house in Denmark were forgotten as she revelled in the security of watching without being seen. She lifted her right hand, slowly, from the pad, pressed her palm around the grip and tickled the trigger with her index finger.

The PGM sat heavy in the dirt as Fenna rested her cheek against the tubular stock. She had waited two cold nights and almost two scorching days for this moment. The instructor had told her to watch and wait. With no radio communication, Fenna would have to decide when and if to shoot. She was on her own, he had said. Fenna thought back to the last training session before deployment.

"If the conditions are less than perfect, don't shoot."

She nodded, wiping her sweaty fringe.

"And stop doing that," he said. "The slightest movement will get you killed."

"Okay," she said and tucked her hands in the pockets of her cargo pants.

"You are using live rounds, and I know you can shoot, but the metal plates we have set up are proportionately small. They are about the size of a human head, but they are smaller than you think." The instructor looked up from his position beside a prone sniper student. "If in doubt, don't shoot."

The instructor patted the student on the shoulder and moved out of the way to allow the young man's sniper-observer to slide into position. Fenna listened to the observer, a Marine like his partner, as he called out the ranges and talked the sniper onto the target.

She flinched at the report of the rifle as the sniper fired, the three men standing behind her snickered. The tiny hairs on her arms stiffened despite the heat.

The instructor was watching her, "Everything all right, Konstabel?"

"Yes," she said and took a breath of hot desert air. "I'm fine."

The memory of the second and third reports of the Marine sniper's rifle jogged a succession of images through her mind as she relived the shoot-out at the Arctic schoolhouse, right up to the moment when the whip had cinched tight around the Greenlander's throat, and Dina had broken her neck with a snap.

Thoughts of Greenland and the pre-deployment training receded and she let her finger slide from the trigger. Her cheek slid down the stock as the driver flicked the butt of his cigarette into the scrub beside the road and positioned himself behind the wheel. The door closed with a metallic thud and the Cherokee accelerated along the road.

"Fuck," she said, as the vehicle disappeared and the rush of adrenalin in her veins dispersed and was gone, right when she needed it the most. The click of a stone behind her, to the right, made Fenna turn her head. It was the last movement she made before a pair of size sixteen desert boots pounded into her back and her forehead crunched into the dirt.

"Hello, Blondie," the Gunnery Sergeant said, his voice rasping like the desert. "Having fun?"

Fenna bit back a remark as the man shifted his position and twisted her body beneath his, pinning her arms with his knees. She spat dirt from her mouth and watched the big man grimace as he struggled to pull plastic ties from his back pocket, relaxing the pressure on her arms. She managed to worm one arm free, the desert floor cutting into her flesh. He turned, just as she gripped a rock in her hand and slammed it into the side of his head.

"Fuck you, Gunney," she said, as he tumbled off her body. Fenna scrabbled to her feet and kicked him in the groin. He moaned, she kicked him again in the head, and then, a third time, planting the sole of her size five desert boots in the centre of his chest. She ignored the Gunnery Sergeant and collected her equipment, slipping her arms through the straps of the empty hydration pack, closing her notepad and stuffing it into the cargo pocket of her trousers, before pushing the rubber caps over the ends of the scope and slinging the rifle over her shoulder. The evening chill descended quickly, cooling the sweat on her back. She tugged a buff from her trouser pocket and slipped it over her neck. She took one last look at the Gunnery Sergeant and took a breath. It was time to move.

After just three paces she lowered the rifle and carried it in the ready position. She had no secondary weapon, choosing to travel light, and relying on her experiences in the Arctic to help her through the chilly nights. The heat of the day was the problem, but now she had been compromised, she needed to move.

The escape route she had originally planned to use was too predictable. *If the Gunney could find my position*, she mused, he would have figured out her escape route too. Counter-sniper teams at the Desert Training Center worked in groups of four on the ground, with a drone in the air. *That's how they found me*, Fenna realised. She filed that thought for later; she would tell the instructor, away from the other students. The gravel slipped, giving way under her feet, slowing her descent of the ridge. There was movement in the valley below, so she slid to a crouch behind a spiny bush.

The voices of the men below her chattered up the side of the canyon. *No noise discipline. Why?* A bullet snapped above her head and she realised why the men were so undisciplined.

A distraction, she thought and pushed off along a tiny game trail to her right. Another snap of a suppressed shot made her duck and she pushed harder, racing down the track, the heavy tube gun tugging at her arms. Two more snaps and a crack of an unsuppressed rifle forced Fenna behind a boulder. She raised her rifle and rested it on the flattest part of the desert rock. She pressed the soft flesh of her shoulder into the butt, and sighted on the military vehicle in the canyon below, aiming for the hood of the engine. Compared to the tiny metal plates she practised on, the Humvee was a massive target. She focused and pulled the trigger. The report was loud and the recoil satisfying. Fenna smiled as she pulled back the bolt and chambered another round. The empty shell casing tumbled onto the path and down the side of the canyon. *Another item lost*, another penalty point against her.

She rested the barrel of the PGM in the crook of her left arm, pulling it to her chest as she traversed the slope, following the track, stumbling only once, before she slid to a stop. The shadow of a man moved in from her right and levelled a short-stocked M4 carbine at her chest.

"Fenna," said the man holding the assault rifle.

She frowned and let the weight of the rifle tug at her arms. "We..." she started.

"We're not supposed to use names?" The man laughed. He took a step onto the track and shifted his position into a firmer combat stance. "Having fun in the desert, Konstabel?" he said.

"Yes," she said and turned at the sound of men grunting as they scrabbled up the canyon side.

"We haven't got much time."

"No." Fenna felt the pinch of her frown as she tried to remember where she had met the man.

"Don't."

"Don't what?" she said and squinted in the gloom at the man's face. The desert paint he wore was mixed with dust and obscured his features, but his voice was measured, smooth, familiar. "Toronto?"

"Yes."

"Nicklas Fischer?"

"Yes," he said and Fenna caught the flash of a smile.

"When did you..."

"No questions," he said, looking past Fenna. She caught the frown on his face, followed by the full impact of the Gunney's fist as she looked behind her.

"Blonde bitch," the Gunnery Sergeant said, and he hit her again.

Chapter 2

The Cherokee returned, its headlights flickering back and forth as it bounced up the gravel track and crunched to a stop behind the Humvee. The rear of the military vehicle cut the Cherokee's light in half, illuminating Fenna where she knelt, wrists bound and the Gunney's fingers gripping her hair in a fist. He jerked Fenna's head back, greeting the Cherokee's passengers with his prize as they exited the vehicle. The driver lit another cigarette and watched her through the smoke as he exhaled.

"What's wrong with the Humvee?" the shorter of the two passengers asked. His companion stared at Fenna.

"Bitch put a bullet through the engine block," said the Gunney.

"Why?"

"Fuck'd if I know."

The man bent down in front of Fenna and gripped her chin in his hand. "Konstabel, isn't it?"

"Yes."

"You realise this is an exercise?"

"Yes."

"Then why did you destroy US Army property?"

Fenna jerked her chin out of the man's grip and looked up, squinting in the glare of the headlights. She recognised his hair from her observations through the rifle scope and idly wondered if he had washed his hands since pissing in the desert.

"Konstabel?"

"I was being pursued. It felt like the right thing to do."

"Oh, that's rich," the man said and laughed. "The

Major is going to love you."

"The Major is back?" the Gunney asked.

"Yep, and the barracks to the east are now off limits. Make sure your people stay clear." The man scuffed his shoes in the dirt as he stepped away from Fenna. He paused and looked at her once more. Fenna caught his eye and the curious angle at which he cocked his head. "You know," he said, "we get all kinds here. Soldiers, sailors, even airmen. *Men* – all of whom understand the chain of command, and obey the rules. Yuma is a privilege. Officers get sent here before promotion, operatives before a mission, assets before an operation. You're in a category all your own, Konstabel, a foreign national with a phoney rank and a fake hair colour."

"Thorough though," the Gunney said and tugged at Fenna's hair.

"Either way, you're still a piece of ass in Uncle Sam's backyard." He spat on the ground. "Let's see what the Major makes of you. I'd like to see how you're going to settle the bill for that," he said, pointing at the Humvee.

The man nodded to his companion. They walked past the Cherokee and stood to one side of the gravel road. The Gunnery Sergeant tugged Fenna to her feet with a firm grip of her hair, and marched her to the back of the vehicle as the driver flicked the butt of his cigarette into the scrub and climbed in behind the wheel. Fenna banged her head as the Gunney pushed her into the rear of the vehicle.

"It'll be the *Sonoran Shuffle* for you, if the Major has his way. I'll make sure to find you the right partner," he said and slammed the door shut.

"All set?" said the driver, as he looked at Fenna

CHRISTOFFER PETERSEN

through the rear-view mirror.

"I guess," she said and squirmed into a sitting position. She caught a glimpse of Nicklas as he passed in front of the vehicle, the light flickered across the dusty webbing cinched and strapped across his body. Fenna thought he paused to nod in her direction. *A flash of sympathy, perhaps?* But then he was gone and the driver shifted the Cherokee into gear and backed down the slope. He used the side mirrors, and she watched as he corrected the vehicle's course with small adjustments of the wheel.

"What's the *Sonoran Shuffle?*" she asked, as the Cherokee bounced up and over the lip of the desert road leading back to base.

"We had a bunch of Brits here once," the driver said. "A while back. Paratroopers, I think. They introduced us to *Milling* – sixty seconds of controlled aggression." Fenna caught his eye in the mirror. He continued. "Sure, we had our own version, but the boss, back then, was the son of an engineer, and he liked the idea of the milling process – grinding and shaping something with a rotating tool. The *Sonoran Shuffle* is Yuma's name for a minute's worth of shit-kicking." She could tell he was smiling. "Of course, it's officially frowned upon, and therefore fully endorsed by the Army. It's also, usually, same sex, but for you, I think the Major will make an exception."

"Great." Fenna leaned back on the seat, arching her back to make room for her bound wrists.

"How heavy are you?"

Fenna glanced down at her body. The year with the Sirius Sledge Patrol in Greenland, the 10k runs along the beach in Denmark, and the first two weeks of orientation at Yuma had trimmed whatever fat she might once have had. Her curves were curbed and her breasts and bottom were firm to non-existent. "Fifty kilos?" she said and shrugged.

"What's that in English?"

"Oh, about 110 pounds, give or take."

"Christ," the driver said and whistled. "Well, at least I know where to put my money. Good luck, Konstabel."

He was quiet for the remainder of the journey back to base, just flashing his headlights as two Humvees passed on the road to pick up the rest of the team.

"This is where you get out," he said, pulling to a stop outside the office block.

"Can you open the door?" Fenna asked. She watched as he shrugged out of the driver's seat and helped her out of the vehicle. "Maybe take these off?" she said, turning to show him her wrists.

"Better not," he said before shutting the rear passenger door. "The light's on. Just go right in."

Fenna waited until the driver had pulled away in the Cherokee. She stared at the light shining in the Major's office and wondered why the base was run by a Major and not someone with a higher rank? She stepped onto the deck, walked to the door, and pushed it with her shoulder. It opened with a creak and she stepped inside.

The Major's aide turned away from the wall-mounted television and the CNN report questioning the latest in a long line of military budget cuts. He looked up at Fenna and nodded for her to enter. *Another man*, Fenna noted. The Desert Training Center at Yuma was, it seemed, practically off-limits to women. She knocked on the door and walked in.

The Major pressed his fingers on the loose pages on his desk as Fenna closed the door behind her. He said nothing, and Fenna remembered she should probably salute. With her wrists bound all she could do was shrug her shoulders. The Major sneered and shook his head. He looked down at his papers and rearranged them.

"You're the Dane?" he said.

"Yes, sir."

"Sir?" The Major looked up. "I suppose I should give you credit for remembering that little formality." He shuffled the papers into the top drawer of his desk and sat down on his chair. Fenna noticed a manila folder beneath the Major's battered briefcase. He smiled when he realised she had seen it. "That's you," he said and lifted his briefcase to pick up the folder. "Do you know what it says about you?"

"No, sir," Fenna said and watched as he opened it.

"Nothing," he said and let a single piece of paper flutter to the desk. Fenna studied the man's hands as he picked up the paper. His hands were gnarled and scarred, like his chin and the left side of his face. She guessed he was a veteran who had been in combat, although the lack of decoration or photographs on the walls suggested he didn't crow about it.

A soldier's Major, she realised. *They'll do anything for him*. She turned her attention to the paper in his hands as the Major began to read aloud.

"Konstabel Fenna Brongaard," he began and then stopped to slip the paper back inside the folder. "That," he said and tapped the folder with a stubby finger, "is my warrant to do whatever I want to you, short of having you killed." He waited for Fenna to speak. She noticed a tic of irritation pinch his scarred cheek as she remained silent. "Something I find very difficult to understand." He stood up and walked around the office, circling Fenna as he spoke. "How tall are you?"

"Five and a half feet."

"Weight?"

"About 110 lbs."

"Unit?"

"I can't say, sir."

"Can't?"

"Under orders..."

"Fuck your orders, Konstabel," he said and stopped in front of her. The Major stabbed Fenna's breastbone with a bent knuckle.

"I don't like spies," he said, emphasising each word with a stab to Fenna's chest. She tried not to gasp. "Christ, I could drop you onto the floor with my finger." He took a step back. "What are you being trained to infiltrate? An orphanage? Hah," he said and forced a second laugh before leaning against his desk. "You know Jarnvig? Personally?"

"Yes, sir," Fenna said and remembered the day at the summer house, on the beach in Denmark, when he had ordered her to the desert.

"He obviously thinks highly of you. This is only the second time a Dane has been sent here, and the first time it's a woman."

"You don't like women, sir?" Fenna asked and then bit her tongue. Her body stiffened as he tensed. She waited for him to stab her again with his knuckle, but, instead, he laughed and she relaxed as his shoulders shook.

"Do I like women?" he said and shook his head.

"Yes, Konstabel, I like women. And, I have to admit, I like looking at you, even though a few extra pounds wouldn't go amiss. What I don't like," he said and scowled, "is when women fuck around with my camp and my equipment. You," he said, jabbing his finger toward Fenna, "fucked up a perfectly good Humvee. And now," he said, as he slid off the desk, walked around it, and yanked open the top drawer. "I have another fucking woman – Miss Fucking Anonymous Beauty Pageant drop-out. Apparently, she needs a whole fucking wing of the base to herself."

Fenna caught the frown wrinkling her forehead and tried to relax as the Major tossed the papers in front of Fenna, including a large colour photo of the woman. He paused as he looked at the photo.

"Pretty, eh?"

"Yes, sir."

"And now I have two pretty girls distracting my men." He picked up the folder and gestured with it toward the door. Fenna walked beside the Major as he escorted her out of his office. "Of course, the difference is," he said and shoved the folder beneath Fenna's arm, "I can do whatever the fuck I want with you."

Fenna clamped the folder to her side and stumbled into the centre of the outer office as the aide stood to attention.

"Dowd," the Major said.

"Yes, sir?"

"Do we have any Brass visiting at the moment?"

"No, sir."

"Good," he said and nodded at Fenna. "Schedule a *Shuffle* for midnight tonight." The Major snorted at Fenna, turned and walked into his office. The building shook a little as he slammed the door and the aide sat down at his desk.

Fenna waited for a moment and then realised she was dismissed. She ignored the aide and walked out of the outer office and onto the deck. She let the door close behind her and then stepped onto the road leading to her quarters.

A figure slipped out of the shadows by the side of the office and jogged to catch up with her. She turned, recognising Nicklas; the moonlight catching the crusts of the camouflage paint flaking on his cheeks and forehead.

"You met the Major then?" he said and cut the ties around her wrists with a pocket knife.

"Yeah, he's a real gentleman," Fenna said. She realised she had been creasing the folder. She relaxed her grip and rubbed her wrists.

"Your orders?"

"My death warrant."

"From Jarnvig then?" Nicklas said and reached for the folder. He let out a short whistle as he read the letter inside.

"Bad?"

"Let's just say you should be pleased your time here is limited."

"Why? What do you know?"

"Not so much. Only that you're to leave in two weeks," he said. "That's why I'm here."

"To keep an eye on me?" she said and laughed.

"To keep you alive," he said and nodded at the letter. "Jarnvig has written one of his *no special treatment* letters."

"You've seen them before?"

"I've *had* one before."

"Nicklas," Fenna said. She stopped as a black SUV drove through the gates, slowing as it drove past the office and Fenna heard the driver tell the passenger behind him to wind up the window. As the smoke glass purred upward and obscured the interior, Fenna caught a glimpse of blonde hair, short, like her own. She waved and was rewarded with a brief smile from the beauty pageant drop-out.

"Cut it out," Nicklas said and pressed Fenna's arm to her side with a firm hand.

"What?" she said, as the SUV continued past them.

"Forget about it."

"Forget what?" Fenna took an irritated step away from him.

"Forget about the girl," he said and tugged Fenna in the direction of the barracks.

Chapter 3

Nicklas guided Fenna from one shadow to the next as he led the way to her barracks. *He knows this place*, she realised and caught his arm as he paused at the passing of another Humvee. He frowned as Fenna let go.

"What?"

"The Major said I was only the second Dane to train at Yuma, and yet you walk around this place as if you've been here before."

"Three times," he said. "This is my fourth."

"But you're Danish."

"I was, but they think I'm Canadian, at least my mother is," he said and gestured for Fenna to follow. "Come on. They'll be looking for you soon."

She followed Nicklas across the main road dissecting the base and onto the deck of the barracks reserved for women stationed at Yuma. Before the arrival of the blonde in the SUV, she had been the only one. Fenna stepped around Nicklas and pressed her palm against the door.

"Listen," he said, "about the *Shuffle*."

"I've been beaten before," Fenna said. "I'm not worried."

"But this isn't about being beaten, this is a test, the kind used to determine combat suitability, showing your team that you can turn on the aggression when needed, and give it all you've got."

"No-one is on my team here, Nicklas. I won't be fighting alongside any of them."

Nicklas paused to look at Fenna as the light from a passing vehicle caught her cheek and she blinked in the glare. "One day you might."

Fenna shrugged. "I got the distinct impression that Jarnvig plans to send me to places on my own."

"Even more reason to prove that you're one of them, to give them a reason to want to come and get you." Nicklas paused. "Operators making it to this level work within a fairly small community. You will meet some of these guys again. You don't want to piss them off with stupid stunts." Fenna caught the edge in Nicklas' voice and stiffened.

"Stupid stunts?"

"The Humvee," he said. "It was reckless. Your shot could have gone wide, hit one of the men."

"But it didn't," she said and pushed the door open.

"I'll see you after the *Shuffle*," Nicklas said as Fenna walked into the barracks. "I have a secure, online briefing scheduled with Jarnvig in an hour. I'll have more information for you then."

Fenna let the door swing to a close and waited until she could hear Nicklas' footsteps in the gravel, just a metre or so beyond the thin barrack walls. She clenched her small fists and pressed the base of her palms into her eyes.

"Fucking men," she whispered, and then, louder, "Fuck all men. All of them." She let her fists drop to her sides, spun around and tilted her head to study the metal locker pressed against the wall. She reached out and yanked it onto one of the four corners and it spun onto the floor. She imagined Nicklas pausing at the crash and she grinned, running her tongue across the film of grime on her teeth. She hadn't brushed them in days.

She spent the next hour sitting on the edge of her bunk, tracing the rough knots of the wool blanket with her fingertips. A bulb began to flicker at the far end of the barracks and Fenna lifted her head to look at it. It blinked twice with a *pling* before settling into a dull glow. She tapped her fingers on her head to the rhythm of each blink and pling until the filament finally gave up and that end of the barracks was lost to the shadows. It was there, in the dark frame of the doorway, that Fenna saw the figure of a young Greenlandic woman swing from a cord lashed around her neck.

"Stop, Dina," Fenna said. "I can't deal with you right now."

The Greenlander twisted in the doorframe. The fingers of her hands splayed away from her body. They were thin, delicate. Fenna remembered clutching them in her own as she dragged Dina away from the men, away from Burwardsley.

Fenna took a breath and forced herself to stare at Dina, to draw her back inside her mind, from one dark place to another. Dina's hair whisped in the desert wind that coiled around the base, blowing through the barracks from the open door at the opposite end of the long room. Fenna looked up and away from Dina, and into the fierce eyes of the Gunnery Sergeant as he pushed a large plug of tobacco into his mouth, positioning it between his gum and top lip with his thumb.

"Busy?" he said and strode into the barracks. The thud of his boots drilled along the wooden slats of the floor. "Only, there's a dance tonight, and you're invited." He stopped a metre from Fenna and sucked at the tobacco. Fenna watched the Gunney as he spat a leaf-flecked brown gob of saliva onto her right boot. "Shall we dance?" he said and grabbed her arm.

"Get your fucking hands off me," Fenna said and slipped free with a jerk of her arm as she stood.

"Whatever you say, bitch," he said and pressed his face into hers. Fenna wrinkled her nose at the sweet smell of tobacco that brushed against her face as he spoke. "But come the end of the night, you'll be too fucked to fuck. The Major and I agreed that you get to dance twice, maybe even three times tonight. That's the going price for a Humvee," he said and shoved Fenna in front of him. He stayed there, just two paces behind her, all the way to the door of an old warehouse. The outside lights were smashed; the glass bowls of the lamps were cracked and filmed with desert dust. A blue light filtered through the gaps between the boards in the walls, and Fenna caught herself, fascinated for a moment by the striped building, and then the image was lost as the Gunney yanked open the door and shoved her into the neon blue hell.

Fenna found herself in a den of dust, drink and wide-eyed devils. They whooped as the Gunney pushed her all the way to the ring in the centre of the den. He lifted the slack hawser rope looped around each of the four oil drums, one in each corner, and shoved Fenna forward. She stumbled and the devils cheered. Fenna caught single words cast into the ring, lifted her chin and searched the men's faces, chasing the words as they were nudged around the spectators.

"Bitch."

"Cunt."

"Pussy."

They laughed at that one, spluttering cheekfuls of light beer over each other, pressing grimy dollar bills into the bookie's hands, and jostling for a better view in the four-deep throng of military men.

"Men," Fenna mouthed and shook her head. She took a breath of fetid, sweaty air and scanned the faces once more, lingering over Nicklas' as he lifted a bottle of beer to his mouth and stared at her. His eyes focused, intense, oblivious of the men around him, and the bookie tugging at his arm and spilling his beer. Fenna watched as Nicklas wiped his chin and pushed the man away.

"It's your loss," the bookie said, with a flick of his head in Fenna's direction. "But then I wouldn't bet on her either."

Fenna caught the movement of Nicklas' eyes as they flicked away from her and focused on the arrival of two men. She watched the Major enter the den, his aide one step behind him. The Gunney raised his arm and the men hushed.

The attention of the men diverted away from Fenna to centre on the Major. She realised they didn't just respect him, they revered him. She faced him as he nodded at them and smiled.

"Where's my beer?" he said and the men whooped and raised the beers in their hands as his aide thrust a dew-budded *Budweiser* into the Major's hand. He took a long slow slug of beer and raised his bottle. "Yuma," he cried and they roared back at him.

"Yuma."

"Gunney," the Major said, when the men were finished. "Are we going to dance tonight, or what?"

"Yes sir," the Gunney said and raised his hands for quiet. The men hushed as the bookies tugged dollar bills from the last show of hands and folded them into their notebooks. A man belched and tossed his empty bottle at Fenna, only to be pulled out of the den by two large men, Military Police that had been lurking at the rear of the crowd. Fenna relaxed for a second at the sight of them, until the largest of them returned and unbuttoned his shirt. He handed it to his partner and stepped over the rope and into the ring.

"Our first dancer," the Gunney said.

"Are you sure, Gunney?" the Major said and made a point of gesturing toward the difference in height between the MP and Fenna. "I thought we agreed on three dances for our Little Mermaid."

"Yes, sir," the Gunney nodded as the MP winked at Fenna. "I suggested the Sergeant start with a light Tango, sir."

"Very well," the Major said. "When you're ready, Gunnery Sergeant."

The hush that descended around the ring tugged at Fenna's resolve and she remembered Burwardsley with the kukri blade pressed into her back in Greenland, Bahadur's backhand, and the weight of the fat lawyer, Lunk, as he forced the air from her lungs with his body on the bathroom floor of *The Ice Star.*

The spectators pressed their bodies against the rope between each of the four oil drums. She was trapped inside a ring of sweaty desert fatigues and the leers and jeers of men of differing ages, races, and ranks, united in the ecstasy and promise of a one-sided fight with a defenceless girl. *Me,* Fenna realised and shuddered at the realisation that these men didn't baulk at beating girls or, better still, seeing one getting a beating.

The Gunney raised his hand once more, and Fenna caught a glimpse of Nicklas as he took a step back from the wall of men, his eyes lasered to her face. He nodded, once, but it was enough. Fenna dropped her shoulders and bent at the knees, just a touch, as she squirmed her boots in the dirt and faced her opponent.

"Let the dance begin," the Gunney shouted, and Fenna caught the single ring of a bell before the MP thrust his fist at her chest.

Lazy, Fenna thought as she stepped away from the MP's attack and let his own momentum propel his body past her. *He thinks he's fighting a girl*, she mused and aimed a kick at the side of the man's knee. She felt her boot connect and then leapt back as he buckled. The MP grimaced as he spun around, reeling a little to one side, enough for Fenna to land a punch to his head and kick the man in the groin. He groaned and she stepped back again, only to have a man wrap his arm around her chest and butt her in the back of the head.

"Fists only, bitch," the man said and shoved her back into the centre of the ring. Fenna's face took the full brunt of the MP's fist as he ploughed his knuckles into her nose and she felt the pump of blood as it cascaded onto her chin and chest. The men roared and the MP pulled back his fist and punched Fenna a second time.

The monkeys chattered and whooped as Fenna fell from the jungle canopy, through the upper and mid layer of branches, past fluorescent-scaled snakes coiled around thick mossy trunks, past the fingers and vines of tree monsters tugging at her hair, until she landed on the fetid floor of the jungle with a thump, the air emptying from her body like a jet exhaust, as a troop of monkeys pummelled her body with hairy fists and squealed in her ears. Squealing for blood, beer, and money.

Fenna ratcheted the jungle air into her lungs, arched her back and pressed her shoulders into the floor. She waved at the monkeys, slapping her hands at their faces, teeth and claws until the jungle fell silent, and the desert air returned. The blue light was replaced with a brilliant pin-prick of white, as rough fingers prised her eyelids apart, first her right, and then her left. The light disappeared with a click and she felt the fingers wipe her mouth and nose free of slime. And then she remembered, it wasn't slime, it was blood. The dirt encrusted in the blood from her nose scratched at her skin as the hands, as gentle as they were rough, cleared her nostrils so that she could breathe. Fenna opened her eyes and blinked to focus on Nicklas' face.

"Hello, Konstabel," he said.

Fenna closed her eyes and licked at the dry blood on her lips.

"Water?"

"Beer," Nicklas said and she felt the glass mouth of a bottle rest against her bottom lip. She let the first mouthful dribble over her lips and chin. She rinsed her mouth with the second and swallowed the third. Then she sat up and groaned.

"I hate men."

"I know," Nicklas said and pulled her to her feet. "Let's get you home."

"Home?"

"Well, your bunk for starters. You have a long day ahead of you."

"It's Saturday tomorrow."

"Yes."

"I have the day off."

"You did, yes. But, not any more," Nicklas said and gripped Fenna around the waist, as he walked her toward the door. "Jarnvig wants me to brief you on your mission."

"Tomorrow?"

"Yes."

"But..."

"Yes, I know," Nicklas said and pushed the door open with his foot. "It's your day off."

Chapter 4

The jungle was silent but for the soft pummel of drums behind Fenna's eyelids. The desert air, dry and warm, blew in through the open window, and she felt the blood crust as it dried inside her nose. Saturday's light was harsh and she was not inclined to open her eyes for any man, beast, or God. No one was going to force her to face the world, but then the mattress of her cot shifted as someone sat down, and she knew that Nicklas had arrived to ruin her day. He was gentle, as he pressed his hand around her arm to wake her, but he was persistent, oblivious to her pain, *the bastard*. Fenna tried to roll away from him, but the drumming on her eyelids increased and she lay back down and forced her eyes open, the rheumy sleep sticking to her lashes and requiring more effort than she felt she had.

"Fenna," Nicklas said. "It's time."

She grunted and pulled free of his grip. Fenna blinked in the light and tried to ignore the drums and the image of the jungle from the night before. Nicklas laughed and she focused on his face. The camouflage paint was gone, and the combination of a clean shave and the sharp morning sun accentuated his jawline.

"You laughed?"

"Your eyes," he said.

"Like two piss holes in the snow? I can imagine," she said and lifted one hand to her nose. She pressed her finger to her cheeks and explored her swollen nose.

"Don't," Nicklas said, "best to leave it."

"You're probably right." Fenna let her hand fall to her side and pushed herself into a sitting position.

The drums beat again, as she squirmed on the cot and she felt a stream of fresh blood trickle from her nose and onto her lip. "Tissues," she said, pointing at a pile of napkins on the desk.

"*Taco Bell?*" he said, as he stood up and picked up a wad of napkins. He pressed them into her hand.

"Can't a girl have secrets?" Fenna said and wiped the blood from her nose.

"Yes, but not today." Nicklas dragged a chair from the desk to the side of Fenna's cot and sat down, opening a folder as he crossed his legs. "I got this from Jarnvig. It's your mission," he said and looked at Fenna. "At least, part of it. I'm still waiting for more details."

"So you're my handler?"

"Sort of," Nicklas said and shrugged.

"And the Major doesn't know?"

"Doesn't need to know either. You've been through the basics already. The DTC specialises in insertion and extraction, weapons, sniping, spotting and communications." Nicklas flipped through the contents of the folder. "Jarnvig wants you to take a tracking course at the end of next week, but you're to start your specialist training on Monday."

"Dancing lessons?" Fenna said and tossed the bloody napkin onto the floor.

"No," Nicklas said and laughed. "Although, I thought I would give you a few hints later."

"Great." Fenna sighed and inspected the napkin for blood. Nicklas laughed again and she shot him a look. "What?"

"I never thought *panda eyes* could be so sexy."

"That's a line if ever I heard one."

"It's not a line, Konstabel," Nicklas said. Fenna

caught his gaze and snorted a fresh trickle of blood onto her upper lip. She considered telling him to fuck off, but then she remembered the same intense look on his face right before the military policeman knocked her out with a second punch to her face. She returned Nicklas' look until he looked away. He coughed, shifted his position and read aloud from the folder in his hands. "Investigation techniques, criminal and covert. Oh, and Chinese."

"I prefer *Taco Bell*, but thanks for the invitation."

"Funny," he said and shook his head. "You start Chinese lessons Monday evening."

"On the base?"

"No, actually," Nicklas said and flicked the pages back and forth. "Off base for some reason. It doesn't say."

"I'll find out."

"You'll need a driver. It's in Phoenix."

"That's a long drive for a Chinese lesson," Fenna said and frowned.

"Two hours each night for the next week. You're going to be busy."

"Apparently." Fenna swung her legs around and placed her bare feet on the wooden floor. They were pale compared to her bronzed arms, neck, and face. She glanced at her boots, spotted with blood and dusty from the two days and nights in the desert. She looked at Nicklas. "Can we look at that over breakfast?"

"Sure," Nicklas said and stood up. "We'll drive into Yuma."

"You have a car?"

"I have a Humvee," he said and smiled. "It goes with my rank."

"Captain?" Fenna said, as she noticed the brass crown pinned to Nicklas' collar.

"Inspector," he said. "I almost lost it after your stunt with Humble."

"Stunt?" Fenna said and laughed. She pressed her palms to her eyes for a moment as the drummers picked up the tempo. "I didn't kill him, *Inspector*. I haven't killed anyone."

"No," Nicklas said. He tucked the folder under his arm and pointed at Fenna's boots. "Put them on. We can talk about Humble another time. Let's get some breakfast."

Fenna padded across the floor and tugged her boots over her bare feet. She wrinkled her nose as she bent down and took a careful sniff of her armpits, the blood caked in the lining of her nostrils was not enough to disguise the rigours of the past few days in the desert and the stench of the *Sonoran Shuffle*. "I stink," she said.

"Do you want to take a shower?"

Fenna finished tying the laces and stood up. She laughed, softly this time, and looked at Nicklas. "Breakfast first."

"Come on," Nicklas said. "I know a place. You'll fit right in."

Nicklas bumped the Humvee up a narrow track and over a low rise; *Freddy's Diner* was a rusted airstream camper nestled, within the brush at the end of the track, on the banks of the *Gila River*. Fenna cranked open the passenger door and waited. She watched Nicklas as he approached her, noting the casual cut of his fatigues, his shirt tight around his biceps.

Get it together, Fenna, she scolded herself. *He's not the first man you've worked closely with*. She stopped mid-thought as the image of Oversergent Mikael Gregersen flickered into her mind, the ice hanging from his red beard, a stark contrast to the desert heat. Fenna pushed Mikael's image away, hoping that Dina's would also stay hidden, silent, but then she was always silent, and would remain so, forever. *Just let me enjoy breakfast*, she pleaded to her demons. *After that, you can plague me all you want.*

"Everything all right?" Nicklas asked.

"I'm fine," she said. "Let's eat."

Nicklas led the way through the spiny scrub and across a wide deck of desert-bleached wood, splintering beneath the first of two steps into the diner. A man greeted Nicklas as they entered and tipped his *Diamondbacks* cap in the direction of the table at the window at the front end of the airstream. The heat inside the trailer was even more intense than outside. Nicklas wiped his neck with his hand and waited for Fenna to sit before sliding onto the seat opposite her.

"Freddy," he said, with a nod towards the man in the grimy baseball cap, "spends any spare cash on trips to see his wife in Phoenix. He can barely afford the medication, so…"

"No air conditioning."

"That's right. But what Freddy's lacks in comfort, it makes up for in privacy." Nicklas placed the folder on the table. "We won't be disturbed, and Freddy doesn't speak Danish."

"All right," Fenna said, as Freddy shuffled over to their table.

"What'll it be?" he said.

"Two burgers and cokes," Nicklas said before Fenna could respond. "Coffee to follow."

"You want pie?" Freddy glanced at Fenna. "It's good."

"We want pie then," she said.

"Could use some fat on those bones." He studied her eyes for a moment and then nodded at Nicklas. "He did that?"

"No," Fenna said and smiled.

Freddy leaned forward, closer to Fenna. "But could he have stopped it, eh? That's the question."

"Well…"

"Well, nothin', miss. I'll make sure he pays," he said and paused to squeeze Nicklas' shoulder. Fenna heard him whisper, "Thanks for the help the other day, son."

"You're welcome, Freddy. You only have to ask."

"I know," Freddy said and gave Nicklas' shoulder another squeeze. Fenna watched the old man shuffle back to the counter and disappear into the kitchen area. At the sound of a knob of fat sizzling on the hot plate, Nicklas opened the folder and started speaking in Danish.

"You're going back to Greenland. Flying into the capital, Nuuk, three weeks from now."

"What will I be doing?" Fenna said and savoured the words. It had been a long time since she last spoke Danish.

"That," said Nicklas with a frown, "is where it gets complicated. I can tell you what I know." He shuffled the papers inside the folder to find the one he wanted. "You will be acting as a company representative, on a fact-finding mission attached to a Chinese delegation currently in talks with Tunstall

Mining Consolidated."

"Sounds English," said Fenna.

"It is, but they have Chinese investors. A man called Hong Wei is the leader of the delegation. You will be accompanying him and his liaison from the Greenland Self Rule government and the Department of Natural Resources in Nuuk."

"That all sounds great, Nicklas, but I know nothing about mining…"

"Hence the crash course in geology in Copenhagen the week before you fly out," he said.

Fenna shook her head. "Great. Jarnvig thinks of everything."

"He says you're a fast learner, wrote as much in your profile."

"And so what if I am?" Fenna said. "Why am I going to be a go-between for the Chinese and the Greenlandic government?"

"Because," Nicklas flicked to the last few pages in the folder, "there is another matter." He slid them across the table to Fenna and tapped his finger on the letters highlighted in bold.

"LOMROG?" Fenna said and frowned.

"It's the acronym for a research expedition exploring the *Lomonosov Ridge off Greenland*, a joint scientific venture with an international crew of Swedes, Danes, Norwegians, and Canadians. I have the field report for you to read back at the base."

"Have you read it?"

"Skimmed it. The report is relatively recent, the expedition vessel returned to Sweden late last summer." Nicklas paused. "The sea ice conditions were poor – or good, depending on how you look at it. There was plenty of open water and so they could have stayed out longer."

"Where were they?"

"About 100 miles from the Pole."

"And why did they come back?"

"Something about equipment malfunction, and a dead crewman."

At the sound of Freddy arriving with their food, Nicklas collected the papers inside the folder and placed it on the seat next to him. Freddy served their meal and winked at Fenna as she smiled at the tulip-shaped tomato beside her burger.

"Enjoy," he said. "I'll be out on the stoop if you need me."

"Sure, Freddy," said Nicklas. "Thanks."

"You're welcome," he said and left them alone. Nicklas took a sip of coke.

"What were they researching?" Fenna asked.

Nicklas swallowed and set his glass down on the table. "The continental shelf. You must have heard about this when working with Sirius?"

"Yes," Fenna reached for her burger. "If Denmark can prove the shelf extends from Greenland to the North Pole, then we can claim it," she said and took a bite. "This is good."

"I know," Nicklas said and smiled. "UNCLOS – another acronym – the *United Nations Convention on the Law of the Sea* gives a claimant, in this case Denmark, a period of fourteen years to prove they have a claim on the Pole. With the current thinning of the ice, and the retreating coverage…"

"Whoever owns the Pole can control sea lanes and navigation routes," Fenna said and paused. "It hurts when I chew," she said.

"Take smaller bites," Nicklas said and picked up

the folder. Fenna watched as he pulled out the last paper. "There is a hearing scheduled for the end of June. The research from the LOMROG expedition is going to be a central part of the evidence in proving that Greenland is not connected to the Pole, and that Denmark has no more right to the sea lanes around it than, say, Russia."

"Or Canada," said Fenna and remembered the extent to which Humble's splinter group had tried to humiliate the Danish sovereignty mission in Greenland.

"It's not Canada we need to worry about, not at the moment."

"Who then? The Chinese?"

"The Chinese have a delegation on the Arctic Council. They are observers only, but have a growing interest in the Arctic, not least for oil and minerals."

"And Danish agents posing as mining company reps."

"Exactly," Nicklas said and grinned. "For a nation with no geographical ties to the Arctic, they are committed, with one ice breaker…"

"The *Xue Long*," Fenna said.

"And the *Haibing*, which is under construction," Nicklas said, with a quick flick through the papers. "The Chinese are very interested, and are already negotiating the building of a mineral mine in the mountains north of Nuuk, in Godthåb Fjord."

"The Tunstall mine?"

"Yes."

"And that's where I'm going?"

"Yes, but your brief is more specific." Nicklas paused. "The Field Report suggests that data was spoiled by a member of the expedition, and that the results are inconclusive."

"So they can't be used."

"No, not unless the nature of the spoiled data can be re-evaluated."

"I don't follow?" Fenna said. "Is Greenland connected to the Pole or not?"

"The data says it's not."

Nicklas turned his head at the swing of the screen door as Freddy came back in and prepared a fresh pot of coffee. Fenna took a small bite of her burger and waited for him to continue.

"Jarnvig thinks the data is fake, that the so-called malfunction of the machine is fake."

"And he thinks the Chinese are behind it?"

"That's the theory," Nicklas said and nodded.

Fenna mused over the implications, and the memory of the *Xue Long* entering Canadian waters unannounced several years ago. That incident alone had forced the Canadians into an escalation of military activities and patrols in their Arctic territories; it had also culminated in the death of her patrol partner, and Dina. *And it was almost the death of me*, she thought as she swallowed. A Chinese foothold in Greenland could be used as leverage for a greater Chinese role in the Arctic, she realised.

"And Jarnvig wants me to find out the truth?" she asked.

"Not exactly," Nicklas said and lowered his voice as Freddy approached with their coffees and pie. "He wants you to find the researcher who falsified the data, before the hearing." He paused and leaned forward. "Jarnvig thinks the Chinese have turned someone on our side," he said. "There's a traitor among us, Fenna, and your job is to expose him."

Chapter 5

Fenna wound down the Humvee window and let the warm air scour the grime from her face. She enjoyed the flick of her hair against her skin, and ran her hand through her fringe. Nicklas was silent and Fenna thought she caught a glimpse of him looking at her, but when she turned, he was focused on the road. The glimpse was gone, but she slid her fingers through her hair one more time, laughing at herself when she saw her reflection in the Humvee's mirror. *Get over yourself, Fenna,* she thought. *These are hardly come-to-bed eyes.* She smiled again as the thought flushed her cheeks and she tried to remember the last time she had lusted for a man.

"Too long," she said, as Nicklas turned his head toward her.

"What is?"

"Nothing," Fenna pressed the heel of her right boot against the solid wheel arch in front of her. She closed her eyes and let her mind wander in the desert as they continued along Highway 95 towards the base.

Nicklas slowed the Humvee as they approached the entrance to the DTC. He flashed his ID card and leaned back so Fenna could do the same. The guard nodded for them to pass. Nicklas drove beneath the raised barrier and onto the base. Fenna took a moment to prepare herself for going back to the barracks, but Nicklas continued past them, slowing to a stop by the side of a dishevelled warehouse. Fenna recognised it, even without the blue light leaking out between the wood panels.

"Why are we here?" she asked.

"Dancing lessons," Nicklas said and got out of

the Humvee. Fenna stared at him as he shut the Humvee's door and waited for her to get out. She climbed out of the vehicle and slammed the door.

"I'm hardly ready for this," she said and scowled.

"But you need it," he said and signalled for Fenna to go inside.

The wind licked tiny clouds of dust from the heels of her boots as Fenna walked up to the door and yanked it open. She squinted into the dim interior, stepped inside and waited. She watched as Nicklas found a length of wood to prop against the door.

"The lock's broken," he said. "Come on."

"I don't like this place," Fenna said, as she followed him to the dusty ring in the centre of the warehouse. She remembered the screech of the monkeys, the fetid taste of sweat and testosterone as she ducked under the rope and stood opposite Nicklas. He grinned and pulled his shirt off.

Fenna's eyes adjusted to the soft desert light creeping in through the holes in the tin roof. She watched the dust motes as they filtered down on shafts of light to settle on Nicklas' body. She traced the shadows that cut his body into muscle, ribs, a scar here, a patch of burned skin there. The drumming behind her eyes was lost as her heart beat faster, thudding against her chest.

"Forget about this area," Nicklas said and traced his finger around the muscles on his flat belly. "Fat or muscle, you won't get the effect you're looking for with a punch to the stomach. Not with a soldier, not with these guys." Nicklas tapped his breastbone with his knuckle. "Here. This is where you want to hit. Maximum effort," he said and let his hands fall to his sides. "Now," he said and squared his feet in the dirt.

"You want me to hit you?"

"I want you to try."

"All right," Fenna said and took a step forward. She made a fist with her right hand and extended the knuckle of her middle finger. Nicklas stepped to one side, turned sharply and caught Fenna's arm in the crook of his own. He closed his left hand around her fist and started to bend it back on itself.

"Fuck," Fenna said and jerked to her right.

"Kidneys," Nicklas said. "Ignore the pain. Go for the kidneys."

Fenna grimaced and slammed her left fist into Nicklas' back.

"Lower," he said and grunted when she made contact. He bent her hand again. Fenna's wrist consumed her focus and she twisted in his grip. "Again."

Fenna ignored the pain in her wrist and slammed her fist into Nicklas' back, lower this time. He grunted and twisted his back away from her. Fenna bent her left leg and kneed him in small of his back.

"Better," Nicklas said with another grunt. "Keep going."

She tried but the pain in her wrist overwhelmed her. He spun her onto the ground and her body went limp. Dust pillowed from the floor as she slammed onto it. He let go of her and slapped at her hands as he sat astride her chest.

"You're always going to be weaker," he said. "You're never going to win a fight if you let them get close. Keep your opponent at a distance. Always."

Fenna spat dirt from her mouth, squirmed her heels into the dirt and arched her back, trying to propel him away. She glared at Nicklas.

"Forget it, Konstabel. I'm at least 50lbs heavier than you. You're pinned."

"Then what do you suggest?" Fenna said. She felt a fresh trickle of blood leak from her nose. With her arms trapped beneath Nicklas' knees, the blood trickled down her left cheek.

Nicklas lifted one hand and wiped the blood away with his thumb. The scratch of his skin was familiar. His eyes, brown – almost black in the dim light – settled on hers. Fenna felt his knees lift from her arms, as he positioned them on either side of her body, and Fenna, silent, her blue eyes locked on his, arched her back, her hips brushing against his inner thighs.

"Konstabel," Nicklas said, his voice hoarse.

Fenna said nothing. She arched her back again and he pressed down into her. She spread her arms at right angles and pressed her fingers into the dirt. Fenna ignored the pain in her eyes, her nose. She heard her breaths rasp in and out of her mouth as she arched her body again and he matched her movement. Fenna licked her wind-chapped lips and sniffed at the air. It was hot. Moist. She was on the floor of the jungle again, and she succumbed to its feral nature as he unzipped his cargo pants and Fenna reached down to unbutton and squirm out of hers.

The dust of the ring clung to their skin as sweat beaded their faces, glued Fenna's hair to her cheeks, and ran in spasmodic streams as Nicklas thrust his way inside Fenna and she pushed to feel him deep inside her. Fenna purged the violent and dominant images of man from her mind and lost herself in Nicklas, in the fusty dirt of the ring. *The dancing lessons are over,* she thought as she caught him mid thrust, cupped his balls and rolled him onto his back. Fenna straddled him until he closed his eyes and groaned. She felt the jungle, smelled it as it enveloped her, the vines curling around her legs, her arms, her ribs, constricting her breathing, until the jungle withdrew and she let herself slip onto his chest, content, for the moment, and Nicklas opened his eyes.

Fenna felt another stream of blood trickle onto her chin and she wiped it with the back of her hand. Nicklas took her hand, her blood smearing into the cracks in his rough skin. Fenna sat back on his thighs as he lay down in the dirt. She felt him inside her, limp but warm, and smiled.

"You're pretty," he said. "But…"

"But?" Fenna said and dug her knuckles into his stomach.

"But beautiful when you smile."

"Hah," she said and moved as if to roll off him.

"Stay," he said, and moved his hands to her hips.

"Can't," she said with a glance toward the door.

"No-one's coming, Konstabel."

"How do you know, *Inspector*?" Fenna shook her head and laughed.

"I don't … care," he said and reached up to caress her cheek. Fenna turned her face and took his finger between her lips. "I wouldn't," he said and pulled his finger out of her mouth. "Not clean."

"I don't care," she said and closed her teeth around his finger, biting until he complained. Fenna released him and Nicklas slipped his hand to her breast, smoothing his palm over her dusty thermal top, searching for her nipples. "They're tiny," she said, as he rubbed her nipple to a hard bud.

"I don't care."

"You're my handler," she said. "Aren't you?"

Nicklas nodded and said, "And do you like the way I *handle* you, Konstabel?"

"Yes," Fenna said and slipped onto Nicklas' chest. She felt him slide out of her as she kissed him. Her eyes hurt, and she closed them. Her nose ran and she ignored it. Her heart hammered and she felt it. Nicklas stirred beneath her and she anticipated it. The jungle enveloped Fenna once more and she lost herself in the wild beat of its drum.

The canteen was empty when Fenna entered. She had revelled in the shower that gave her a chance to scrub the stubborn desert grime from her body and now she was ready to eat. Nicklas was gone for the evening, and she realised she didn't even know where he slept. The thought amused her as she helped herself to a meal from the fridge and took her tray into a corner, choosing to eat in the shadows. The anchor of a late night talk show on the television was berating the President for his short-sightedness on defence job cuts, and the need for a strong, capable military in an increasingly volatile world. Fenna was almost finished when the door opened and the beauty queen walked in. Two sturdy men accompanied her, one on either side. They studied the rows of empty tables and chairs and Fenna shrank deeper into the shadows. The men nodded for the girl to help herself and walked out of the canteen to wait outside. Fenna watched her walk to the fridge, and, when she was looking for a seat, she whispered to her, "Hi."

The girl was startled, but Fenna continued.

"Sorry. Come and join me." She beckoned to the

girl, who took one step and stopped.

"I'm not supposed to," she said and glanced at the door.

"How long do you have?"

"They usually give me fifteen minutes."

"Then I'll be gone in ten," she said. "Sit with me."

The girl took one more look at the door and then, with a breath, walked over to Fenna's table. She slid her tray onto the table and sat down. Fenna smiled and studied her face. She was a natural blonde. They shared the same glacial-blue eyes.

"Fenna," she said and held out her hand.

"Alice," the girl said.

"We're the only two girls on the base. How old are you?"

"Nineteen."

"I'm twenty-four," said Fenna. "They keeping you busy?" she said, looking toward the door.

"I'm really not supposed to talk about it."

"I understand," Fenna paused as Alice started to whisper.

"They want me to do something, and I'm pretty sure it's bad, but they won't tell me what it is."

"You don't have any idea?" Fenna said and leaned forward. Alice shook her head and slipped her pale arms either side of the tray. Fenna noticed that her hands were trembling and she placed hers on top of them and squeezed. "It'll be all right," she said.

"No," said Alice. "I don't think it will."

Chapter 6

The base was quiet when Fenna slipped out of the kitchen. Alice intrigued her. The way she constantly checked towards her minders, encouraging Fenna to leave after only seven minutes, during which time she had said little, only stared at Fenna's eyes, and taken tiny bites of the sandwich on her plate. She had flinched when Fenna leaned across the table to smooth a lock of her hair from her face.

"It's okay," Fenna had said. "I won't hurt you."

"You won't?"

"No, I promise," she said, "us girls have to look out for each other."

"And you'll look out for me?"

"Yes," Fenna said and clasped Alice's hand. "Do you eat at the same time each night?"

"Yes."

"Then I'll be here, in the shadows."

"Okay," Alice said and Fenna caught the beginnings of a smile.

"I'll see you tomorrow night," Fenna said. She squeezed Alice's hand, and then slipped out from behind the bench and into the kitchen. Fenna looked back from the doorway, but Alice turned away, chewing small mouthfuls of sandwich as she stared at the door. Fenna left through the back entrance.

The two of them shared a similar build, but where Fenna's skin was tanned and tight, Alice's was pale and smooth. *Cute*, Fenna realised. *Pretty and innocent. The kind older men go for,* she thought and felt sick at the thought of Richard Humble.

A cascade of thoughts plagued Fenna as she crossed the grounds of the base. She half expected to see Dina hanging in the doorway, or Mikael grinning from behind the uprights of the Sirius sledge, the dogs wagging their tails, anxious, anticipating his commands. Fenna pushed each image aside, spinning through the cruel carousel in her mind before it settled on one image, Dina. *Always Dina.* Fenna, her hand on the screen door, closed her eyes and tried to push the carousel on to the next image, Maratse, his cigarette rolled into the gap between his teeth, but Dina's face remained.

"I'm sorry," Fenna whispered, as she let the door close behind her. It clapped against the wooden frame and Fenna sank to her knees. She opened her eyes and blinked. There was Dina, twisting from the beam above Fenna's bunk, and, for a moment, the Greenlander's almond face paled, her cheeks swelled a fraction and her eyes opened, changing from black to brilliant blue. It wasn't Dina's long black hair she saw, but short hair, curled into a blonde fringe. Fenna gasped when she realised it was not her own face staring back at her, but another – Alice. Then Dina returned, twisting silently three full turns before Fenna turned the carousel in her mind, stopping it on a single image, an iceberg locked into the ice, extending from the coastline and far into the Greenland Sea. She stared at it until the white surface of the berg consumed her and everything and everyone was gone. Fenna was alone.

She stood up and dragged her pack to her bunk, tugging the LOMROG report out from the back of the pack. She flicked through the first few pages, familiarising herself with the Swedish author's name, Lars Johansson and his Danish colleague Karl Lorentzen. She crawled beneath the blanket and folded her pillow in half, lay on her side and drew her knees toward her chest. She skimmed over the academic descriptions detailing the remit of the expedition, and focused instead on the opening sentences of the report. Johansson was wasted as a scientist, surely his true calling was writing. She absorbed his descriptions of patchwork plates of ice, hinged with elastic tongues of black water, desperate to freeze, thwarted by the movement of the plates, and the curved bow of the icebreaker rising up over the ice and cracking it beneath its monstrous displacement. Fenna forgot the desert, the pain behind her eyes, only to wake as the report slipped from between her fingers and slapped onto the barrack floor. She set the alarm and pulled the blanket up and over her head. She needed to sleep.

The canteen at breakfast reminded Fenna of the jungle floor of the ring. The taint of testosterone hung heavy over the tables of men, who were sweating and coated in dust from a morning run through the desert. She recognised some of the faces as they looked up from their meal, elbowing each other in the ribs, nodding and sneering in her direction as she passed. The counter-sniper team sat at one end of the table closest to the serving area. Fenna stopped as the Gunnery Sergeant extricated himself from the bench and made his way toward her, the tread of his boots heavy on the floor. Fenna picked up a tray and faced him.

"Konstabel," he said and stopped in front of her. The men at the table behind him leaned around each other to watch. He gave them a threatening look and they turned away.

"*Konstabel?*" Fenna said, as he looked at her. She tilted her head. "Not *bitch*, or *pussy*? What about *cunt*?"

The Gunney laughed. "Save it for the ring," he said and nodded at the soldiers queuing at the serving counter. "Major wants to see you after breakfast," the Gunney said, as he walked away. Fenna let out a breath and joined the line.

She ate alone at the same corner table she had sat at the previous evening. She looked up from her meal and scanned the soldiers for a glimpse of Alice, chiding herself for even hoping she might see her. She twisted around as the bench creaked beneath the weight of someone sitting down.

"She's not here," Nicklas said, as he opened his carton of milk and drank from it.

"I know," Fenna said and sighed. She pushed her spoon around the muesli in her bowl. "Where did you sleep last night?"

"The same place I always do. Why?"

"It occurred to me," she said, "that I don't know where that is."

"And that bothers you?"

"No," Fenna said and smiled. "I'd just like to know. That's all."

"So you can make a booty call?" Nicklas said and laughed.

"God," she said and caught herself in the act of slapping him on his arm. Fenna let her hand drop to her lap. "No," she said. "I don't do booty calls."

"Shame," said Nicklas. "If you did, I might be more inclined to tell you where I slept."

Fenna hid her smile behind a spoonful of muesli, chewing over the thoughts that tickled her mind.

"I have to see the Major," she said, as Nicklas

46

finished his milk. "Should I be worried?"

"No. He's just going to give you a car, and a driver."

"Chinese lessons?"

"Tomorrow night, yes. But before that, you'll need to get over to the quartermaster and draw some more kit."

"It's Sunday."

"He'll be open."

"And what do I need?"

"Here's a list," Nicklas said and tugged a slip of paper from his pocket. He handed it to Fenna, pausing as he caught the eyes of the counter-sniper team watching them.

"We've become an object of interest," Fenna said and took the paper.

"You were the moment you arrived."

"And you?"

"I'm Canadian, remember? We're never interesting, just polite. No," he said, shoveling egg onto his French Toast, "you're the item of interest, and they are hungry. Watch yourself, Fenna."

"I'll be fine," she said and slipped the list into her pocket.

"You're not going to read it?"

"After I've seen the Major." Fenna stood up and picked up her tray. "I'll see you later?"

"No," he said and shook his head. "I have to leave for a few days."

"Jarnvig's orders?"

"No, Toronto's. I'm lucky enough to have two masters. I'll see you when I get back."

"Okay," she said.

"Fenna?"

"What?"

"You're getting better, but I think more dancing lessons might be in order," Nicklas said. He grinned and stabbed his fork into the toast. Fenna caught the smile on her face and wrangled it into a frown.

"I'm not so sure about that, Inspector," she said and smirked at the flash of insecurity in Nicklas' eyes. She walked away from the table, conscious of the eyes following her all the way to the door. She knew Nicklas' gaze was among them, and the thought lifted her step all the way to the Major's office.

The woman sitting on the chair against the wall of the outer office was older than Fenna, her clothes tighter, her perfume sweeter. She caught Fenna's eye before the aide stepped out from Major's office and closed the door. Fenna caught a glimpse of a man talking with the Major and recognised him. It was the same man that had confronted her in the dirt beside the Humvee in the desert, the one that had warned the Gunney and his men to stay away from eastern barracks.

"That's three women on my base," Fenna heard the Major bark through the thin wall. "And damn it, this one is a fucking hooker."

"Exotic dancer," the woman said, as Fenna looked over at her. "I'm not a hooker."

Fenna shrugged and walked over to the aide's desk as he called to her.

"Konstabel."

"Yes?"

"The Major has arranged a car and a driver. You'll be picked up at 18:00 hours each night from Monday. The car will wait for you at the main gate.

You're to be back by midnight. If not, the guards have been instructed to hold you at the gate."

"Really?"

"Yes," the aide said and smiled. "Really."

Fenna nodded and turned to leave.

"Just one more thing, Konstabel."

"Yes?" she said and looked at the aide. She noticed the smile on his face as it broadened into a smug grin that filled his cheeks.

"The Major instructed me to remind you that you are invited to a second dance this evening." Fenna's stomach churned as the aide's grin widened. "He hopes you will come suitably dressed."

"Hey," said the woman. "I thought I was the only one dancing?" She moved to one side to look around Fenna at the aide. "Nobody said nothing about dancing with a partner." She paused and made a point of appraising Fenna's body. "No offence, honey, but your body and," she spun her finger around her face, "those black eyes n'all. I just don't do no kinky stuff."

"Don't worry," Fenna said and took a step toward the door. "I dance alone."

Fenna pulled the crumpled slip of paper from her pocket as she walked to quartermaster's store. She listened to the woman protesting as she was ushered into the back of a black SUV. Fenna watched for a moment and then focused her attention back to the paper – Jarnvig's shopping list.

"Interesting," she said and smiled as she scanned the different items.

The quartermaster didn't smile when she handed him the list. He whistled and scratched at flakes of skin on his parched head. He caught Fenna's look and explained, "Had a barbecue yesterday. Forgot my cap."

"Okay," Fenna said and placed her hands on the counter between them.

"This will take a while," he said. "Some of these things... Well, we have them, but they haven't been used in I don't know how long. You might want to take a seat."

Fenna nodded and sat down on the bench opposite the counter. The quartermaster whistled for a second time and then looked at Fenna, deep wrinkles furrowing his brow.

"I'm probably not supposed to ask," he said.

"But?"

"But," he said and nodded. "Why would you need an M1 Carbine? Those things are ancient. I mean, we have a couple, but..."

"It's a Greenland thing," Fenna said and smiled. The carousel in her mind clicked and there was Maratse, grinning behind the wheel of a Police Toyota Rav4 as it sped across the ice. Fenna let the image linger as the quartermaster disappeared into the strip light interior of the stores to rummage around the lockers and shelves. She found an empty chair and pulled the LOMROG report out of her pack, losing herself once more in Johansson's lyrical description of the Arctic, and his unhurried detailing of life on board the Swedish research vessel *Odin*.

The quartermaster returned faster than he had anticipated, forcing Fenna to tuck the report back inside her pack, and to find room for the various items he had assembled from her list.

"You'll have to sign for all of it," he said. Fenna nodded. "And," he said as she picked up the pen, "that makes you responsible for it."

"So if I break it...

"You bought it," he said and shrugged. "I don't make the rules."

"That's okay," Fenna said, as she shouldered her pack and picked up the carbine. "I don't often follow them." She turned away before the quartermaster could respond, smiling as she stepped out of the stores and into the afternoon heat. *It would be dark soon*, she realised as she walked toward her barracks, anticipating with pleasure a little feminine contact. *Alice*, she thought. *I wonder what you have learned today?*

Chapter 7

The base was dark and quiet but for the muffled beat of rock music coming from the barracks beyond the canteen. Fenna put down the LOMROG report and checked the equipment that she had arranged on her desk and bunk. She had spent most of the evening cleaning the carbine. *The quartermaster was right*, she had mused, *it was a relic*. But neither the carbine nor the scientist's field report held her interest. It was getting late, and the canteen would be empty. Fenna checked her watch. The dance, she imagined, would start at midnight. She tugged on her boots and slipped out of the barracks.

Fenna entered the canteen through the kitchen door. The emergency exit sign cast a green glow above the doors and she saw the familiar shadows of Alice's protection detail. She pressed her palms against the swing door and pushed it open a crack. Alice was at the table, a half-empty glass of milk in her hand as she nibbled at a sandwich. Fenna slipped inside and padded over to her.

"I thought you weren't going to come," Alice said, as Fenna sat down.

"Sorry. I lost track of time."

"It's okay."

"How was your day?" Fenna asked.

"Actually," Alice said and smiled. "It was a lot of fun."

"Fun?" Fenna said and tilted her head. The wry smile that tugged at Alice's lips caught her attention.

"Kinda naughty."

"Now I'm interested." Fenna leaned forward. "Tell me."

"Well," Alice said and placed her sandwich on the table. She licked a crumb from her lips, glanced at the door and then whispered, "This woman came. She was older than you. A dancer." Fenna nodded, she knew exactly who the woman was.

"And?"

"She taught me to lap dance. You know? Like in a strip joint?"

"Yes, I know," Fenna said and frowned. "Did they say why?"

"No," Alice said, "that's the thing. They haven't told me anything. They just give me classes in different stuff and expect me to do it."

"What kind of classes? Apart from lap dancing, I mean."

"There's gym, for one. They have me out running a lot."

"In the desert?"

"Yeah," Alice said and shrugged. "I like it. It's the only time they let me outside in the daylight. Although we're up so early…"

"You don't meet anyone."

"That's right. But it reminds me of the dawn at my daddy's favourite place, in Washington state," she said. "In the Cascades."

"He has a cabin there?"

"Kind of. He was a mountaineer. He got sick – cancer – and he'd spend every night talking about this cabin, way up on the top of a mountain – an old lookout hut on top of the North Cascades." Fenna listened as Alice continued. "When I was seventeen, daddy got better for a little bit – even the doctors were surprised. So we went up there."

"To the lookout?"

"Sure," Alice said and grinned. "Scariest thing I ever did in my life. There's all these ladders, and you climb through the clouds..." Fenna lifted a finger to Alice's lips and she lowered her voice. "The ladders go all the way to the top, some 7,000 feet high. Then there's this amazing cabin – it looks like it's going to fall apart, but people look after it, and it's still there. You can see all around it, for miles." Alice sighed. "The climb nearly killed him. He wasn't ready. And when we came down, well, he died, just a few weeks later. I held his hand, right at the end, describing the cabin over and over, until he stopped breathing. Until his body just stopped."

"It sounds like an amazing place," Fenna said and took Alice's hands. She squeezed them, smiling as Alice squeezed back.

Alice slipped her left hand free of Fenna's and wiped a tear from her cheek. She glanced at the door. "They'll come in soon."

"I'll go," Fenna said. She reached out and smoothed Alice's cheek. "You're okay though?"

"Better now. I still don't know what I'm doing. They tell me nothing. There's no TV. They took my Smartphone the day they picked me up."

"I know the feeling. They took mine too. You're cut off from the world."

"Pretty much."

"Okay," Fenna said, as Alice pulled away. "I'll see you tomorrow night."

"I hope so," Alice said and smiled. Fenna slid back on the bench and melted into the shadow of the corner, as Alice emptied her tray at the counter and walked toward the door. One of the men opened it for her and she walked past him. She didn't look back.

Fenna waited several minutes, mulling over the strange classes Alice was taking, before standing up and making her way to the kitchen. She padded past the stoves and hotplates and opened the door. A warm draft of desert air tousled her hair as she stepped out into the night, only to be replaced by a cloth sack pulled over her head that blotted out the stars and, when the opening was tightened around her neck, threatened to turn that breath of warm wind into her last. Fenna struggled and was rewarded with a knee in her stomach. She doubled over and sprawled onto the deck as rough hands bound her arms behind her back and she heard the all-too-familiar snick of plastic ties as they locked her hands together.

"Get her in the truck," said a man, and then she felt more hands on her body. They clamped around her ankles, jammed into her armpits and lifted her. Fenna was weightless for a brief moment before her chin cracked on the metal bed of a pick-up and the metal gate hit the soles of her boots as it was slammed shut. Doors opened on both sides of the vehicle and it rocked as the men got in. The engine coughed into life and Fenna slid across the metal bed as the vehicle roared off the base and onto what she imagined was a side road, her knees and elbows jarred as the pickup bumped up the track.

Fenna fought to calm her breathing and tried not to retch as the oily cloth pressed against her lips and teeth with each breath. Dark scenarios raced through her mind.

She struggled onto her knees and half slid, half rolled to the gate at the rear of the pickup. It pressed into her back when the vehicle crunched through another pit. As the driver accelerated out of the hole, Fenna arched her back, straightened her legs and pitched backward out of the bed of the pickup. She landed on her shoulder, gritting her teeth at the crack of bone on the compacted grit and rock of the track. The vehicle continued and Fenna scrabbled to her feet.

"Move," she breathed and stumbled to one side. She continued in the same direction until the ground disappeared beneath her, she then fell a metre and a half. She laughed as she landed on her feet. Grit and dirt tumbled onto her fingers and she explored the earth wall behind her back and leaned into it. Fenna twisted her head for sounds of the vehicle and thought she heard the muffled shouts of men searching both sides of the track.

"Fuck," said a man. His voice was pitched higher than the others. Fenna didn't recognise it. But a second voice caused her stomach to tighten.

"She won't get far." Fenna recognised the southern drawl of the Gunnery Sergeant. She held her breath and leaned into the earth, willing it to envelop her. "Let's get back."

"Gunney?" said another man. "We can't leave her out here. What if she talks?"

"About what, dick wad? She knows nothing, there's nothing to tell," the Gunney said. Fenna could almost feel the tremor of his boots as he walked around the vehicle. He raised his voice. "Konstabel," he said. "Do yourself a favour. Stay the fuck away from the girl."

Fenna held her breath and tilted her head to listen, willing her heart to slow down, and for the pulse of blood in her ears to quieten. At the sound of doors slamming she let out one ragged breath after another. As the pickup bumped and grinded through a four-point turn and then accelerated down the track, Fenna became aware of her bladder. She waited until the vehicle was gone and flexed her wrists within the plastic ties. She almost laughed at how loose they were. *The plastic is too thick for small wrists*, she thought as she wormed her left hand free of the loop. She closed her eyes and was, for once, grateful of her skinny frame and low body fat.

I might have a flat chest, but being skinny has its advantages, she mused, ignoring the taste of motor oil inside the black cloth sack, she raised her hands, brushed the dirt from the skin, and felt for the plastic tie around her neck. With all the movement, from bouncing around the bed of the pickup and tumbling over the gate and off the track, the cloth skirt at the opening of the sack was loose. She pulled it off, tossing it to one side as she took a gulp of air. Fenna took two more long, deep, breaths before running her hands over her body to check that the bumps and scratches were nothing more than superficial.

"I got off lightly," she whispered and sighed.

"That," said a voice with an unmistakeable lengthening of the letter A, "is a matter of opinion, Konstabel." The shadow of the Gunnery Sergeant grew as he left his concealed position behind a boulder and took a single step closer to Fenna. She held her breath as he scuffed the toe of his boots in the dirt. "What do you say, *bitch*?"

Fenna didn't trust her voice to carry over the first wave of tremors rippling through her body. She clenched her fists and let her arms fall to her sides.

She took another breath when she realised the Gunnery Sergeant had not moved since he startled her.

"You didn't go back in the truck," she said.

The Gunney shook his head. The white of the moon glistened in his eyes, his pupils huge, round, and predatory.

"Smart."

"I've been around the block," he said. "I know a few things."

"Enough to send your buddies back to base."

"No witnesses."

Fenna nodded, slowly. *I've been here before*, she reminded herself. *But last time I had a gun.* She let out an even breath and the Gunney caught her staring at his waist. He made a point of turning on the spot before facing her again, his hands folded in front of his crotch.

"I'm not armed, Konstabel," he said.

"I can see that," she said. "I'll be missed."

"Accidents happen."

"But I'm not American. My country would start an inquiry, ask questions."

"You don't have accidents in Denmark?" the Gunney laughed. "I find that hard to believe."

Fenna tried a new tack. "But there are people at the base," she said, looking in the direction of the arc lights blazing in the distance. Cones of light pointed inward, outward, but nowhere near Fenna. She was in the dark, again.

"Oh, that's right," he said and took a single step forward. He stopped when Fenna flinched. The Gunney smiled. "Your friend. The *Canadian?*"

"Yes," said Fenna.

"I know a lot of Canadians," he said. "I go hunting there a couple times a year."

Fenna waited. She worked on her breathing as the Gunnery Sergeant took another small step toward her. She reached one hand behind her back and felt the earth wall just centimetres away. She took a handful of dirt and slid her hand to her side.

"He's been recalled."

"Fuck," Fenna breathed.

"Seems they… the real Canadians… have some issues with double agents. Just like we do."

"I don't understand?"

"You don't? Then you're not here to spy on us? It's just a coincidence then?"

"Coincidence?"

"You meeting with the girl, late at night, in the canteen."

"Alice…"

"Shit, Konstabel," the Gunney ran his hand through the tight stubble that was his hair. "Don't they teach you anything at Danish Spy School?" He lowered his hand and slipped it inside his pocket. When he pulled it out, his fingers were wrapped around a short blade with a thick metal ring, like a trigger guard, protecting his index finger. "Let's imagine that this," he said and waved the knife at the desert scrub surrounding them. "This is Spy School and Rule One is…" he paused. "Well, it's gotta be the most important fucking rule there is."

"Okay," Fenna forced herself to focus on both of the Gunney's hands, his stance, and the look in his eyes, and not be distracted by the knife flashing in the moonlight. "Rule One," she said, as she leaned forward, changing the balance of her weight from her heels to her toes.

"Rule One is never give information voluntarily, and never ever *after* you've just been told that your enemy knows you are alone."

"Are you my enemy, Gunnery Sergeant?" Fenna asked, her voice level, despite the thunder in her chest.

"Hah," he snorted. Fenna noticed that the knife sank as he shifted on his feet. "What do *you* think, Konstabel?"

"I think," Fenna tightened her fingers around the dirt in her right hand. "We've moved beyond dancing."

"Yeah," the Gunney drawled, "that's about right."

He lunged forward and Fenna released a cloud of grit into his face.

Chapter 8

The Gunnery Sergeant spat as the desert dirt clung to his lips and caked his eyes, blinding him for a brief moment, long enough to piss him off, and just long enough for Fenna to strike. She pushed off the earth wall behind her and let the momentum carry her left fist, middle knuckle extended, between the Gunney's arms and into his solar plexus. Fenna cried out as she felt her knuckle crack. She caught her breath as he faltered onto his heels. Fenna ignored the pain in her hand, bent her arm, and swung her elbow up, screaming as it caught the top of his chin, the impact snapping his head up and back. She reeled and stopped to regain her balance as her opponent stumbled one more step, and then a second, away from her.

Press your advantage, Fenna imagined Nicklas would say, and she did, slamming the toe of her boot into the Gunney's crotch as she cradled her left hand in her right. The Gunnery Sergeant grunted but only for a moment. He twisted his knife hand, palm upward, extended his reach and slashed at Fenna's calf muscle as she withdrew her foot. The knife nicked at her skin and caught on the collar of her desert boot, startling her. The Gunney recovered his stance, shifted his weight onto the balls of his feet, and lurched toward her. Fenna moved backward only to catch her feet in the exposed roots of desert scrub and sprawl to the ground. She cried out in pain as she broke her fall with her injured hand.

Fenna gritted her teeth and rolled toward the earth wall as the Gunney pounced. He cursed when he landed on the ground and not on Fenna's back as he had planned. Fenna scrabbled to her feet, ducking to the right as the Gunney slammed his knife hand toward her, burying the blade in the earth. She wondered at his aim and, after a quick glance at his face, she realised his eyes were still smarting and the fine desert dust was clogging his vision.

You'll always be weaker than your opponent, Nicklas' voice reminded her. *Be smart, Fenna*, she added. Fenna spun around the Gunney's back as he worried the knife out of the earth wall. She pummelled his kidneys with her right fist, and, in a move that was as surprising as it was savage, she butted him in the left eye with her forehead as he twisted toward her.

"Bitch," he said, and then she butted him again, and a third time until her head began to throb and the blood from the tear in his skin above his eye blinded him once more. The Gunney pushed at Fenna with a blind sweep of his left arm as he jabbed the knife where he thought her body should be. Fenna moved around him and punched him in the kidneys again, the thunder of her heart and roar of the blood through her temple lost in a funnel of intensity that guided her hand and purpose. *Put him down*, she mouthed, again and again until the Gunnery Sergeant sank to his knees.

Keep going, Fenna. Nicklas' voice said from somewhere in the desert, off to her left, maybe her right – she resisted the urge to look. *He's down. Keep him down.* Fenna bit back the pain and shoved the Gunney's head down with her left hand. The stubble of his hair rasped against her palm. She curled the fingers of her right hand into a fist and punched the base of his neck. She did it again, her left hand creeping down the Gunney's forehead and curling beneath his brows to keep his head up as she hit him one more time. The big man slumped to the floor and Fenna took a breath.

She took a step backward and flicked her hair from her eyes. Striped with blood, sweat, and desert dust, her fringe clung to her forehead and she wiped it to one side. Her fingers trembled and she clasped them together only to realise it wasn't just her fingers, but her whole body. She felt her knees, twitching to an unfamiliar rhythm, the pulse of the desert, of battle, and her first real *Sonoran Shuffle*.

You know what you have to do, Fenna, Nicklas' voice chided her.

"I know."

He would have done the same to you.

"Yes," she said, and then, angrily, "I know."

Then do it.

Fenna took a single breath and held it as she stomped forward. Her knees thumped into the dirt beside the Gunnery Sergeant. Fenna exhaled as she reached across his body and yanked at the knife looped around his index finger. She swore as the trigger ring caught on his knuckle, forcing her to lean across him and use both hands to pull it free. She pushed off him and swallowed as he let out a single groan.

Hurry, Fenna.

"Fuck off, Nicklas," she waved her hand in the dark space behind her.

Get it done.

"I know," she said as she sank onto her heels. Fenna could feel the grip of her desert boots as they gnawed at the thin layer of fat in the flesh of her bottom. She wiped a tear from her cheek with the back of her left hand and cursed at the pain of the forgotten knuckle.

Fenna.

"Yes," she said and reached for the Gunney's shoulder.

Kill him.

"Yes," Fenna heaved the Gunnery Sergeant onto his back. She curled the finger into the trigger guard of the knife and thrust her right hand forward. The tip of the blade slipped into the Gunney's windpipe and Fenna gasped at the burst of air that slipped out as she withdrew it. The Gunney's eyes opened. Fenna pressed her left hand over them and jabbed the knife into his throat until his chest was bloody, his lungs were empty, and the desert was still but for the soft sobs that tumbled out of her body.

Good, Fenna, Nicklas' voice said. *Good. It is done.*

Fenna half imagined Dina to drift through the night and arrive on a desert wind to admonish her, but the Greenlander was silent and unseen, for once. Mikael was absent too. Her demons, it seemed, had decided to leave her alone with her thoughts. Only Nicklas was determined to plague her, and he wasn't even dead.

Fenna, his voice said. *You need to move.*

"I know," she curled her arms around her knees, her bottom cooling on the desert floor. The knife, sticky and sweetened with blood, dangled from the crook in her finger. "Give me a moment. Please."

A moment then. No more.

Fenna let the desert's breath lap at her face and twist the fringe of her hair. The blood dried as she let one moment pass into another. She moved her chin up and down her right knee with exaggerated movements of her jaw, as if the silent shapes she formed might become words and tell her what to do.

"I killed a man," she said, as her stomach spasmed and she retched on the desert floor. Fenna wiped her mouth with the back of her hand and flicked her eyes toward the Gunney's bloody body. Now the act of burying him forced her into action. She pushed his body tight against the earth wall, clawing at it until he was buried in a thin layer of desert. She rubbed the last of the dirt from her palms onto her bloody fatigues and slipped the Gunney's knife inside her belt. The handle pressed into the small of Fenna's back as she walked and she was surprised how reassuring it was.

You have a plan then?

Nicklas again. Fenna ignored him until she was back on the road and headed in the direction of the base. It shone like a beacon before her. She preferred the shadows.

Fenna?

"Yes, I have a plan, Nicklas," she said aloud. Her voice fragmented on the wind. It was stronger now, flicking at her fringe. It felt good.

And what is it?

If Fenna had wondered at the personification of her thoughts, she didn't let it show. Her face was set, and determined. She picked idly at a patch of blood drying on her cheek. Her left hand dangled by her side, as she adjusted her step to the throbbing in her knuckle.

It's not broken, you know.

"What?"

Your finger. The knuckle is dislocated. That's all.

65

"Oh," Fenna said and stopped. She wrapped her right hand around her middle digit, gnawed her bottom lip into a bight of flesh and bit down as she pulled and straightened her finger.

Better?

Fenna imagined Nicklas smiling as she stifled a stream of curses. She tasted blood on her lip, spat on the ground.

"Nicklas," she said.

Yes?

"Fuck off."

He was silent then and Fenna's thoughts were her own. She needed to plan her entry onto the base so that she could collect her gear. The carbine could be a problem.

It's too big, she thought. *I can't conceal it, and I can't fly out of here with it.*

Flying. The thought of getting away unnoticed was her primary goal. Flying out of the States was a distant and luxurious dream.

"Jarnvig, he'll get me out. He needs me."

That thought occupied Fenna the last hundred metres to the perimeter of the base. She crouched behind a patch of thick desert scrub at the first rise of the track she had been bumped along only a few hours earlier. She wondered where the Gunney's soldiers might be, but a quick scan of the immediate area revealed no sign of the pickup. There was little activity beyond the blue glow of a monitor projected onto the far wall of the guard's office. She selected her route and counted the paces she would have to take, using the shadow patches beneath the eaves of the offices, the canteen, and the barracks. She took a breath, stood up, and moved.

The first patch of open ground would be dangerous. The glare of the lights threw her shadow in a slow arc on the ground as she moved out of one light sphere and into another. She ran, her breath escaping from her lungs through pursed lips as she reached the deck of her barracks. The first of the bruised boards creaked, she waited three heartbeats, and then opened the screen door and walked inside.

Her gear was still strewn across her bed, the rifle rucking the blanket into ridges, the spotting scope and sight still in their cases. She padded across to the desk, opened the top drawer and pulled out the LOMROG field report. She tucked it inside the desert-ravaged daypack that was hanging by dusty straps from the back of the chair. She put several items into the pack, pausing at sounds beyond the walls. First, the yip of a desert fox, then the slap of the desert wind as it toyed with a loose shutter on the barrack opposite her own. She crossed to the bed and slipped the sight and scope inside the pack, the leather was warm beneath her fingertips.

She lingered over the M1 carbine, her fingers brushing the folding metal stock. A slow smile tugged at the corner of her mouth as she remembered Maratse and their wild dash across the sea ice, the policeman grinning behind the wheel, revelling in the madness of it all.

She packed spare clothes, together with energy bars and a bottle of water. She carried the pack around the bed, knelt in front of her footlocker and spun the combination lock. She rested the lid against the foot of the bed and tucked her personal effects, passport and wallet inside the pack. The memory of the handle of the Gunney's knife pressing into her back made her pause for a moment, her forehead resting in the crook of her arm as she gripped the locker lid. She took a breath and closed it. Then, closing the buckles of the pack she slipped it over her shoulders. She took one last look at the carbine on the bed before tightening the laces of her boots and walking toward the door.

The desert night welcomed her with a flick of dust that brushed her trouser legs and deposited another layer of Yuma dirt on her boots. She looked beyond the administration block of the DTC and squinted at the gate in the distance. She shook her head, tightened the straps of her pack and looked toward the track she had walked in on, the one with the body she had buried halfway along it.

Her first kill.

"But maybe not my last," she said, quietly, tasting the desert on her tongue. It was time to leave the States, it was time to go north.

Chapter 9

Shadows grew in the pre-dawn light, the personnel on the base would soon wake. There was no sign of the Gunney's thugs as she stepped onto the deck. She gave a moment's thought to Alice, picturing her briefly before tossing the image aside.

"Get it together, Fenna," she whispered, her words blown away by the desert wind. Another step and she was at the edge of the deck. She scanned the buildings and roads around her for sign of the black SUVs, synonymous with the young girl and the mystery surrounding her education and training.

Fenna's backpack pressed the handle of the knife into her back. She slipped her hand beneath the pack, removed it, curled her finger into the circular guard beneath the blade and took a breath; the surface of the knife and the handle still tacky with blood.

The sound of the knife plunging in and out of the Gunney's throat festered in Fenna's mind, the soft cut of flesh, the rasp of air as it raspberried out of the man's lungs. *They will be looking for him soon*, she reminded herself.

A second voice pushed the image of her first kill out of her mind.

Time to go, Fenna.

"I know," she said, with a slight nod. "But the girl…"

Was never your concern.

Fenna shook her head and gripped the knife in her right hand, she could feel the layer of blood pressing into the creases of her palm.

And neither was Dina. You have to let them go. Save yourself.

69

"For the good of the mission? Hah," she said, her voice low. "That's Jarnvig talking."

And what if it is? You need to move, Fenna. Now.

The sky lightened, the shadows lengthened, and Fenna stepped off the deck and slipped between the barracks toward the track. She skirted the offices and, ducking between the shafts of light she left the base. She stopped at the first rise and looked back.

"I'm sorry, Alice," she said, closing her eyes for a moment before tightening the straps of her pack and walking off the track and onto a game trail. It had been widened by the passage of soft desert boots, the kind preferred by snipers and spotters, the same as the ones she wore. She knew it led over the mountain, and that two more – one twisting east, and the second west – would lead to the road. Fenna had already decided on Phoenix, but a payphone at a truck stop or diner was her priority. She slipped the knife into the space between her belt and her cargo trousers and picked up the pace heading west.

As the gradient increased she relaxed, her breathing easing into a familiar rhythm. She let the rigor of the trail free her mind, suppressing her thoughts and the chiding from Nicklas, focusing instead on the desert and the potential for ambush and capture. She spotted the dust of the first roving patrol – four men, lightly armed, returning to base – and altered her course, using the contours of the slope and the tracks of desert predators to box the patrol and slip past them unnoticed. They seemed relaxed, she reasoned, and guessed that the Gunney had yet to be missed. Fenna turned west and glimpsed the highway, as she crested one rise before dipping into a gully.

She paused in a patch of dense scrub and removed her pack. She pulled out the water bottle and took a sip, her eyes scanning the desert. Her boots were dusty, blotched with dark patches of blood. She knelt down to smear dirt over the evidence of her kill, wrinkling her nose as she smelt her stale sweat. Fenna lifted her hand and studied the dirt and blood beneath her nails. She spared a little water to rinse the tips of her fingers, sucking the stubborn blood from her thumbnail.

Time, Fenna.

"I know," she whispered.

Sun's almost up.

Fenna screwed the cap of her water bottle and shoved it inside the pack. She took out the spotting scope and placed it on the ground, shrugging the pack onto her shoulders and tightening the straps. Then, as she bent down for the scope, there was a sound of stones trickling down the side of the slope, about four metres from her position. She sank to the ground, one hand on the scope, the other reaching for the knife in her belt.

She peered into the scrub, her heart pumping, her breathing shallow. She willed her body to still. At the sound of a second trickle of stones, Fenna held her breath, her eyes lasered on the area immediately in front of her.

A small black nose pressed out of the scrub, followed by the sleek contoured cheeks of the desert fox. Fenna kept still but for the twitch of a smile on her lips. The fox, one paw in the air, stared at her and she was rewarded with a moment of wild curiosity wrapped in lupine eyes that reminded her of her sledge team, of Lucifer, Betty and the wolf. The wind

71

dusted down the side of the slope and flicked the blonde fringe from her forehead. The fox bolted and Fenna let out her breath. She checked the periphery, relaxed her grip on the handle of the knife and slowly straightened into a standing position. The sounds of the fox receded and she picked her way up the slope, settling into a prone position to study the highway below her.

She scanned the highway through the scope, following the path of an old and bruised Ford Bronco, as it turned into a diner roughly one kilometre north of her position. *I can be there before he finishes his coffee*, she reckoned, and pressed the rubber caps onto the ends of the scope.

Be smart, Fenna.

She checked her surroundings before picking a route to the highway, leaving her concealed position and moving swiftly down the slope, small clouds of dust billowing up from beneath her heels, like cobras rearing for a strike. The clouds dissipated, the dust twitching into the wind, invisible to all but the sniper team the Gunney had ordered to watch the road before he had bundled Fenna into the bed of the pickup. She didn't see them, nor think to look for them as her goal shifted, and time trumped caution. She let the terrain determine her speed and raced down the desert hill and ran parallel to the highway.

She was in the sniper's sights as she crossed the highway and settled into a jog toward the diner, the spotter calling out the ranges as she closed on the dusty parking lot. A Greyhound bus saved her, throwing up dust and grit as it passed. She squinted through the bus's wake and pressed on as the sniper lifted his finger from the trigger and waited for his spotter to call it in. She slowed to a brisk walk past the Bronco. The sniper watched as she smoothed the worst of the desert from clothes, slapping the dust from her palms before she reached for the door and entered the diner.

You can't stay long. You have to keep moving.

"I know," she mouthed, as she walked inside. She smiled at the waitress and looked around the tables, nodding at the man she presumed to be driver of the Bronco, his cap, shirt and jeans as ragged as his car, his face as dirty as her own.

"You're up early," the waitress said. "Coffee before you look at the menu?"

"Sure," Fenna said, as she dropped her pack from her back and slipped onto a seat at the table nearest the door. She brushed her hair from her forehead with one hand as she picked up the menu with the other.

"I'll be right back," the waitress said and walked to the counter. Fenna was tempted by the thought of breakfast, but a glance at her watch reminded her she needed to keep moving.

"So," the waitress placed a large mug in front of Fenna and filled it half full of coffee. She reached into her apron and tumbled tubes of sugar and creamer onto the table. "Anything else?"

"Um, what's fast?"

"Fast? You in a hurry, darlin'?" she peered at Fenna's face. "Some fella comin' after you?" The waitress flicked her eyes at the parking area beyond the smoke-hazed glass behind Fenna.

"Maybe," Fenna said and shrugged.

"The chef has eggs on toast, ready to go. How about that?"

73

"Yes. That'll be fine." Fenna cupped her hands around the mug, sipping at the coffee as the waitress scribbled a note on her pad. When she walked away Fenna turned her attention to the driver. She noticed he had finished his breakfast. *Damn*, she thought, only to relax when he lifted his hand for more coffee. He nodded in her direction as the waitress wove between the empty Formica tables to give him a refill.

As Fenna turned to look out of the window, a blur of movement in the distance on the highway caught her eye. She recognised the familiar shape of the black SUVs she had seen on the base and tapped her fingers on the table. The driver coughed as her drumming increased to match the tempo of her heartbeat.

"Hey," he said, but Fenna ignored him. She scanned the room, the parking lot, the desert to either side of the highway. Her head flicked from side to side, oblivious to the man until she noticed him standing beside her, the mug of coffee in his hand, a frown on his forehead, and, to Fenna's delight, his car keys held loosely between wrinkled fingers. "You okay?" he said and leaned down toward Fenna.

Fenna looked up and studied the man for a second.

"Your eggs are ready," the waitress called out, making her way over to the table.

Fenna turned her attention back to the driver, grabbed the top loop of her pack and swiped the man's keys. "Sorry," she said, as she twisted out of his reach. The waitress stumbled as Fenna charged past her, through the door and onto the parking lot. She could hear the man give chase as she sprinted to the Bronco. Fenna wrenched the door open and tossed her pack onto the passenger seat. She slammed the door shut and thrust the key into the ignition, grateful as the engine caught on the first turn.

"Hey, what the hell do you think you are doing?" the man shouted, as he reached for the door handle. Fenna looked straight ahead, shoved the gearstick into drive and slammed her foot on the accelerator. The Bronco lurched forward as its owner banged on the side of the vehicle. Fenna glanced at him in the mirror as he gave chase, stopping and wheezing at the entrance to the parking lot. She accelerated onto the highway and bumped the Bronco over the central reservation and onto the northbound lane.

She straightened the vehicle and willed it to go faster than the SUVs she could see in the rear-view mirror. While the Bronco lurched from gear to gear, the SUVs seemed to glide along the tarmac, the wheels barely kissing the surface. Fenna spared one second for a wistful thought of the carbine lying on her bed in the barracks before tightening her grip on the wheel and wrenching it to the right. The Bronco protested as she slammed on the brakes and skidded onto a track leading deep into the desert.

"Come on," she screamed, as the Bronco juddered over the first twenty metres. She glanced down at the gearstick, shifted it into first and whooped as the old Ford remembered its purpose and bit into the track with chunky tyres and an automobile heart that was part combustion engine part warhorse.

Fenna prayed that the SUVs were as unsuited to off-roading as they were suited to the highway. She whooped again and pushed the Bronco through second and into third, the gravel pebbling the underside and panels reminding her of bullets. Then the rear window shattered beneath a long burst of automatic weapons fire.

Chapter 10

Fenna grabbed the steering wheel and ducked as safety glass plastered the back of the seats, scratched at her neck and lodged in the tangled strands of her dirty hair. She took a breath, recovered, and stomped on the accelerator, the Bronco lurched forward and Fenna swung the aging off-roader around a sharp bend to the right. A second burst of 9mm blistered the desert to the left of the vehicle, dirt and dust pluming under the impact. The track dropped beneath the wheels and Fenna guided the Bronco in a mad descent to the bottom of a shallow gulley. It handled well despite its age and Fenna spared a thought for the owner, only to forget him again as the lead SUV loomed large in the rear-view mirror and Fenna heard the growl of its engine beneath its massive hood. She risked a glance over her shoulder and through the shattered window but the windows of the SUV were smoked and the driver remained anonymous. *But no less lethal,* she surmised and willed the Bronco to go faster.

"Come on, girl," she yelled and leaned into the steering wheel.

The back end of the Bronco reared as the SUV rammed into it. Fenna yelled a second time as the Bronco threatened to flip, the rear wheels spinning free in the air almost a metre higher than the hood. She felt a twinge in her back as the Bronco touched down and the worn suspension failed to compensate. Fenna recovered, gritted her teeth and shuffled the sole of her boot back onto the accelerator pedal and knuckled down, riding the Bronco as it bucked down the track.

Fenna.

The voice caught her by surprise and she flicked her eyes to her right as if Nicklas was in the passenger seat beside her. She imagined him to be nonchalant, the epitome of calm, a true inspector of the Royal Canadian Mounted Police. And then she remembered he was a spy, a PET agent like herself. She flipped him a mental finger and ignored him.

Fenna. The road.

"Fuck off, Nicklas. I'm busy," she said and gripped the wheel. A quick glance in the rear-view mirror confirmed what she already knew – the SUV was still there, black and ominous. She spared an idle thought as to who might be behind the wheel. *Was it the Gunney's men, or Alice's minders?* And then Nicklas' voice punctured the thought and captured her attention.

End of the road, Fenna.

"What?" Fenna said and looked up. "Oh."

Fenna eased up on the accelerator. The receding growl of the SUVs motor confirmed that her pursuers knew she was cornered, trapped – again. She scanned the track as the Bronco sped down the last five hundred metres. There was a wooden building, shanty-like, on either side of the track, and a larger structure – a tired and worn plywood cabin – in the centre. It marked the end of the road. Fenna thought for a second, gripped the wheel and accelerated toward it.

What are you doing, Fenna?

"I could ask myself the same question," she said. "But somehow I think I already did."

And?

Fenna grinned, and, in that moment, for one

joyous second, she forgot the wake of dead in her near and distant past, she ignored the chiding of her subconscious. In that brief moment, and for however long she had left before the end, Fenna chose to live.

"I'm tired of running."

But the cabin?

"Tired of being chased by men," she flicked her eyes to the mirror. The lead SUV had pulled back, the second had stopped, blocked the track and disgorged men with long rifles from its interior. Now all her focus was on the track and the cabin at the end of it.

You're not going to…

"Yes," she said. "And you had better get with the programme or get the fuck out." Fenna accelerated, squeezing the last, the richest, and the most precious drops of power from the Bronco's combustion engine – a gas-guzzling product of the eighties. "C'mon, girl," Fenna said and slapped the steering wheel with her palm. "Let's see what you've got."

Grit blasted the side panels of the Bronco. The motor roared. The cabin loomed. Fenna yelled.

"Do it," she screamed and shut her eyes as the front wheels of the Bronco bumped up and over the shallow deck with a crunch of desert-husked wood. The timber walls imploded in a cloud of splinters and dust. Nails, embedded in the panels and freed from the structure, clawed at the Bronco, as it careened through the one-roomed hovel, carrying the prospector's bed clinched beneath the bumper. Fenna opened her eyes a second before the Bronco burst through the rear of the structure and bounced onto a narrow ledge of flat ground. The bed crumpled under the front wheels, a blanket wrapped around the left wheel, its tattered tail twisting and slapping at the driver's door.

"Fuck," Fenna said, as the desert dropped from under the front of the Bronco and she was airborne again, her foot pounding on the brake pedal, her head slamming the top of the steering wheel as the old Ford bounced down a boulder-strewn slope and into a dry river bed. Fenna screamed the whole way down, biting her tongue and tasting blood as the Bronco's hood concertinaed upon impact with the dry bank of the river. The engine stalled and she slumped back in the seat. She blew the air from her lungs until the pressure in her chest told her she was alive and that she needed to breathe.

"Okay then," she said, after a long breath of dust-drenched air. She opened the door and slid out onto the river bed, leaning against the side of the vehicle until her legs stopped trembling. Fenna looked up at the splintered remains of the cabin, cursing at the sight of two men scrambling down the slope, rifles bobbing in their grasp. "Time to go," she said and climbed back into the Bronco and slammed the door.

The engine caught on the second turn of the key and Fenna blessed the ground its owner walked on. She shifted into reverse, cringing at the sound of the suspension grinding on the axle. With a last glance at the men behind her, she shifted into first and tickled the accelerator with her boot. The Bronco limped forward under protest, the screech and grind of metal on metal increasing in tempo and pitch as Fenna willed her bloody and beaten charge forward, drifting to the centre of the river bed. The Bronco bled oil in a spattered and broken line behind it, an easy trail to follow, but Fenna dismissed the thought in favour of the lone house on the horizon.

"They must have a phone," she said and shifted into second gear. The Bronco responded with a reluctant judder and the hiss of water boiling out of a burst radiator. Oil purged from the motor as Fenna accelerated into third. She ignored the crack of rounds as the men behind her punctured the tail gate with well-placed shots designed to intimidate her and remind her that they had not given up, whoever they were. She dipped her head to look up at the house at the top of the slope, in the bend of the dry river.

Fenna drove the Bronco as far as she could before it died, parched of oil and water, another desiccated husk of life succumbed to the desert. She pulled her pack from where it was lodged in front of the passenger seat and considered her own fate, preferring the thought of a quick cold death to a dry, hot one.

"Thanks, girl," she said as she climbed out of the Bronco. She tugged her pack onto her shoulders and jogged to the base of the slope before picking her way up and around the boulders to the house. The phone lines strung from the roof were a good sign. She opened the screen door and broke the lock of the main door with a kick. Once inside, she squinted in the gloom of what she imagined was a seldom-used office belonging to the highway maintenance company, the heavy jackets and dusty boots confirmed as much. Fenna found the phone on the desk and lifted the receiver. She dialled zero for an outside line and punched in the number she had memorised so many months earlier. The line crackled and buzzed, as if protesting the distance of the call, and then she heard a familiar voice answer with the flat guttural tone of Danish. For that moment it was the most beautiful voice Fenna could ever remember hearing.

"Jarnvig?" she said and waited.

"Yes?"

"It's Fenna."

Jarnvig grunted and Fenna imagined him shifting position. She glanced at her watch and realised, with the time difference, he was likely finishing his shift. It would be early evening in Denmark.

"I thought we agreed you would never call this number."

"We did."

"And yet?" he said and added a silent rebuke in the weight and length of his pause. "What do you need?"

"Help. A ticket out of here. Safe passage…"

"Stop, Fenna," he paused again as Fenna took a breath. "Where are you?"

"In a house, north of the base."

"Why?"

"I killed someone," she said, tapping her hand and flicking her gaze from one window to the other as she waited for Jarnvig to process the information.

"Anyone important?" he said.

"You're not going to ask why?"

"I would say *who* is more important right now. If I know who, then I might be able to help."

"Might? Fuck, Jarnvig…"

"Who was it, Konstabel?"

Fenna told him. "It was me or him," she added.

"Which begs me to ask the question *why*?"

"Because of the girl, Al…"

"I don't need to know her name." Jarnvig cut her off. "I thought I ordered you to leave her alone?"

"Nicklas said…"

"He was relaying my orders. Damn it, Fenna…"

Fenna whirled at the sound of gravel crunching beneath what she imagined were large military boots outside the house.

"I don't have much time," she said.

"And neither do I," Jarnvig said and cursed. "I need you in Nuuk, not some American Black Site in the middle of the fucking desert."

"Jarnvig," Fenna said and stared at the window.

"What?"

"They're here."

A tall man, his biceps larger than Fenna's neck, steadied his M4 carbine in one hand as he waved his finger at Fenna, motioning for her to hang up.

"Stall them. I need time."

"I can't," Fenna said, as the man's partner entered from the door at the front of the house. Fenna turned in a slow circle to face him. He stalked around the furniture toward her.

"I'll get someone to you, Konstabel. Just hang in there. Keep breathing."

Breathing was fast becoming an art form. The man yanked the phone from her hand and pulled a black hood from his belt.

"Put it on," he said, as he tossed it at Fenna. She caught it and held it in front of her. "Now," he said as the man with the M4 walked in.

"We could talk about this," Fenna said and twisted the hood between her fingers.

"Tell that to the Gunney," the man said.

"He's here?" Fenna said and arched her eyebrow.

"Funny," the man said and drew his pistol from the holster attached to his chest rig. "Now put on the fucking hood, Konstabel, before I put a bullet through your pretty little skull."

"Do it," his partner said and jabbed the barrel of his M4 into Fenna's shoulder. Fenna resisted the temptation to twist and grab the carbine, favouring instead the brief moment of calm before the inevitable storm.

"All right," she said and lifted the hood to her head. Nicklas, she mused, was silent for a change, and it was then that she realised he had always been silent, and that she truly was alone. The man behind her tugged her pack from her back as soon as her head was covered. Fenna stumbled forward and into the butt of her captor's pistol, as she fell into another kind of blackness, one that she knew only too well.

Chapter 11

The thick hood muffled the sounds of activity inside the SUV, but Fenna knew the men were rifling through her gear as the driver drove off the gravel strip in front of the house and onto the highway. Fenna toyed with the ends of the plastic strips the men had used to bind her wrists. She had lost count of the number of times she had been bound in this way. It was almost laughable.

"Laugh it up, Princess. We'll see how funny you think it is when we start your interrogation."

"You don't have to interrogate me. I'll talk."

"Sure you will, but we want to have a little fun first," the man said. Fenna recognised his voice and pictured the man with the M4, the one who had poked her with the barrel.

"Perks of the job," said the other man. Fenna heard him grunt and flick through the pages of the LOMROG report. "What's this?"

"Bedtime reading," she said, and tensed in anticipation of the man striking her, but he seemed more interested in the report than her sarcasm. Fenna realised that they had yet to lay a hand on her. The thought festered in her mind beneath the hood, occupying her thoughts and distracting her from the driver's curses as he slammed on the brakes. Fenna's head pounded into the passenger seat, as the men opened doors and leapt out onto the highway. She could hear the click and clack of weapons being readied and the concise and confident commands the men exchanged.

"What's going on?" she asked, only to realise that the SUV was empty. The engine growled and she twisted her head to the left to hear the growl of the second SUV just a few metres away.

"Behind us," a voice said. Fenna assumed it was one of the men from the second SUV. Fenna dipped her head, pinched the hood between her palms and tugged it off. She blinked in the noon-day sun and scanned her environment in all directions.

The SUVs were blocked by three white SUVs in front and two vans behind. Her captors were outnumbered at least two to one, and the desert air was heavy with the taint of testosterone and tension. Fenna slipped out of the SUV and leaned against the side.

"Get back in the vehicle, Princess. This will all be over in a heartbeat." The man Fenna realised was the leader didn't even look at her, his finger feathering the trigger of his M4 carbine as he leaned into the hinges of the passenger door. The driver assumed a similar position on the opposite side of the vehicle.

"Who are they?" she asked.

"Unknown, but I'm guessing they're not friendly," he said.

"Not to you anyway." Fenna looked beyond the roadblock and noticed a police patrol car slowing traffic to a stop a few hundred metres further up the highway. A quick glance behind her confirmed that they had done the same in both directions. The operation had a surgical Scandinavian feel about it, *or Canadian*, she realised as she scanned the men for a glimpse of Nicklas. They were wearing masks and helmets, but she recognised the stance of one man, the way he held his automatic rifle as he approached the SUVs.

"That's far enough," the leader said. "Unless you

want lead for lunch?"

"Just want to talk," the man said and Fenna smiled as she recognised his voice.

"So talk," the leader said, before quietening his voice and addressing the driver. "If this fool so much as breathes wrong…"

"Got it, boss."

Fenna watched as Nicklas tugged his mask down to his neck, slung his rifle and removed his helmet. He waved and indicated that he intended to approach.

"You ditch your weapon, you can come closer."

"All right," Nicklas said and lowered his rifle to the ground. "But I'm keeping my sidearm."

"Sure you are. All buttoned up and snug in that fancy holster." The leader slung his weapon over his shoulder and rested his arms on the sill of the open window. "What do you want to talk about?"

"The girl," Nicklas said and nodded at Fenna.

"Okay."

"Both of them."

The leader tensed. Fenna watched as he straightened his back. He moved one hand from the window to the pistol strapped in a holster around his right thigh. "You might want to reconsider that, Inspector."

"So you know who I am? That's good," he said and took another step closer. Fenna couldn't see the leader's face, but she doubted he returned Nicklas' smile. He unsnapped the holster and closed his fingers around the pistol grip. Fenna shuffled forward, closer, but a voice behind her whispered for her to stop.

"Let my boss talk, unhindered," the man with the M4 said, "and I might just let you live." Fenna nodded. "Good. Now let's hear what your boyfriend has to say."

"Let's hear it, RCMP, before I lose my sense of bipartisanship." Fenna noted the man's hand did not stray from his pistol.

"My friend, the Konstabel," Nicklas said, with a gesture toward Fenna, "is too curious for her own good."

"On that we agree."

"But she knows nothing. I can promise you that."

"Promises? Shit, Inspector, promises mean nothing to me."

"That's right, of course," Nicklas said and nodded. He looked up at a glint of metal high up in the sky. "Are they with you?"

"Unlikely." The leader glanced at the drone circling above them. He looked at Nicklas. "We're wasting time. Get to it."

"The Konstabel is important to us, to the group I represent. She is needed in the north."

"And?"

"And I have been instructed to inform you that, when the time comes, you have our support."

"Really?"

"Yes."

"We have your support?"

"Yes," Nicklas said and crossed his hands in front of the buckle on his webbing belt.

"You can confirm that?" said the leader, as the man guarding Fenna fidgeted. The tension ratcheted up another notch and the leader slipped the pistol from his holster.

"You're going to get a call. Any second now."

"Boss?" Fenna's guard said, as the leader's mobile

phone burred in his pocket. Fenna watched as he used his left hand to answer the call, holstering the pistol as he listened and nodded.

"Let's go," the leader said, as he pocketed his mobile and slid into the passenger seat. The man behind Fenna shoved her away from the SUV, reached inside, and threw her pack onto the highway. The wheels were moving as he tossed the LOMROG report out of the window. Nicklas' men made a hole in the roadblock as the SUVs roared past him and disappeared in the direction of the DTC. Fenna shook her head and frowned as Nicklas picked up his rifle, tucked his helmet under his arm and walked toward her.

"Fenna," he said, as he cut the ties around her wrists with a folding knife from his belt.

She glared at him. "What the fuck was all that about?"

"I could ask you the same thing. Jarnvig certainly wants to know."

"Jarnvig?"

"You called him."

"And you were pretty quick to get here," Fenna said, pulling her arm away as Nicklas guided her to the side of the road, away from the traffic released by the police behind them. "I thought you had been called away. Far away."

"Far enough," Nicklas said and shrugged. "Besides," he said and grinned. "You passed the test."

"The test? What fucking test?"

"Your first kill."

"What?" Fenna clenched her fist and raised it. Nicklas dropped his right hand to the grip of his pistol.

"Stand down, Konstabel."

"Stand down?" Fenna spat in his face. She took two steps toward the desert before wheeling, and jabbing her finger at Nicklas. "I killed a man."

"Yes," Nicklas said and wiped his face with his hand.

"With a knife…"

"Yes. A knife. You're operational now. Congratulations."

"Congratulations?" Fenna gripped her hair in her fists. She yelled as she tore out two chunks of dirty blonde hair. "Would you have congratulated him, the Gunney, if he had killed me? Would you?" she said and cast the hair into the wind. Several strands caught in the Velcro of Nicklas' vest and he plucked them free, twisting Fenna's hair between his finger and thumb as he answered.

"No," he said and sighed. He let his hand drop, the hair still pinched between his fingers.

"He could have killed me."

"Yes."

Fenna trembled as she took a step closer to Nicklas. He let his right hand fall from his pistol. Her hair twisted in the wake of the cars speeding past them, the wind buffeting her body.

"What about us? Was that a test too?"

"No."

"So you fuck on your own time, Inspector? How convenient," she said, her bottom lip quivered.

"Fenna…"

"No, Nicklas," she said and shook her head. "No." Fenna walked past him, picked up her pack and the report and strode into the desert.

"Fenna," he called after her.

"Stay out of my head, Nicklas," she said and continued walking. Sooner or later, she realised, she would have to stop, or they would force her to. Her mission was waiting. But right now, *right fucking now, they can wait*, she told herself. Fenna let the wind dry her tears as they streaked down her cheek.

"A test," she said. "It was a fucking test." Fenna stopped and looked back at Nicklas. "And what about Alice?" she said, but either the wind took her words or Nicklas had been ordered not to hear them.

Fenna found a flat boulder and sat down. She let the pack fall onto the ground between her dusty boots. She kicked at the straps, flicking them into a straight line pointing toward the highway. She untied her laces and removed her boots. Her bare feet were blotched with dust and dirt, her toes black beneath the nails. She bent forward to pick at the dirt with her fingers, rubbing her toes until they were red, raw, and warm to the touch. They stung, but Fenna rubbed them one more time, then stood and squirmed the soles of her tiny feet in the sand, the dead and dry skin rasping from her feet and into the dirt. *My DNA*, she mused, *part of the desert now.*

She looked up as Nicklas picked his way around the boulders toward her. She placed her hands in her lap and watched him as he approached. "Come to take me away?" she said, as he stopped in front of her.

"Those are my orders."

"From whom? Jarnvig?"

"Amongst others, yes," he said and let his hands fall to his sides.

The wind carried a wisp of red dust between them, coating his boots and tickling her skin.

CHRISTOFFER PETERSEN

"Fenna," he said.

"What?"

"What happened in the boxing ring, that wasn't Jarnvig…"

"I know," she said.

"It was me," he said, his voice rasping like the sand across her feet.

Fenna looked up at the gleam of metal, circling, droning above them.

"Did you hear me?" Nicklas said.

"Yes," she said. She got up and shouldered her pack, nodding toward the men waiting for them on the highway. "I'm ready now."

The City

COPENHAGEN, DENMARK

Chapter 12

BRITISH AIRWAYS TRANSATLANTIC FLIGHT

Fenna braced her hands, palms flat, against the sides of the space; she had to bend her elbows. The walls thrummed beneath her fingers and the sensation of movement, erratic, undisciplined, and violent, tugged at her stomach. She looked up at an insistent knock at the door.

"The seatbelt sign is on," said a voice, muffled, on the other side of the door. "You must return to your seat."

Fenna ignored the woman. She slid her palms up the walls and stood up. She held onto the sink, glancing at herself in the mirror and focusing, of all things, on the chestnut roots of her hair pushing the blonde strands further from her scalp.

I'll have to colour it again, she thought.

Fenna averted her eyes from the reflection. She didn't want to confront the killer she had become. *I passed the test.* The thought flickered through her mind as the flight attendant thumped her fist on the door.

"I'm going to have to open the door if you don't return to your seat."

Fenna sat down on the toilet seat and waited.

Her memories of the chatter and bustle of two American airports, the smell of coffee and food stalls, restaurants and terminal cafés competing for customers turned her stomach once more as the Boeing 777 aircraft, a *British Airways* transatlantic flight, was buffeted by another bout of turbulence. *It's like sledging*, she mused. *Long stretches of smooth, rapid ice, followed by short, intense sections of challenging geography – the shifting peaks of the ice foot along the coastline, a steep gulley, a wolf.* Fenna's thoughts centred on the wolf, and, for a few precious moments, she forgot her nausea, sidelined her murderous thoughts, and pictured the lanky gait of the white Arctic Wolf, its black eyes reminiscent of the polar bear – two obsidian orbs pressed into a white furry face. The wolf's face was lean, like its body, a stark contrast to the bulk of the bear. Fenna considered her own body, the tight muscles pressing at her skeleton-hugging skin. She was the wolf, loping alongside the bear, her boots secured in the bindings of her skis, Mikael towering above her to her right, the wind abrading their faces with snow needles.

I'm going back, she thought as the flight attendant unlocked the door and scolded her with official-sounding words that Fenna chose not to understand.

"In future," the woman said, as she escorted Fenna to her seat. "When the seatbelt sign is on…"

Fenna ignored her as she squirmed past the passenger sitting by the aisle, lifted the belt buckle and flopped onto the seat. The flight attendant tutted and wove her way back to her seat by the exit. If Fenna had been bothered she might have withered under the woman's glare, instead she wiped her hand across her face, buckled the belt across her lap, and reached for the bottle of water she had tucked into the mesh pocket in front of her.

"You don't fly well?" said the passenger on her left, the teenage girl on Fenna's right was hidden beneath a blanket, and Fenna envied the girl's indifference to the turbulence and the activity around her.

"Sorry?" she said, facing him, an African

American she imagined to be in his sixties.

"Flying," he said. "You don't like it?"

"It's okay," Fenna said and shrugged. "I'm not usually bothered by it. I've just had a rough time lately."

The man turned in his seat and held out his hand in greeting. "Solomon," he said and shook Fenna's hand. He frowned as she let go. "That's a strong grip for a pretty child such as yourself."

"Yes," Fenna said and smiled.

"You have a name to go with that grip?" he said and made a show of massaging his hand.

"Yes." She laughed. "Fenna," she said and paused to smile at the look on Solomon's face. "I'm from Denmark."

"Well," he said and relaxed back in his seat. "I never met nobody from Denmark before."

"Now you have," Fenna said and took a sip of water.

"And what do you do, child?" he said with a glance at Fenna's clothes and a nod at her hands. "I'm thinking you don't work in no convenience store."

"No. I'm in the military," Fenna said. *I can't hide it*, she realised.

"Ah," he said. Solomon closed his eyes for a moment and Fenna stared at the husks of white whiskers, the salt in his peppery stubble. The corner of her mouth twitched and she hid her smile behind the lip of the bottle as Solomon opened his eyes.

"My son," he said. "He was in the military. He sent me letters all the time. Then," Solomon said and reached for Fenna's hand, "he stop. You know, child? From the one day, to the next. The letters just stop." Fenna squeezed Solomon's hand. He took a breath and looked at her as he spoke. "They sent me his things, what he had left, in his locker or some such. There was one last letter. He stay writing, right up to the end." Solomon chewed at his lip. Fenna squeezed his hand one more time. "He done good by his family, my son."

"What was his name?"

"Jesse," Solomon said. The wrinkles around his eyes spread, splayed like slender toes as he smiled. "Jesse Solomon Patrick Owens."

"Patrick?"

"Yup. Mama, my Mary, she stay Catholic all this time. Even now, still Catholic."

"Why isn't she with you?" Fenna asked as Solomon squeezed her hand and let go. He gripped the ends of the seat rests as if he was about to stand.

"Oh, she don't travel too well. Besides," he said and turned to Fenna, "my family said said it was best I go alone."

"Go where?"

"Germany," he said. "My son died in Germany." Solomon chuckled for a moment. "You was thinking Afghanistan, wasn't you?"

"Yes."

"You ain't the first. But no, he died in a training accident. He was drivin' a tank somewhere east of Germany. Estonia, or some such." Solomon leaned back in his seat. "The whole world is squaring their shoulders, getting' ready for a spittin' competition, and my son died for it."

"I'm sorry," Fenna said and pressed her hand against Solomon's arm as he nodded.

"I know you are, child," he said and turned his head to the side. He smiled at Fenna, flicking his eyes once at the seatbelt sign as it disappeared with a low ping. "Family is never more important than when there is none. I just wish I knew that before. I might have taken this trip before he died." Solomon shook his head and sighed as he pushed himself out of his seat. He stopped in the aisle, resting his hands on the seat backs for balance. "My turn to visit the tiny John," he said and winked.

She watched him go, tugged the in-flight magazine from the mesh pocket, and, now that the turbulence had disappeared, made herself comfortable. Fenna flipped through the magazine, stopping to read the article predicting the beginning of the end for the American President's administration. According to the article, his popularity was falling further than predicted, even among his staunch supporters and members of his own party. *Defence cuts*, Fenna thought as she closed the magazine. *There's one place I wouldn't miss if he cut it from the budget.* She looked out of the window, but the vast stretch of sea below looked uncannily like sand, and the desert, and her actions in it, occupied her for the remainder of the flight.

HEATHROW AIRPORT, ENGLAND

Fenna bought Solomon a coffee while they waited for a connecting flight from Heathrow Airport. She lost herself in the details of his family, picturing the pranks he and his brothers played as children, smiling at the scolding they had received from his mother, wincing at the slipper his father had used later that same night. *Family.* The thought lingered in her mind, as she remembered her father, and the time they had spent together before he died, in Afghanistan.

Fenna enjoyed another hour of Solomon's company and then he had to leave to catch his flight. She hugged him when he left. She had no choice. The big African American wrapped his arms around her slight frame and pulled her close.

"I don't know where you is heading, child, but be safe."

"I will," she said. "And thanks."

"For what?" he said, as he let go of her and extended the handle on his walk-on baggage.

"For our conversation," Fenna said. "About family."

"Conversation?" Solomon laughed. "Child, a *conversation* requires two people to talk. I done all the talkin'. But you a good listener, and it's me that should be a thanking you." He winked and tipped his baggage onto the back wheels. "You take care now, child. And if you're ever in Washington State," he said. "Well, there ain't too many Solomon Owens in the phone book. You be sure to look me up."

"I will," said Fenna as Solomon waved and walked away. She sat down as he turned the corner and took a sip of coffee. She tipped the paper cup to drain it. She sat for another five minutes and thought about her extraction from Arizona, and her re-entry to Denmark. *If there is a watch list for agents going off the reservation*, she mused. *I don't seem to be on it.* Fenna slid her pack out from under the table, shouldered it, and made her way to the departure gate.

KASTRUP AIRPORT, DENMARK

The flight from London to Copenhagen was too short for Fenna to see the new Jason Bourne movie to the end, but she watched it anyway. *The CIA doesn't need a foreign state to fight*, she thought and shook her head, *they're too busy fighting themselves*. Analysing the movie helped Fenna distance herself from the close-quarters fighting, the quiet grunts and gasps from the combatants, the hiss of air leaking from a punctured throat. Fenna gripped the armrests and, closing her eyes, she forced the image of the Gunney from her mind as the aircraft began its descent. She opened her eyes again as the wheels kissed the runway and the pilot taxied to the gate.

Per Jarnvig was waiting for her as she got off the plane. He guided her around and through passport control without a word. He ushered Fenna into a small office in the customs area, closed the door, and gestured for her to sit at the table.

"This room is secure," he said and plunged Fenna back into the world from which she had escaped with Solomon. She waited for him to sit down.

"I just want to say…" she said and stopped as Jarnvig lifted his hand.

"Don't," he said. "It's done. You passed the test."

"A man died. I killed him."

"Yes," Jarnvig nodded. "And passed the test." He smoothed his hands on the table. "It's time to move on, Konstabel. I need you to move on. I need you in Greenland."

"So I can kill another man?"

"If necessary," he said and shrugged. "Yes."

"I thought you were going to train me as an

investigator. That's what I signed up for."

"No," Jarnvig said and shook his head. "The minute you decided to board that plane to Toronto, and pull the trigger on Humble, you agreed to do whatever job I deemed necessary." Jarnvig tapped a finger on the table. Fenna focused for a moment on his groomed nails, so different from her own. "You showed real grit in Greenland," he said. "I call it potential, and when I recognise that in a person, I'm compelled to do something useful with it. Your career with the Navy is over, Konstabel. You could never have returned to the Sirius Patrol, not after Mikael's death."

"I didn't kill him," Fenna said and jabbed her finger at Jarnvig.

"We have established that, and I believe you. But let's get something straight, Konstabel. When I tell you to do something, you do it, to the letter. If I tell you to kill someone, or if the situation requires it, you do it. Without pause. Without question. Do you understand, Konstabel?" Fenna leaned back in her chair and splayed her hands on the surface of the table. "Because if you don't…"

"I understand," Fenna said and stared at Jarnvig.

"Good," he said and rested his hands in his lap. "Now, tell me what you know about the LOMROG expedition."

Chapter 13

Per Jarnvig was a thorough man. During the first two hours of her briefing in the tiny customs office Jarnvig focused on tiny details buried within the LOMROG report, as if he was teasing threads from a shirt, only to push them back in, one millimetre at a time, until the garment was still a shirt, but essentially rewoven. The configuration was the same, but the layered meaning and significance of each thread was known and its place in the garment understood. Fenna knew it was for her benefit, but she wished the process would go faster.

"Tell me again about Dr Johansson," Jarnvig said. He paused at a knock on the door. Fenna brightened at the smell of the fresh coffee and breakfast rolls a customs officer brought in on a tray. "Thank you." Jarnvig waited for the man to place the tray on the table, gesturing for Fenna to help herself. He started talking again once the man had left and closed the door. "Dr Johansson?" he said and reached for his coffee.

"He was enthusiastic," Fenna said, wiping butter from her lips with the back of her hand. "His report is optimistic. It's part field report, part nature book…"

"And another part mystery suspense."

"Yes. About halfway through the expedition."

"The report was originally intended to be posted online in the public domain," Jarnvig said and reached for a roll. The crusty exterior cracked into jagged flakes as he cut into it with the serrated teeth of the thin plastic knife; Fenna was reminded of sea ice breaking up in June along Greenland's east coast.

"Obviously, his superior..."

"Dr Peters. The Canadian," said Fenna.

"Yes," Jarnvig said, "she put a stop to that." He put down the knife and peeled a greasy square of cheese from a paper plate on the tray. Fenna noted that he used no butter and realised she was hungry. She took a second breakfast roll from the tray and waited for Jarnvig to continue. "Johansson's report took on a different character after the midway point of the expedition, when the first data started to come in. What is your take on that?" Fenna tried to recall the particular section of the report and reached for her pack. Jarnvig stopped her with a raised hand. "Let's see what you can remember, shall we?"

"Is this a test?" Fenna said, as she sat back in her seat. Jarnvig took a bite of his roll. "All right," she said. "Johansson was convinced that someone had tampered with the instruments." She paused, waiting for Jarnvig. He took another bite. "The Kongsberg EM 122 multibeam echo sounder in particular."

"Go on."

"As Johansson explains, the data is recorded within a known reliable range. The report was very clear about the margin of error, but..."

"The readings were way beyond that."

"Yes. Johansson believed the machine needed to be recalibrated."

"And he approached Dr Lorentzen."

"Because he is the so-called authority on the MBES," Fenna said and smiled. She realised she was enjoying the step-by-step process of analysing the details of the report. She had, she remembered, been impressed by Johansson's style of writing, his descriptions of standing at the bow of the *Odin* as it broke through the ice, plying the northern waters, heading for the pole. When his style had changed, she found the reading less interesting, reminding her more of the science texts at Gymnasium. But then the report shifted character again, beyond the initial documentation of the problems with the MBES, to a series of speculations and deductions, as Johansson focused on his conviction that the instrument had been tampered with. She forgot about her jetlag, brushed a flake of bread from her chin and cupped her hands around the paper cup of coffee. She leaned over the table and grinned. "Lorentzen went from scientist to suspect," she said.

"Over the course of three days."

"By which time they were approaching the most northerly boundary of the operating area."

"You mean the pole."

"Yes."

"So?" Jarnvig said and took a sip of coffee.

Fenna looked away for a moment. She tried to recall the next sequence of events, enjoying the test for what it was, enjoying the lack of testosterone and sweat. This was the kind of investigating she had assumed Jarnvig wanted her to do. *And I could be good at it*, she thought as she faced Jarnvig.

"Johansson was convinced that, even with the margin of error, the data would reveal that Greenland's continental shelf was connected to the North Pole. So were his colleagues."

"What do we know about Johansson?"

"He is Swedish. In his forties. Married with three kids. A career scientist, mortgaged beyond belief," Fenna said and grinned. "I'm sure his wife despairs, but loves him for it."

"I am sure she does," Jarnvig said and allowed a faint smile to creep across his lips. "And Lorentzen?"

"Dr Karl Lorentzen. Danish. Unmarried." *Attractive*, she remembered.

"And highly respected in the community. Lorentzen has been the so-called expert on the continental shelf for the past five years. He is an established scientist, and a regular publisher of articles for the Danish Polar Center." Fenna sipped her coffee as Jarnvig continued. "I met Lorentzen on two occasions, although I doubt he will remember me. He is popular at functions, and has an attractive personality to match those good looks of his." He paused and looked at Fenna. "You read his profile?"

"And saw the picture," Fenna said, smiling at the memory.

"Good," Jarnvig said and leaned back in his chair. He waited for Fenna to finish her coffee. "He is based in Nuuk, seconded to the Department for Natural Resources. He has an office there. He divides his time between the office, holding talks at Katuaq, the cultural centre, and giving lucrative lectures to tourists on the cruise ships visiting the capital." Jarnvig paused as Fenna sat up straight in her chair. "I have checked the location of *The Ice Star*, Konstabel." He smiled as Fenna relaxed. "It is currently in the Bahamas."

"It wouldn't have mattered," she said, as she pushed the paper cup between her fingers.

"We both know it would," Jarnvig said.

Yes, Fenna thought, *it would have*. She remembered the dank hold and the cold metal deck as Dina, beaten, bruised, and bloody, had pressed her naked body into Fenna for warmth. She remembered the elephantine image of Lunk, the bandage ballooning the side of his head as it covered the ear she had perforated for him when he had tried to rape her on the bathroom floor, and, finally, the boom of the shot that killed him as it reverberated around the hold, the gun steady in Dina's hand. Fenna gripped the paper cup, crushed it in one hand and nodded at Jarnvig. "Good," she said and nodded for him to continue.

"When Lorentzen is not charming tourists and politicians," Jarnvig said, as he appraised Fenna with a casual glance, "he acts as an advisor to the Chinese representatives, currently in talks with Tunstall Mining Consolidated."

"The Chinese are in the process of buying Tunstall?" Fenna said and smiled. *I'm okay now*, she thought. *Back on track.*

"Yes, Tunstall carried out the original geological surveys, at great expense."

"But they can't afford to begin operations."

"Few private companies can," Jarnvig said and tapped the table. "The standard operating procedure is to make a good show of it and deplete the company funds to show a maximum level of commitment…"

"And hope to be bought out by a larger company?"

"Or country."

"China."

"Exactly." Jarnvig gestured at Fenna's wrinkled paper cup. "More coffee?"

"Yes," Fenna said and waited as Jarnvig sent a text on his mobile. The LOMROG report was the only reading material she had while she was in the desert. She looked at the mobile in Jarnvig's hand and wondered if she had been deprived her own for security reasons, or to keep her in the dark and pique her curiosity. *If it was the latter*, she mused, *it had worked*. Her mind swirled with the different threads she and Jarnvig had teased out of the story. *I'm in. I'm invested. So let's cut to the chase and get started.* Fenna felt the fatigue of flying lift from her shoulders and she straightened her back. Jarnvig looked up. When Fenna smiled, so did he.

"Konstabel?" he said and pocketed his mobile.

"I was thinking about the Chinese, and the mining site."

"Isukasia," said Jarnvig. "There has been some confusion around the name, but the proposed site for the iron mine is on the edge of the ice sheet, north of Nuuk, in the mountains at the top of Nuuk fjord."

Fenna frowned and shook her head. "I'm not familiar with it."

"And why should you be? Sirius patrols in Northeast Greenland. Beyond looking for new breeding stock amongst the sledge dogs on the west coast, Sirius have no business in Nuuk."

"But the headquarters for Arctic Command are in Nuuk," Fenna said.

"Yes, and I want you to avoid them at all costs."

"Then what exactly do you want me to do?"

Jarnvig turned at a knock on the door. Fenna recognised the routine, and waited until the customs officer had exchanged the empty tray for a new one with fresh coffee. Jarnvig continued once the officer had left the room.

"China was afforded observer status on the Arctic Council in 2013. There is no doubt that China is paving a road to the Arctic. They have recognised the wealth of raw material in Greenland, and they are in a position to fund operations, such as Tunstall. The quest for oil might have dipped out of the media spotlight – it's too expensive and technically challenging for limited rewards, but the Chinese plans to invest in Greenland have stirred up the Greenlandic government, and the environmentalists - including a lot of Danes, I might add. The Chinese plan includes wild propositions of a new harbour, a new airport, and a new city for the Chinese workers. There will be few jobs for Greenlanders, but, potentially, a lot of investment, and likely benefits for the Greenlandic elite. If anything comes of this, it will put Greenland on the map and confirm China as a major player in the Arctic."

"I can see that, but where do I fit in?"

Jarnvig paused for a moment to pull a thin folder from his briefcase and place it on the table. "The LOMROG expedition, as you know, was funded as a means of confirming, once and for all, who owns the North Pole. The Russians have claimed it, but the evidence is weak. LOMROG should have put an end to that. Two weeks from now, a representative of the Danish Government will present the findings of the LOMROG report to the UNCLOS hearing, convened to satisfy the Danish claim to the Pole. We believe…"

"We? Who's *we*?"

"Konstabel?"

"Sorry," Fenna raised her hands in apology.

"It is believed," Jarnvig said and continued, "that the Danish representative will present the LOMROG findings as they are, currently, with no mention of any discrepancies, or appeal for more time to launch a new expedition."

"So," Fenna said, "effectively giving up Denmark's claim to the Pole?"

"Yes," said Jarnvig. "Now, whereas that might be attractive in some circles – maintaining sovereignty over Northeast Greenland is a challenge at best, but doing the same as far as the Pole will require a serious amount of funding…"

"But the potential financial rewards through shipping routes…" Fenna suppressed a shiver as she recalled Humble's words and his motivations aboard *The Ice Star.*

"Given the current warming of the climate and the retreat of the sea ice," Jarnvig said and nodded. "Yes, there is potential there, which is why we are convinced that our Danish representative, unbeknown to him, is being influenced by a foreign power."

"The Chinese."

"Most likely, but unconfirmed. That's where you come in."

A jolt of adrenalin surged through her at the prospect of a new mission. A real investigation, she realised, was just what she had been looking for. *A chance to prove myself, on a level playing field for once.*

"As you already know, you are going to join Lorentzen, as a representative from Tunstall Mining Consolidated."

"Hah," Fenna snorted. "I'll be exposed in a heartbeat."

"Hence the intensive geology course tomorrow."

"Yes, Nicklas mentioned that. And afterward?"

"You must find evidence to support Johansson's theory that the instruments were tampered with. You have to prove the link between the Chinese and the representative at the UNCLOS hearing."

"Is that all?" Fenna said. She suppressed a wry smile, as she wondered where to start.

"No. Not quite," said Jarnvig. Fenna waited as he opened the folder and pushed it across the table toward Fenna. She studied the grainy image of a man sprawled on the deck of a ship. There was blood on the deck. "If you recall the notes at the end of the LOMROG report, you'll remember that the report never did get posted online."

"Yes," Fenna said as she studied the photo. "I guessed it was something to do with Johansson's accusations." She moved closer to examine the photograph and tapped the image with her finger. "The metal object sticking out of the chest." She looked up. "Is that the tip of an ice axe?"

"It is." Jarnvig said, and added, "The rest of the axe, the shaft and the adze, is hidden beneath the body. It was written up as a freak accident, but it is clear that the axe penetrated the man's body from behind, with enough force to puncture his sternum." Jarnvig waited as Fenna looked up. "You'll recall, from the report, that it was published posthumously."

"Posthumously? I missed that."

"Yes," Jarnvig said as he leaned forward to tap the centre of the photograph. "You're looking at the body of Johansson. About twenty minutes after his death."

Fenna studied the photograph as Jarnvig removed his finger. She noticed the striations of blood frozen to the deck, the look of anguish pasted to the man's face, and the impression of a boot, the ridges of its sole preserved on the deck, frozen for all to see.

"Find Johansson's killer, Konstabel. Bring me substantial evidence…" Jarnvig said, his voice faltering for a moment, "and I will put Lorentzen away for good."

"You think it is him?"

"I have my suspicions," Jarnvig said. "Do it quickly, and I'll get the Pole for Denmark."

"For Greenland," Fenna said, her voice a whisper, as she studied the dead Swede. *Another body on another ship*, she said to herself. *It's like* The Ice Star *all over again.* The thought lingered as Jarnvig pulled the folder from beneath her fingers and closed it. *Here we go again.*

Chapter 14

COPENHAGEN, DENMARK

Copenhagen in spring buzzed like any other major European city. Fenna tried to ignore the bustle on the street beneath her hotel window, choosing instead to enjoy the lazy day ahead of her, before her meeting with the geology professor later in the evening. She curled her leg over the duvet, trapping the thick quilt between her knees. The traffic continued to tease her with the occasional hiss of a large vehicle – a bus or a lorry – interspersed with the wail of a two-tone siren and the single ring of a bicycle bell. She smiled at the bell, and the next one, imagining a street twisting with steams of confused tourists, and a steady stream of Danes plying the international waters, armed with shrill bells and sharp tongues. Fenna had never liked the city, but from her hotel room overlooking the train station and Tivoli Gardens, she revelled in a sense of familiar comfort and let the twinges of patriotism tug her out of bed. She wrapped a sheet around her body, her elbows pressing the thin material into sharp angles as she padded barefoot across the carpet, pulled back the curtains and looked out onto the activity below her. The coffee machine with a built-in clock alarm filled the room with Radio P3's playlist, insignificant banter, and the smell of coffee.

"I could get used to this," she said and smiled. "Better than a barrack in the desert."

She thought about Jarnvig's methods as the coffee brewed, the way he sent her into the desert, to train, fight, and kill. *To kill*, as if she was a real secret agent, an assassin, being hazed, hounded, and herded, funnelled into the nastiest and narrowest phase of her training, squeezed into a tight corner and expected to kill or be killed. *Well,* she mused, *I killed. And now I'm here.*

The coffee machine beeped and she let the sheet slip to the floor as she walked into the kitchen area of the room. Fenna used the same cup from the night before and filled it to the brim. She eyed the plastic *Matas* shopping bag on the counter and smiled as she took her first sip of coffee. She pulled down one corner of the bag and chuckled at the result of Jarnvig's shopping expedition. The bag contained hair dye and an assortment of make-up. She put down her cup, picked up one of the boxes of dye and walked into the bathroom, but the headlines of the hourly news made her stop.

"Strong criticism of the American President continues, as more military bases are marked for closure in the White House's unprecedented budget reforms, the first ever to target American military spending to such a degree under a Republican President."

Fenna closed the bathroom door, turned on the shower, and drowned out the radio broadcast with a deluge of hot water.

Once she was showered and towelled dry, she waited for the mirror to demist enough to see her reflection and apply the hair colour. She opened the packet while she waited, pulled out the product and stopped.

"Black?" Fenna sighed and looked in the mirror. "I'm going to have to do it all," she said, with a glance down the length of her body. She recalled the folder Jarnvig had given her on leaving the airport, her profile and the physical description of her new alias. She must have glossed over the part that said she had black hair, and suddenly it made sense that Jarnvig needed a new photograph for her passport, something he had requested as he dropped her off at the hotel. Fenna shrugged, read the instructions and applied the product to her hair. When she was done, she used the scissors from the complementary sewing kit to tidy up her fringe.

Jarnvig had left a new suitcase in the hotel room. It contained a selection of clothes fit for a young geologist, jeans, t-shirt, and a figure-hugging fleece. The worn-in boots surprised her; she wondered who might have the same size feet to break in her boots.

"And the rest of my outfit," she said, as she took a closer look at her clothes. Jarnvig, it seemed, was a stickler for details and was leaving nothing to chance. She tied her boot laces, grabbed her pack and her copy of the LOMROG report, pulled the key card from the unit by the door and left the room. Two minutes later and she was on the street among the tourists, and walking past the entrance to Tivoli and the Hard Rock Café. Fenna drank in the air of the city and found she preferred it, for the moment at least, to the dry air of the Arizona desert. She spared a brief thought for Nicklas, and then pushed him out of her mind and into a mental compartment labelled: Jarnvig's Puppets. There was room in that headspace for more than one, she realised, and was suddenly conscious of her new hair colour, her newly fashioned clothes, and her new mission. The thoughts occupied her all the way to the University of Copenhagen's Department of Geosciences and Natural Resource Management, on Rolighedsvej. She stopped a couple of students and asked for directions to the main lecture theatre, nodded her thanks, and set off for her evening class. Fenna paused to use a passport photo machine, slipping the photos for Jarnvig inside her pack before hurrying to class.

The students moved differently to the tourists, with an almost imperceptible balance between purpose and procrastination. Fenna bumped past the students in the corridor outside the main lecture hall for the natural sciences, waited for a line of students to exit, before slipping past them and hovering by the door as she scanned the room. She recognised her tutor from the description Jarnvig had given her. She knew he was at least twice her twenty-four years, but he seemed to be in good physical shape, and, given she knew his specialist area of study, Fenna imagined she knew why.

Greenland did that, she thought, as she made her way between the rows of seats all the way to the lecture stage and pulpit. The man looked up as she sat down on a seat in the front row.

"So you're the reason my wife is cooking for the kids tonight?" he said and grinned.

"Is that a bad thing?"

"They'll survive, and Carina will appreciate the extra cash." He walked forward and extended his hand. "Anders Nielsen," he said, as he greeted her.

"Fenna."

"Do you have a second name?"

"Yes," she said and stood up. "When do we start?"

"All right," Anders said and scratched at the stubble on his cheek. He frowned for a moment and then said, "What do you know?"

115

"About geology?"

"About Greenland."

"I know more about ice than rocks."

"That's a start, a good one, considering that the one has significantly shaped the other." He paused. "I understand that this is a rush job, like cramming for an exam."

"Yes."

"Then why don't you tell me what you need to know, specifically, and I can help you from there."

Fenna returned to her seat and pulled a notebook from her pack. "Tell me about mining in Greenland."

"Specifically?"

"Everything," Fenna said and opened her notebook. She scribbled notes as the geologist talked, stopping when he stopped, pausing to clarify a point before he rambled on to the next topic. There were slides, and Fenna stood up when the projector froze and needed to be restarted. The last image before the screen went blank was of the mountains to the north of Nuuk Fjord. Fenna stared at it and realised how much she missed Greenland. Anders fiddled with the remote control and the image disappeared. Fenna suppressed a sigh.

I'll see it again, she thought. *Soon.*

"This will take a moment," Anders said. He gestured with the remote to his right. "There's a coffee machine at the end of the corridor," he said. "Be sure to press the plus symbol for extra strength, otherwise it tastes like dishwater."

On the way back from the coffee machine, a paper cup in each hand, Fenna studied the students loitering in the corridor after class. *I could be any one of them*, she mused, as she passed couples and small groups. She imagined a life of academia, the occasional field trip, and the little she knew of things like peer-review and publication, remembering stories she had overheard between lecturers at her old Gymnasium, and the snobbish ways of academics. She opened the door to the auditorium with her shoulder and smirked at the thought of working in the field alongside any one of the students she had passed in the corridor. She could feel the muscles in her arms, her thighs, the strength in her fingers, the ones she had used to kill a man. Academia, all of a sudden, didn't seem so bad. She walked down the shallow steps and handed one of the cups to Anders just as he clicked the next slide into focus.

"Isukasia," she said, as she recognised the shadow of mountains, the contours, and the proximity of the ice sheet beyond it.

"That's right," Anders said and frowned as he looked at her. "You've been there?"

"No," Fenna shook her head. "Tell me about it."

"It's a hot subject right now," he said, as he walked away from the projector and onto the low stage beneath the large image. He straightened his arm and pointed, clicking the remote with his other hand. "Granite, mostly, like the majority of rock formations and features in Greenland. The difference here," he said, is what you can't see, the story told in the geology of the land, beneath the surface." Fenna listened as he told her about the millions of years required to create the ore that, if mined, could be forged into iron, and then steel, the building materials of a nation with ambition, a superpower for the twenty-first century. "It's interesting," he said, after he had finished flicking through the slides, "when you consider the activities of the current leader of China."

"What do you mean?"

"The way he's courting the Arctic countries at the moment. He visited Alaska recently." Anders paused to laugh. "I mean, Alaska. No politicians ever visit Alaska, not since the gold rush, back in the age of the frontier."

"Greenland is the new frontier," Fenna said, setting her empty cup down on the seat next to her.

"You believe that?"

"Yes."

Anders nodded, "So do I." He walked off the stage and sat next to Fenna. "So, tell me," he said. "Why all the urgency?"

"I don't know what you mean?" she said and fought to control the buzz of adrenalin his words induced. "I'm studying for an exam, and if I pass…"

"You'll get your promotion. Yes," Anders said and waved his hand. "I remember your boss explaining it to me." He stared at Fenna as he finished his coffee. She waited as he turned the empty cup between his hands. "My wife Carina, is also a geologist," he said.

Here it comes, Fenna mused, as he smiled and studied her face. *That clever moment when he thinks he has figured it all out. Should I put him out of his misery or…*

"She said you're not interested in iron and you're certainly not cramming for a promotion."

"Oh?" Fenna said and smirked.

"She said it would be about oil, and that you are here to sound me out and to get my professional opinion for a reduced consultancy fee."

"Is that a problem? I thought you said your wife would appreciate the extra cash?"

"I did, and it's not, but now that I have met you," Anders said and paused. He turned to point the remote at the projector and clicked forward one more slide. Fenna flicked her eyes to the screen, taking a moment to pause as she processed the image of a man standing in front of an orderly ridge of white triangular tents, pitched in a line close to a small helicopter and a row of fuel barrels, ubiquitous to the Arctic, the waste product of one geology expedition after another. The man in the foreground, standing with his arm around Anders Nielsen's shoulder, could not have looked more comfortable with his surroundings, the pink glow of the late Arctic sun flushing his bronze complexion as he grinned through the swathe of mosquitoes at the camera. Fenna recognised Lorentzen from the profile photograph Jarnvig had given her and she turned her attention back to the geologist.

"Oil is a dead end for the time being," said Anders. "But if you want to get your promotion, you should be talking to that man, not me."

"But I'm talking to you," Fenna said.

"Yes, and that's what I tried to tell Carina."

"What?"

"The real reason you are meeting with me, late in the evening, the night before you fly to Greenland."

Fenna took a breath and raised her hands in a clueless gesture. "You're going to have to spell it out," she said.

"I've known Karl Lorentzen since University. We graduated in the same year, and have been on three major expeditions together. I even led one of them." Anders paused to smile. "Your boss knows that much, even if you don't."

"So tell me what it is I want, and we can stop guessing," Fenna said and shrugged. "You seem to know that I'm getting on a flight tomorrow – something I didn't. What else do you know?"

"I know that without an endorsement from me, you're never going to get a meeting with him, let alone the chance to be his chaperone when he visits Isukasia at the end of the week." Anders smiled, as Fenna worked hard to disguise the surprise threatening to encompass her whole face. "We're a small community of geologists who specialise in Greenland," he said. "As much as I like and even admire Karl, he is still a pompous ass with an inflated ego."

Fenna laughed, relaxing and letting her hands fall into her lap. "So," she said, "if I wanted your endorsement, would you give it to me?"

"Yes, and something else, for free."

"And that is?"

"A friendly warning," he said and took a moment to study Fenna's face. She blushed as his eyes drifted down her body before returning to her face. "Karl is an incorrigible man in his early fifties. His looks have probably accelerated his career just as much as his knowledge. You should be careful, Fenna *with-no-last-name*, Karl has a reputation for destroying the careers of peers and competitors, and there is a wake of pretty women in his past, all of them young, all of them who have changed course and career." Anders stood up. "Karl uses people he finds useful, and takes advantage of those who can satisfy his career needs, or his sexual ones. He is a cautious and calculating man," Anders said and shrugged. "I'm sorry to say this, but I hope you are stronger than you look, because he is going to eat you alive."

Fenna paused for a beat and hoped the surprise she revealed earlier was enough to hide the spark of excitement she felt pricking beneath the surface of her eyes. She nodded once and cleared her throat. "Thank you," she said and stood up.

"You're welcome," Anders said, as Fenna shook his hand, shouldered her pack and brushed past him. He called after her just as she reached the door. "You never asked if I will do it," he said.

"Do what?" Fenna said and turned to face him.

"Endorse you."

Fenna felt a rush of energy through her body and embraced it, smiling as she looked down at the professor standing by the projector. She prepared her voice, searching for just the right tone of attitude and assertion.

"I think, professor, I'm my own endorsement."

Fenna left whatever geology she had gleaned from her private session with the professor in the auditorium. She knew how she would tackle Lorentzen, how she would approach the investigation, and how she would root out the agent sabotaging the Danish polar agenda. What pissed her off, she realised as she walked off the University campus and entered the steam of early evening tourists, was the thought that Jarnvig had set her up, in the desert, in the lecture hall, even in the airport when he practically gave her his blessing to go to Toronto with a loaded gun in her luggage. What pissed her off was that she had been accomplice to all his machinations, he had played her, and she had let him. She was still fuming when the kiss of rubber on the curb caused a bubble of tourists to burst around her, as a black BMW parked beside her. The rear window rolled down and Jarnvig waved from the seat.

"Get in, Konstabel."

Chapter 15

The driver stepped out of the car and opened the passenger door. Fenna ducked inside and stuffed her backpack in the space between her feet. She buckled her seatbelt as the driver got back in the car, checked the side-view mirror and pulled out into the evening traffic. Fenna turned to face Jarnvig.

"Do you have the photos?"

"Yes," she said and pulled the thin contact sheet from the front pocket of her backpack. She handed them to Jarnvig and leaned back in her seat.

"You're quiet," he said, as he glanced at the photos. "Something on your mind?"

"You," she said and smirked.

"Care to elaborate?"

Fenna considered for a moment the consequences of exposing her understanding of Jarnvig's manipulations, and then she realised that although he might have been responsible for everything since Greenland, he had no part in what happened prior to Mikael and Dina's deaths. *And, very nearly, my own*, she mused. Without Jarnvig's intervention she could be dead, detained, or, at the very least, destitute. *I have a job*, she thought. *I have an income*, although details surrounding her bank account eluded her for the moment. *And I'm going back to Greenland*. She forgot all about Jarnvig, choosing instead to think about Maratse, the policeman, and Kula, the hunter. She thought about her unprecedented contact with the Greenlanders. *Most Sirius patrollers never meet actual Greenlanders in Greenland*, she remembered, *they operate too far north. But, neither do they have high-speed car chases on the sea ice, escape from*

sadists on cruise ships, or have gun battles with private armies.
Fenna smiled. *Unreal,* she thought and turned to look
at Jarnvig.

"I don't know how much I learned from the
professor," she said. "But he has *endorsed* me."

"Good," said Jarnvig.

"Mostly for my looks, of course," Fenna said and
waited for Jarnvig to comment.

He sighed and tapped the corner of the photos
on his knee. "Do you remember when we first met?"

"In Kastrup airport? Yes."

"I said I needed a young woman with your
expertise, and I meant it."

"Because of Lorentzen?"

"He has been on my radar for a while, yes."

"Yours or PET's?"

"When it comes to Greenland and the Arctic I
am PET," Jarnvig said. He leaned forward and spoke
to the driver. "Remember we have one stop before
the airport."

"Yes, boss."

Jarnvig straightened his jacket as he leaned back
on the seat. "We need to get your passport updated.
You and I will stay in the car and discuss the mission
while Møller," he said with a nod toward the driver,
"sorts out your passport." Fenna opened her mouth
to speak and then closed it again. "What is it,
Konstabel?"

"Lorentzen," she said. "You said you have been
watching him for some time."

"I said he has been on my radar."

"But not under surveillance?"

"Not officially."

Fenna was quiet as she processed the

information. She was beginning to put things into order, a timeline of events as it were. *There must be an overlap*, she realised. *A time when Jarnvig became aware of me, and realised...* Fenna paused. She swallowed at the taste of bile in her throat. She felt her cheeks flush. She dug her fingernails into her palms as she clenched her fists. Small as they were, *they can still do damage*. She turned in her seat and fought to control her breathing, measuring out her words, one at a time, for fear of spillage, losing her message, losing control.

"Konstabel?" Jarnvig said. Fenna flicked her eyes to the 9mm pistol he wore in a shoulder rig hanging on the left side of his body. She saw him glance at the driver, and the look that Møller returned in the rear-view mirror.

"You knew," Fenna said.

"Knew what?" Jarnvig shifted in his seat and Fenna felt the car slow as it neared a traffic light at a crossroad. She could see the airport in the distance, but Møller signalled that he intended to turn left onto Saltværksvej. The *tock tock* of the signal light repeated loud in her ears and caught in her throat, she forced her words around it.

"You had Humble under surveillance," she said and waited.

"Yes," Jarnvig said, slowly, with another glance at Møller. Fenna thought she saw Møller shift his position, moving his right hand into his lap as if he was drawing a gun from his own shoulder rig. She pursed her lips and breathed out, raising her hands so that Møller could see them, and then shuffling further back into her seat. The traffic light was still red. Fenna positioned her body so that she could slip her hand around the handle of the door. She turned her attention back to Jarnvig.

"You knew about Kjersing, Humble's man in Sirius."

"I had my suspicions."

"And Burwardsley?"

"The Marine Lieutenant? Yes," Jarnvig said and smoothed a wrinkle from his jeans. "I knew he was in Greenland, aboard *The Ice Star*."

Fenna flicked her eyes toward the traffic light. It was still red, but the movements of the drivers in the cars either side of them suggested it would change soon. She took a breath and turned once more to face Jarnvig.

"Then you knew what Humble was doing, how he was manipulating Kjersing, and…" Fenna almost choked on the next word, a name. "Mikael," she said and felt tears well in her eyes. "You fucking knew what Humble was going to do."

Jarnvig drew a breath as the traffic light changed to amber. He parted his lips to speak, but Fenna had already opened the passenger door. "Fenna," he shouted as the cars behind and to both sides of the BMW blasted their horns, the drivers waving their arms as Fenna wove her way between them, slinging her backpack over her shoulder as she swerved around a cyclist and pounded down the pavement. She ignored the sound of the passenger door slamming and the screech of rubber on the tarmac as Møller swung the BMW around in a U-turn and roared down the street toward her. Fenna ducked down a side street, stopped beside a door and kicked at it until it opened. She put her shoulder to it and burst inside a stairwell leading to the roof of a small warehouse. She pounded up the stairs, barely hearing the BMW braking to a stop in the side street, and Jarnvig's commands as he exited the vehicle, slammed the door, and followed her inside the building. Fenna stopped at the door to the roof, kicked it open, and stepped out into the evening air. Copenhagen hummed with activity, but it was nothing to the rage of emotions buzzing through Fenna's skull. She pressed her hands to her temples as she cut a path around the vents and antennas on the roof, like growths on the canopy layer of the urban jungle.

She stopped and turned at her name as Jarnvig stepped onto the roof. His right hand, she noted, was tucked inside his jacket. He let it fall to his side and straightened his back as he walked toward her.

"Konstabel," he said. "Fenna…"

"You knew they would kill Mikael," she said and pushed her fingers through her black hair. She tightened her grip, as if entwining her fingers in her hair might stop her from beating her handler to death with her fists. That's what he was, she realised, her handler. Not Nicklas, but the real one, the one who called the shots. *And he has been handling me from the very beginning.*

"There was a risk…"

"No," she said, working her jaw as she took a breath, and then, "it was a certainty. You knew the outcome, knew what they would do. There was no risk…"

"The risk, Fenna," Jarnvig said, as he took a small step closer to her, "was losing you."

"Me?"

"Yes," he said. "You."

Fenna let her hands fall to her sides. She shrank to the floor, pushing herself against a vent, the base of her backpack resting on top of it, the straps suspended above her shoulders. Fenna tucked her knees to her chest and wrapped her arms around them as Jarnvig sat down beside her.

"I didn't know about Dina," he said and waited for Fenna to react. She shuffled her feet closer to her bottom, the heels of her boots scraping across the rough surface of bitumen. Jarnvig continued, "Arctic sovereignty is complicated, and expensive. There are many players and, while it might have cooled down for a few decades," he paused to smirk at his own joke, "all eyes are now firmly on Greenland and the lands around the pole. It's like the Great Game of Central Asia in the 1800s, but further north, with more nations involved."

"It's not that I don't understand the bigger picture," Fenna said and lifted her head. "But at my level, sea level, on the ice, with the dogs, with Mikael, it was so much less complicated."

"I know."

"All that changed," she said and looked at Jarnvig. "I'm just trying to find out why."

"I can tell you why, but before I do, I need to know if you are onboard? If I can trust you. If my judgement was correct." Fenna lifted her chin and stared at Jarnvig. He continued, *"The Ice Star* was a good cover for Humble. It gave him legitimate access with very little fall out. But it also made him careless."

"Dina," Fenna said and waited for her to appear, but she was alone on the rooftop with Jarnvig.

"Yes," he said. "But all the while Humble was working to discredit the Danish military presence in Greenland, preparations for the LOMROG expedition were already in motion, and the Chinese were posturing in the capital, seeking a foothold, securing their Arctic future. Mikael and you, your patrol, were tiny pawns on a huge chessboard. But as soon as Mikael was killed and you put Dina on your sledge, you moved up in that game, and…" Jarnvig paused.

"And *what?*"

"That's when I saw a possibility, a big one, to make some moves and to put some new pieces into play."

"Me?"

"Yes." Jarnvig shifted his position and sat opposite Fenna. He bent his knees and rested his forearms on top of them. "I knew Mikael would be killed, that it was a possibility at least." Fenna glared at him, dipping her eyes as he continued. "I knew of you, but only really became interested when I learned that you were not dead."

"And how did you hear about that?"

"From a mutual friend," Jarnvig said and laughed. "Maratse," he said.

"Maratse?" Fenna looked up and, as she lifted her head, the weight of Jarnvig's revelations ebbed for a moment at the mention of the Greenlandic policeman's name.

"He was quite popular for a while. After your high-profile gun battle on the sea ice… Well, let's just say that the Chief of Police in Greenland reached out, and the man he reached out to was me."

"Your story was that it was an anti-terror exercise?" Fenna could feel the skin of her lips tighten.

"Lame, I know," Jarnvig said and laughed with her. "It was the best I could do. You didn't give me

much to work with."

"No…"

"But you certainly caught my attention. The way you reacted, kept your cool. You had a future, if only I could get to you before they did."

"Yeah," she said. "You failed and Dina died."

"Yes, she did."

Fenna flicked a tear from her cheek and listened to the hum of life in the city as Copenhagen pulsed all around them. Seagulls drifted past from the docks, and she followed their flight until they were gone, out of sight, and she was back on the roof, with her future, and possibly Greenland's in her hands.

"So what happens now?"

"That all depends on you," Jarnvig said and picked up a pebble of bitumen from the rooftop. "I'm already invested, and I would be lying if I'm just going to let you walk away from this mission. I've pleaded your case and defended your actions to too many of my superiors, and too many committees, to walk away now. We have a window of opportunity. Lorentzen is on his way back to Nuuk. He is meeting with the Chinese, and all this just two weeks before the UNCLOS hearing. If ever we needed to act it is now. And right now, this very evening, he is in Copenhagen."

"But he'll know that. Lorentzen, if he is half as clever as you think he is, he will already know that."

"True," Jarnvig said and tossed the bitumen to one side. "But he has his Achilles heel." He paused. "For all his fame, and despite his academic reputation, he is a lonely man, Konstabel, and that is our advantage."

"You want me to fuck him? Is that what you

want me to do?" Fenna said and snorted. "Jesus."

"Listen to me," Jarnvig said and pointed at her. "If I wanted to entrap or blackmail Lorentzen, if that's all I wanted to do, I could get a hooker to do that for less than the price of a meal at Noma."

"You're calling me a hooker now? Finally. Now we get to it…"

"Would you shut up for just a minute, Konstabel," Jarnvig said. Fenna looked up as she recognised the edge in his voice.

"Talk," she said and stared at him.

"I meant what I said when I needed a young woman with your expertise. Yes, your looks are a key feature that figure heavily in my plan…"

"And Lorentzen prefers girls with black hair, eh?"

"Yes," Jarnvig said and blustered, "but listen. Your resourcefulness, and, damn it, even your stubbornness, gives you the edge, it keeps you sharp, and I need you to be sharp. Always."

He paused to look away for a moment. Fenna watched him, waited for him to face her. When he did, she could almost read the conflict that had played out in his mind. She waited for him to speak.

"Others have tried to train naïve young women with physical attributes to do a specific job," Jarnvig said. He caught the quizzical look in Fenna's eye and continued before she could explore it. "They have met with various results, few with any measure of success, and most ending in some political debacle."

"But I'm different? I'm not a naïve woman?" Fenna said and shook her head.

"That's not what I said," Jarnvig said, as he recovered, "but you're not the first woman to be recruited from the military. What you do have, something I admire, is an investment."

"An investment?"

"Yes. You are *invested* in Greenland," Jarnvig said and smiled. "Maybe it's the time you spent in the far north. Maybe it's a little of Mikael rubbing off on you... His record said it all – the environment came before any inkling of patriotism. But you," Jarnvig said, noticing the smile creeping across Fenna's face, the glint of cold fire burning in her ice-blue eyes. "You actually care about the people, not just the country."

"I think I found something there," she said, sighing as she looked up. "Despite it all, I think I found peace."

"And would you fight for that, Konstabel? Would you fight for Greenland?"

"Yes," she said. "I would." *I really would*, she thought.

"Good," Jarnvig said as he stood. "Then let's get down to the street. I sent Møller after your passport. He should be finished soon. Then we'll get you to your flight."

"I thought I was leaving tomorrow?"

"You are, but, as I said, Lorentzen is in Copenhagen. There is a meeting at the Clarion Hotel tonight, in one of the airport suites, a kind of reception. Lorentzen is the keynote speaker and you're going to be there."

Chapter 16

The bathroom of the suite at the Clarion Hotel Copenhagen Airport was larger than the combined area of the kitchen and living room of Fenna's family flat in Esbjerg. She ran the taps for the bath and listened to Jarnvig's and Møller's low voices on the other side of the door. Møller, it seemed, was to be Fenna's chaperone at the function of International Geologists, scheduled to begin in the late evening in the *Ellehammer* conference room. He had proved to have more than a passing interest in geology when they were properly introduced after Fenna and Jarnvig had finished talking on the Copenhagen rooftop. *He knows more than I do*, Fenna realised, and was relieved to discover that Jarnvig had fine-tuned her cover story. Tunstall Mining, while too busy to send any senior employees to Copenhagen, did not want to miss anything of interest.

"They are sending you," Jarnvig had explained as he presented her with her evening wear, "to be their eyes and ears at the function. Your cover is safe, Konstabel."

"And my name?" she said. "It's my real name on the passport."

"Few people know what went on in Greenland. I made sure of that. Until you are comfortable with aliases, your real name is safer. Trust me. Now," he said and indicated the bathroom. "If you'll get ready, I will go over the last details with Møller."

Fenna tested the temperature of the water with her hand and tugged off her *geologist disguise,* smiling at the effort Jarnvig had put into weathering her clothes. She stopped laughing when she caught her reflection in the mirror. She wore the trials of physical training in swathes across her skin. Her panda eyes were, with a little makeup, much harder to distinguish than earlier, but if anyone was to see her naked, they would find it difficult to believe she was just a company representative.

"More like a malnourished sex slave smuggled out of Eastern Europe," she said and traced the bruises and the lacerations, the cuts and the abrasions with a finger. But beneath the blemishes on the surface, Fenna knew she possessed a physique to rival even her biathlon days. Patrolling with Sirius, pulling her weight and wrangling forty kilo sledge dogs through unforgiving terrain, had changed her lithe skiing and shooting form into a hardy, wiry body that could take as many punches as it could give. She pictured Nicklas in her mind and remembered the sparring, the kidney punches, and then the sex, in the dust of the desert boxing ring. She switched her attention to the bath before any images of the Gunney, or Dina, slipped past her mental safeguards. Fenna bathed, longer than she imagined Jarnvig would approve. She picked up the reading material he had left by the sink and flipped through the pages, enjoying the thought of him checking his watch and stressing outside the door. *It's time to take control,* she mused and slipped her head beneath the surface of the water.

When her skin was thoroughly pruned, she dried and dressed. When she opened the bathroom door and stepped into the suite, she knew that she had successfully shrugged off one disguise and assumed another. Jarnvig and Møller revealed as much in their expressions. She joined them on the sofa, perching on the edge with her legs pressed together to avoid wrinkling the black cocktail dress Jarnvig had bought for her.

"It's a little loose," she said when he asked.

"Where?" said Møller. Fenna laughed and dropped the façade long enough to confirm she was the same woman who had walked into the bathroom, irrespective of how she looked when she came out.

"Makeup?" asked Jarnvig, as he focused once again on the details.

"No," Fenna said and shook her head, the wet ends of her short hair clung to her cheeks. "That's not what he's looking for."

"Who?"

"Lorentzen," she said and nodded at the folder on the table between them. "Your surveillance report included photos of the women he had contact with. They are, almost without exception, young, skinny, dark haired, flat-chested…" Fenna paused and made a show of gesticulating at her own tiny breasts. "And," she added, "all of them favoured the natural look, with little or no makeup. I have, I'll admit, added some colour around my eyes to hide the last of my desert souvenirs. Otherwise…"

"You look amazing, Konstabel," Jarnvig said and held her gaze for a moment, long enough for Fenna to glimpse a sense of admiration, perhaps even longing. She pushed the thought from her mind and picked up the report. She flicked through it as Møller excused himself to use the toilet.

"Sorry," she said, as he stood up. "I took my time."

"Not a problem," he said, as he walked around the sofa. She watched him as he entered the bathroom, turning her attention back to Jarnvig at the sound of the door locking.

"He seems all right," she said. "Is he PET, or something else, like Nicklas?"

"Nicklas?" Jarnvig said. He reeled for a second as if caught off guard. "Nicklas is more of a liaison to PET than a direct employee."

"And yet, you seem to have full control over him?"

"With the blessing of the RCMP, yes."

"And what am I?" she asked. "Am I an agent?"

"A PET agent, yes," Jarnvig said and reached for a bottle of water on the sofa table. "HUMINT," he said. "Human Intelligence. Not everything can be discovered through electronic eavesdropping. Intelligence agencies still need boots on the ground."

"Or heels," Fenna said and lifted her foot.

"Yes, heels," Jarnvig said and laughed and then went quiet.

"What?"

Jarnvig twisted the cap of the bottle backward and forward. "Fenna," he said. "I read something recently. Heard it, actually, an audiobook, a dramatization of one of John le Carré's books. Have you read any?"

"No." Fenna said.

"He writes spy books – the thinking man's James Bond. There's a passage in the book when the men training a man to go over the wall in Berlin, after the war, talk about giving him a gun, to make him feel safe. They make him carry it all the time – to the pub, on the street. They even have him place it under his pillow."

"And?" Fenna said and shrugged. She felt the

strap of her dress slip from her shoulder and pulled it back into place as Jarnvig wrestled his eyes from the dress strap to her face.

"The night of the operation, when the man, the agent, is being sent behind enemy lines, they tell him he can't take his gun."

"Why?" Fenna said and frowned.

"To put him on edge," Jarnvig said and stared at Fenna. He caught her eye and held it. "To keep him sharp."

"To scare the crap out of him more like."

"If that's what it took," Jarnvig said and looked away. He leaned back, tugging the thought with him until Fenna grasped it.

"So," she said. "You're not giving me a gun."

"No," he said. "I'm not."

Møller opened the bathroom door, pausing to look from Fenna to Jarnvig. He walked to the sofa and stood to one side. Fenna ignored him. Jarnvig focused on Fenna.

"I'm ready," Møller said. "Whenever you..."

"If that's the case," Fenna said, cutting him off with a glance, "then you can leave the gorilla in the suite." She stood up, tossed the folder onto the sofa table and walked toward the door.

"Konstabel," Jarnvig stood up, lifting a finger to silence Møller, and then stepping around the sofa to follow Fenna. She had her hand on the door when he slammed the palm of his left hand against it. "You will listen to me."

"Let go of the fucking door, Jarnvig."

"Not before you listen to me."

"No," Fenna said, turning within the space cordoned off by Jarnvig's body. She knuckled him in the sternum, just enough to put him off balance as she pulled the 9mm from his shoulder rig, turned it for a better grip, and shoved the muzzle into the side of his head. "I'm done listening to men," she said and tapped the pistol against his temple. Jarnvig staggered back and she shifted position, depriving Møller of a clear shot as he levelled his own pistol at her.

"Fenna," Jarnvig said.

"Now it's *Fenna?*" she said and took a breath. "You use *Konstabel* to order me around. *Fenna* when you want to appeal to my conscience, or my emotions. Well, I'm done with that. You have a problem," Fenna said, "a big fucking problem."

"And what is that, Konstabel?" Jarnvig said, as he rubbed his chest.

"You are my handler, but I won't be handled."

"Just remember," he said, "who got you out of Toronto, and out of the desert, Konstabel. Remember that."

"I don't have to," she said. "You did. And you'll do it again, because the thing is…" Fenna paused to lower the gun. "You need me. And right now, I'm the best option you have of gathering intelligence. You said it yourself, Jarnvig. You recruited me, in part, for my stubbornness. And now you have to deal with that." She pointed at Møller. "You send me in there with him, and you may as well flash a sign saying *secret agent in training*, and Lorentzen will be gone. But if I go in alone, with Nielsen's endorsement, this dress, the bobbed black hair, and my body – for what it's worth, and I guarantee I'll have him on the hook before midnight." Fenna stopped to lift the straps of her dress and slide them back onto her shoulders. She looked at Jarnvig, daring him to disagree.

"Okay," he said and waved at Møller to stand down. "You've made your point."

"Good."

"But, damn it, Fenna. You are every handler's worst nightmare." Jarnvig sighed.

"You better believe it," she said and tossed him the 9mm.

"Konstabel," Jarnvig called out, as she turned toward the door.

"Yes?"

"Be smart. Be safe, and be back here by midnight."

"And if I'm not?"

"I'll make sure Møller is sitting in the bar."

"All right," she said. "I'll agree to that."

Jarnvig slipped the 9mm into his shoulder holster. "Good luck, Konstabel," he said. Fenna nodded as she opened the door and stepped into the corridor.

Fenna's adrenalin cooled as she walked toward the lifts. The carpet and the heels she was wearing reminded her of another corridor and another lift, another time and place. She thought of Vienna, trapped as she was in her luxurious lifestyle aboard *The Ice Star. I'm trapped too*, she realised and pushed the thought to the back of her mind as she approached the elevator. The suite was on the top floor of the hotel, giving Fenna time to rein in her heartbeat and prepare herself for first contact with her target. *The last time*, she remembered, *I wasn't prepared for Humble. This time is different.*

"Just keep telling yourself that, *love*," she said aloud, adding the chill of Burwardsley's familiar moniker to chide herself into action. The elevator slowed to a stop on the ground floor and Fenna took a breath as the doors opened with a soft rumble.

She stepped out into the foyer, found her feet and settled into her walk across the tiled floor. The clack of her heels gave her a cadence to work with, and, despite its unfamiliarity, she realised she enjoyed the extra height they gave her, and the looks she drew from the men, seated at the tables in the foyer, pausing in their banter as she passed.

I don't need a gun, she thought as she followed the signs to the *Ellehammer* conference room. *I'm already lethal.*

Chapter 17

The clock on the wall above the stage at the far end of the room showed Fenna she had less than an hour to make an impression on Lorentzen. So far, the only thing the professor's endorsement had given her was a seat at one of the tables furthest from the stage, together with an octogenarian with halitosis and his portly young assistant with roving eyes and a highly inflated ego, based on some obscure geology expedition to which he had been accepted. The drinks, at least, were included in the admission fee.

She saw him the moment he entered the room. A collective hush alerted her to his arrival, and Fenna turned, along with the majority of people in the room, to see the famed geologist and keynote speaker for the evening. She could see how he charmed his way into the beds of women half his age, into the most exclusive clubs, and onto high profile executive boards eager for the chance to share the same space as Lorentzen and to profit by association.

And yet, Fenna mused as he ignored her on the way to the podium, *you are languishing on assignment in Nuuk. Bored. Or is that just a front?* She pushed the thoughts away and listened as he began to speak.

Lorentzen had obviously studied the art of public speaking, Fenna realised, stopping herself for a moment as she, like those around her, leaned forward, ever so slightly, in anticipation of his next word, the punch line, or the lessons learned from his various anecdotes. It was clear that he had been chosen to speak on a variety of subjects dear to the audience's heart. He was among friends, and many of them had shared more than one of his adventures. He made a pointed at and referenced each of them as his speech progressed. It was his last story that sealed her interest in Lorentzen, especially as she knew the source material intimately. There was even a moment when she imagined that he might confess to the murder of Johansson, and her mission would be over. Of course, he did not, but Fenna's inside knowledge, and her appreciation of sea ice and the north, ensured that he had her full and undivided attention. A fact which, even from the podium at the other end of the room, he noticed, pausing to take a sip of water as he did so.

"He's a bit full of himself," the young geologist whispered.

"Shh," said Fenna, as Lorentzen put down his glass and continued with the story.

"The mist was thick with ice when they found the body of my dear colleague, Dr Johansson. His body was layered in a quilt of crystals, they shone in the midnight sun, and I remember being moved, beyond the tragic nature of his death, to imagine a serenity in the scene that, although wholly inappropriate, I chose to focus on, to remember him, in that moment, as I hope you will do now." Lorentzen picked up the glass of wine beside his water and raised it. "To Dr Johansson," he said.

"Dr Johansson," the audience of geologists, journalists and one PET agent chorused.

Lorentzen put down his glass and signalled to the host of the symposium that he was ready to answer a few questions. The first, as Fenna had predicted, concerned the identity of Johansson's killer.

"Something we all want to know, not least his wife and children," Lorentzen said and placed his hands on the sides of the podium. "The circumstances of his death suggest that it was no accident, and, when you consider the goals of the expedition," he paused to gesticulate. "It begs the question, will people kill for the North Pole? Will countries?"

Clever, Fenna thought as the audience murmured in response. Lorentzen had fuelled the conspiracy theorists among them, and she heard the word *Russians* as it filtered down from one table to another, toward the back of the hall.

Lorentzen answered two more questions before thanking the hosts, the Royal Danish Geological Society, and wishing everyone a pleasant evening. He made his way down from the podium to mingle with the geologists standing and clapping as he stepped off the stage.

He was still pressing flesh and charming his way between tables as Fenna, standing at the bar, finished her second glass of wine. She had already dismissed three offers of something stronger to drink when she saw Lorentzen walk toward her, only to be stopped, just a table away, by two geologists and a journalist Fenna recognised from one of the reports Jarnvig had forced her to read while in the bath. Standing next to the journalist was a tall Chinese man. Fenna noted the way he nodded at Lorentzen as he approached, and the grim but civil expression he wore.

"Karl," said the older of the two geologists. "Terrible business on the LOMROG expedition."

"Yes," Lorentzen said, as he shook his hand. "Still, I'm sure we agree that the outcome is much worse, Dr Villadsen? Wouldn't you say?"

"You mean losing the Pole to the Russians?"

"I mean losing the Pole to anyone." Lorentzen looked up as Fenna made her way to the periphery of the table. The men turned to see what had caught his attention, dismissing Fenna with a mixture of bored stares and raised eyebrows. Dr Villadsen ensured Lorentzen ignored Fenna by adding a follow-up question.

"Forget about the Pole for a minute," he said. "What do you make of the Canadians upping their presence in the north? Their Rangers have skidoos and automatic weapons, you know. It's time we upped our ante and showed them a bit of muscle, not just a few young fellas from the Sirius Patrol with a bunch of dogs and an antiquated rifle. What do you say to that?"

"I'd say..." Lorentzen said, pausing as Fenna chose her moment to make an impression.

"That skidoos will never replace dogs and men," she said, as she stepped between the chairs and joined the men standing in the space between two tables. "That's what you'd say," she said, "if you knew what you were talking about." Fenna winked and took a sip of wine, amazed at her own boldness and praying that the thump of her heart could not be seen trembling the skin between her breasts and the low cut of her dress.

"Ridiculous," said Villadsen, as he scowled at Fenna. "I don't care how many dogs you hook up to a sledge, they simply can't cover the distance that a skidoo can, nor can they pull the kind of loads required to sustain a patrol in the high Arctic. Isn't that right, Karl?"

"Well..."

"A single team of dogs can pull enough supplies

to last them a month," Fenna said and took a step forward. "That month can be extended with seal meat caught on patrol, food and fuel for both men and dogs. Tell me," Fenna said and paused to read the man's nametag, "Dr Villadsen, how much fuel can a skidoo carry?"

"I don't know, I would imagine…"

"Imagining won't cut it in the high Arctic. There's no room for miscalculation, nor is there any room for mechanical breakdowns or repairs. If a sledge breaks, the team has the skills and the materials to fix it. If a harness rips, they sew a new one. If a dog is injured in a fight, they sew it up. Same with a teammate. If he gets a tooth infection, his partner pulls it."

Villadsen looked from Lorentzen to the geologist smirking beside him. "I…"

"Don't know? No," said Fenna, "it appears that you don't. But the next time you scowl at a woman as if she is as intelligent as the cushion you pressed your chauvinistic arse on this past hour," she said, with a nod at the man's chair, "you might remember our little chat." Fenna lifted her glass to her lips and drained it. "Cheers," she said and turned toward the bar.

Fenna heard the journalist chuckle as she reached the bar, and the soft voice of the Chinese man as he spoke in English, suggesting that he had understood what she had said, despite not knowing a single word of Danish. She ordered another glass of wine, her third of the evening, and waited for Lorentzen to join her. She didn't have to wait long.

"Do you always do that at parties?" he said as he leaned against the bar and ordered a whisky.

145

"This isn't a party," she said, facing him.

"Fenna," he said, as he read her nametag. "My name is Karl."

"I know who you are," she said and shook his hand. Fenna nodded toward the stage. "Keynote speaker, Dr Karl Lorentzen. It's on the poster."

"Yes," he said. He thanked the bartender for the whisky and turned his attention back to Fenna. "Shall we find somewhere to sit, and you can tell me who you are?"

"I can tell you here," she said and waved her glass of wine. "It's closer to the bar."

"That's because it *is* the bar," he said and laughed.

"It is?" Fenna said and laughed. "I've been here longer than I thought."

"Or not long enough." Lorentzen raised his glass to his lips. He finished it in one and waggled the glass at the bartender.

"Another *Laphroaig?*"

"As long as it's on the house, why not." He looked at Fenna. "Do you drink whisky?"

"No. I get into enough trouble with wine."

"I see," he said. "Do you know who you just insulted?"

"Insulted? I put him in his place," Fenna said, leaning back against the bar. She let her elbow touch his, and, despite the alcohol in her system, she knew he could feel it, just as she knew he was staring at the straps hanging from her bare shoulders whenever he thought she wasn't looking.

"When you reach his age, it's the same thing."

"Good," she said and took another sip of wine. "But he's not the interesting one. Who is the Chinese man talking with the journalist from *Politiken*?"

"You know Henning?"

Fuck. Careful Fenna, she thought. "Oh, I read something of his recently, something about Greenland."

"Yes, he did write a good piece in Sunday's paper," Lorentzen said with another glance at Fenna's shoulder. "Henning is talking to Hong Wei, a representative of the Chinese government. He's here to…"

"Assess the mine at Isukasia?" Fenna said and smiled at the look on his face.

"Okay," he said, as he pushed himself away from the bar. Lorentzen straightened his jacket and stood in front of Fenna. With a quick glance over his shoulder he turned back to face her. "You officially have my attention. Who *are* you?"

"I'm glad I have your attention," Fenna said, a smile played across her lips.

"So tell me."

"You don't know?"

"I don't," he said, and for a moment, Fenna was almost lost in the boyish flicker of failure that settled on his face. Perhaps it was the wine, the satisfaction of putting a pompous old man in his place, or the realisation that she was on the job and off the leash. Investigating, *finally*, and loving every minute of it. "You're going to have to tell me," he said and reached for his glass.

Fenna caught his hand as he rested his arm on the counter. She smoothed her fingers over his skin, hesitated for a second, and then squeezed his hand in hers. He looked at her, and at the glass in her hand.

"I know," she said. "It probably is the wine, but I

really wanted to meet you tonight."

"You did?" Lorentzen said with a raised eyebrow.

"Yes," Fenna said. She removed her hand and caught a little thrill as she recognised the look on his face as he displayed his disappointment. "My name is Fenna Brongaard, and I represent..."

"Tunstall Mining," he said. "Of course."

"Yes," she said and pushed the straps of her dress back onto her shoulders.

"Obviously," Lorentzen said. "It makes sense now. I got the email a few weeks ago, and then Anders' call earlier this evening. I should have put it all together. You'll be accompanying me to Isukasia. Right?"

"That's right," Fenna said, hiding the feeling of irritation that she didn't have any more information for him to tease out of her. "I'm flying to Greenland tomorrow."

"Tomorrow? Then we are on the same flight. You're flying *Nanok Class*? Business?"

"No," she said and frowned. "I'm pretty sure Tunstall Mining want to keep their costs at a minimum on this venture."

"Well, I'll have to see what I can do about that," he said. "I have some good connections at *Air Greenland*. I'll make some enquiries, get you a seat next to me, and Hong Wei," he said, with a glance over his shoulder.

Fenna was surprised at the thrill the name of the airline elicited in her. It had been a long time, but she was returning to Greenland. *Just a few hours from now*, she added and placed her glass, half-full, on the counter.

"You're leaving," he said and gestured at her

glass.

"It's a long flight."

"It's not, actually. It's the wait in Kangerlussuaq that usually takes time."

"Not *Søndre Strømfjord?*" she said. "You used the Greenlandic name."

"Yes," he said and frowned. "And from what you know of the Sirius Patrol, back there, I imagine you to be a Greenland aficionado. Am I right?" he said and pointed in the direction of Villadsen's table.

"I know a few things," Fenna said. "From what I have read, mostly."

"You've never been?"

Fenna paused for a moment as she recalled the cover story Jarnvig had pressed upon her in another folder, also to be read and memorised while she bathed. "Once, when I was a teenager. My daddy arranged it." Fenna almost choked on the word, but realised the girly term might endear her even more to her mark.

"What did he do? Your father?"

What did *he do?* Fenna recalled her real father, the soldier in the Danish *Jægerkorps*, Special Forces. She wondered if he would be proud of her, honey-trapping a Danish national on behalf of *Politiets Efterretningstjeneste*. Her training kicked in and she said, "He fixed photocopying machines, would you believe?"

"I would," Lorentzen said and took a sip of whisky. "You can make a career of fixing anything in the Arctic, photocopying machines included."

"That's what my daddy said."

"Your *daddy?*" he said and grinned. Fenna smiled as he finished his whisky. "I'm guessing he is about my age?"

"I wouldn't know," she said and lifted her chin. "How old are you?"

"Guess," he said.

"Forty?" Fenna said, and then, "Forty-two?" She bit her bottom lip as if she was thinking. If she got too close, she knew, his suspicions might be aroused. And yet, she could tell he was already aroused. She watched as Lorentzen slipped his hands in his pockets. *A casual move*, she thought, *if it wasn't intended to hide his arousal.*

"I'm fifty-one. But," he said and shrugged, "Greenland…"

"Keeps you in shape?" Fenna said. "I've heard that before."

"It's a physical place. You have to be active if you want to do anything, go anywhere."

"I look forward to seeing it again."

"And I look forward to showing it to you."

"Tomorrow, then," Fenna said and removed her nametag. She placed it on the bar, laughing as he stared at it. "It's not my hotel key card," she said.

"I never thought…"

"Yes you did," she said. "And maybe you were even right to do so. But I have a flight to catch tomorrow, and I don't intend to miss it."

"You are a mystery, Fenna Brongaard."

"Yes," she said and turned and walked away.

Fenna knew his eyes followed her across the room. She felt a surge of adrenalin and a flood of different emotions, wondering just how far she would have gone. She was pleased with herself for reaching out and making physical contact. *My fingers on his hand*, she mused. *Electric. And yet those same fingers*, she recalled, *killed a man*. Fenna stopped in the corridor outside the conference room. *Am I going to have to kill him?* Jarnvig's words filtered through her own as she made her way to the hotel bar.

"Whatever it takes," he had said, and she wondered if she could.

Fenna spotted Møller sitting at a table in the corner of the room. She walked past the bar and sat down opposite him.

"Well?" he said.

"You can tell Jarnvig," she said. "That Lorentzen is on the hook and the mission is on."

The Mine

SERMERSOOQ, GREENLAND

Chapter 18

Lorentzen's influence had, in some circles at least, a limited reach. Fenna travelled in economy class from Kastrup Airport to the old American runway at Kangerlussuaq, the hub of almost all air traffic to and from Greenland. She sat next to the window, grateful for the lack of turbulence, and dozed as they flew over Iceland, only to wake as the *Airbus 330-200* turned feet-dry over Greenland's east coast. She pressed her nose to the glass, looking for familiar landmarks, knowing they were too far south for her to see anything resembling the coastline she had patrolled with Oversergent Mikael Gregersen, or the settlement of Ittoqqortoormiit where she had been deceived, detained, and interrogated about his death. *A sideshow*, she thought. *Just another move of another piece on the chessboard in the Great Arctic Game – a game that I'm a part of.*

The steward disturbed her with the offer of a drink, the last chance before landing in Kangerlussuaq. Fenna asked for coffee, nodded her thanks as she cupped her hands around the paper cup and stared at the ice sheet. She sipped her coffee and thought of the hundreds of people who had skied across the ice, from east to west, since Fridtjof Nansen led the Greenland Expedition, reaching Nuuk, then Godthåb, in October 1888.

Why ski when you can sledge? she thought and smiled as the steam from the coffee settled on the window. She was sitting uncomfortably close to the cool panel of the plane's interior, and yet, she was unwilling to distance herself from the comfort of the ice. She adjusted her position and the passenger beside her snapped the sheets of his newspaper and grunted something about flying *monkey class*. Fenna ignored him and pressed her nose to the glass once more.

There was little comfort to be found in the thoughts that pressed to the fore of her mind as she lost herself in the stark, white surface of the ice, it was a blank slate upon which memories of the settlement of Ittoqqortoormiit were served. *The Magician* appeared as she remembered him in the guise of Premierløjtnant Vestergaard – first name *Klaus*. Jarnvig had said, prior to her leaving for Arizona, that *The Magician* was not her concern.

Whose concern is he, if not mine? she thought and leaned back in her seat.

Another piece on the board. Another puzzle. Fenna wondered just how many demons her return to Greenland would invoke. *And how many can I resist?*

The Magician's role in the Canadian plot to sabotage the credibility of the Danish sovereignty mission in Greenland had been both clever and thorough. Fenna considered what she knew of Lorentzen and his involvement in the subterfuge at the Pole, and who was pulling *his* strings. *The Magician?* It wasn't the most ridiculous idea she had ever had. Fenna smiled at the thought and pulled at the thread, teasing her theory into a thin length of cotton, too thin to sew with, but just enough to feel if she was to rub it between her finger and thumb. She finished her coffee, glancing at the man beside her as he grunted again. When she pulled on the different threads she had assembled in her mind, when she tied knots, only to see them unravel, even *when* they unravelled, Fenna discovered a sense of purpose that she did not experience in the dust of the desert, or the sweat of the Sonoran boxing ring. Thinking, investigating, she realised, was delicious, a tangible mental kick that she could easily become addicted to. Whoever she had been on patrol, on the ice, that girl, that young woman – fighting for a place in a man's world – had now found a niche, a seat at the table, stakes in the game. *And what a game*, she thought. *Perhaps Jarnvig had been right to test her. Perhaps, now, she was ready.* She certainly felt ready, and as the *Airbus* began its descent into the canyon on the last stages of the approach onto the runway at Kangerlussuaq, Fenna felt, for the first time, that the job was not just something she could do, that she was trained for, but that she *wanted* to do it, that she *needed* it. The thought buoyed her through the landing, out of her seat, and across the tarmac into the arrivals building of Kangerlussuaq International Airport. It lightened the load, slipped her through security with nothing more than a cursory glance at her fake passport, all the way into the lounge, where she would wait for her connecting flight. It was a rough male voice and a string of words that shattered her confidence and threatened to start a cascade reaction, a shutting down of all systems.

"Nice to see you again, *love*."

Fenna froze for a second, until her training kicked in. It took all her reserve not to strike first. Instead, she tightened her grip on her North Face holdall and turned, slowly, to face the British Marine Lieutenant, the man who had tried so hard to kill her, the man who ordered her partner killed, on his knees, in the snow.

"Burwardsley," she said.

"Hello, Konstabel," Burwardsley grinned, as she

stared up at him. His bulk blocked her view of the nearest exit. *All of them,* she realised. She flicked her eyes to the left and right of his shoulders, stopping when he laughed.

"He's not here," he said. "I left Bad in Britain. I'm all alone."

"Somehow I doubt it," Fenna said and steeled herself to look in his eyes. She studied them, searching for clues, anticipating a reaction, waiting for a strike.

"Honestly, I am here by myself. Sightseeing," he said and grinned. "I always wanted to see Greenland in the summer." Burwardsley shrugged. "Here I am."

"Here you are," Fenna said and tensed. She looked to Burwardsley's right as Lorentzen approached together with Hong Wei.

"Friends of yours?" Burwardsley asked.

"You don't know me," she said and bit her bottom lip.

"It's a bit late for that. They've seen us talking."

"Shut up," she said, drumming her fingers on her thigh. "You're a tourist…"

"As I have been trying to tell you. Christ, you're not very good at this." Burwardsley shook his head and tugged the backpack over his right shoulder higher up his back.

"No, I'm not," Fenna said, as Lorentzen noticed her and waved. She waved back. "But until I figure things out, you're a fucking tourist who mistook me for a guide."

"Whatever you say, *love*," Burwardsley said, and grinned as he dragged out the last word.

"Hi," Fenna said as Lorentzen and Hong Wei stopped beside her.

"I'm sorry I could not find you a seat with Wei and me in Business Class," said Lorentzen. She held her breath as she noticed Burwardsley raise his eyebrow. "I'm sure you would have made an uneventful flight more interesting."

"Interesting?" Burwardsley mouthed.

Fenna ignored him and forced herself to remember the role she was playing – this life versus her old life. *Even though the one is a direct result of the other*, she mused. The thought slipped from her mind as she smiled and said something about not having slept much and needing to recover on the flight. She almost didn't hear Lorentzen's response, tuning in at the last second as she composed herself and did her best to ignore Burwardsley.

"… Air Greenland has to move the chopper to Nuuk for our benefit anyway," he said, and switching to English, "but I'm not sure there is room for your friend."

"My friend?" Fenna said and realised he was looking at Burwardsley.

"Oh, we're not friends," Burwardsley said and repositioned his backpack. "I thought…" he paused as if to remember her name. "Fenna, is it?"

"Yes," she said and lifted her chin, turning her attention from Lorentzen to Burwardsley.

"I thought she was my guide," he said. "I booked a hiking trip and I'm waiting for someone from…" Burwardsley glanced at a carousel of brochures. "Arctic Adventure." Fenna let out her breath as Burwardsley smiled at her. He shook her hand, holding her grip for a second longer than she liked before he excused himself and walked out of the main lobby area in the direction of the cafeteria.

"You were saying something about a helicopter?" Fenna said, as she watched Burwardsley leave.

"Yes, with a female pilot. A Greenlander," Lorentzen said, as he gestured toward the lounge. "She is waiting for us in there. Let me introduce you."

Fenna felt Lorentzen's hand on her shoulder as he guided her and Hong Wei to the lounge. A tall Greenlandic woman, her jet-black hair pulled back and tied in a neat ponytail, stood up as they entered. Fenna caught her breath as she looked beyond the pilot's dark flight suit – an ultra thin drysuit designed to keep her warm long enough for a rescue should they ditch in the sea – and studied her face. *Dina* – the thought flashed into her mind and Fenna's demons were alive again. A slight wrinkle creased the pilot's frown as she stepped forward to greet them. She greeted Fenna first, and it was all Fenna could do to avoid saying Dina's name. They could have been twins – sharing the same soft caramel skin colour, the same burnt chocolate eyes – and yet, the pilot, Panninguaq Korneliussen, could not have been more different, Fenna realised, especially when she introduced them to her son.

"I'd like you to meet Anguteq. He is seven," she said, as the small boy curled his arms around her left leg."

"Anguteq?" Lorentzen said, twisting his tongue around the boy's name as he knelt to greet him. Anguteq shrank behind his mother and Panninguaq, speaking in Greenlandic, said something that made him reach forward for a second to shake the tip of Lorentzen's outstretched hand. The boy looked at the frown on Hong Wei's face and then retreated behind his mother's legs.

"He is shy," said Panninguaq. "His father and I broke up a few months ago and he is…" she paused. "Struggling a bit."

"I'm sorry," said Lorentzen as he stood up.

"I hope you don't mind, but I need to bring Anguteq with us to Nuuk," she said and glanced at Fenna. "I didn't know there would be three of you."

"Oh, I can find another flight…" Fenna said, stopping as Panninguaq shook her head.

"It's not a problem. The service technicians have already installed luggage pods on the skids. There is plenty of room inside the helicopter. Plenty of fuel too," she said, as she appraised Fenna for a moment. "We're about the same weight."

"Yes," Fenna said and smiled at Anguteq. He grinned and hid behind his mother, only to peek once more when Fenna waved at him.

Panninguaq gestured toward a door to the rear of the lounge and encouraged Anguteq to collect his things with a few words in Greenlandic and a pat on the bottom. Fenna caught her smile, as Panninguaq watched her son struggle into the arms of an oversized *Spiderman* backpack. *Not Dina*, Fenna reminded herself as Panninguaq caught her eye.

"We'll be flying in a Eurocopter AS350," said Panninguaq, as she led them along a corridor. Anguteq ran ahead of them, stopping at a security door, pushing and straining against it in mock exasperation until his mother swiped her card through the door lock and interface. Fenna watched as he pushed the door open. They all blinked as they stepped through the door, into the glare of the bright polar sun and onto the tarmac, following the yellow dashes painted onto the surface all the way to the helicopter. It was parked on a large, square trolley, with a tow hitch angled down to the landing pad. Panninguaq nodded at one of the ground crew as he placed a metal step in front of the trolley, took their bags, and helped them up and into the aircraft. Panninguaq guided Fenna into the co-pilot's seat and smiled as she handed her a set of headphones.

"So we can talk," she said.

"Thanks," said Fenna, as she strapped herself in. She turned in the seat to smile at Lorentzen and Hong Wei, as they settled onto the bench seat behind her. Anguteq made a show of helping them fasten their seatbelts, laughing as Lorentzen high-fived him.

Fenna settled into her seat, making a point of keeping her feet off the pedals and her hands off the control stick.

"Don't worry about them," Panninguaq said, as she buckled in beside Fenna. "They will move. Just ignore them. Unless," she said and brushed a loose wisp of black hair behind her ear.

"Unless what?"

Panninguaq grinned, as she pulled on her helmet. She pulled a stick of gum from the top pocket of her flight suit, pushed the microphone out of the way and popped it in her mouth. She repositioned the microphone and tapped it with her finger, indicating that Fenna put on her headset.

"Unless I fall asleep," Panninguaq said, her voice sudden and intimate in Fenna's ear. Fenna heard the Greenlander's light laugh and decided she liked her.

"Thanks," she said and shook her head.

"I thought you needed a laugh. You looked a little preoccupied back in the lounge. You afraid of flying?"

"What? Oh," said Fenna, as she realised the cloud of Burwardsley's sudden appearance had followed her further and for longer than she had thought. "No," she said and smiled. "I'm not actually afraid of anything." *Not any* thing *at least*, she added. *But people. People can still scare the crap out of me.*

Fenna heard Panninguaq laugh, talking to her son in Greenlandic as she flicked through the start-up sequence and talked to the tower. The rotors of the Eurocopterwhined out of slumber and a touch of obstinacy into a roar of motion. Fenna felt the vibrations through her feet, as Panninguaq waited for the helicopter to warm up and the engine to settle into a steady rhythm. The pilot spoke to the tower, twisted the collective and lifted the aircraft into a hover above the trolley with a smooth grasp of the control stick. Fenna spared a glance at Anguteq who was fidgeting between the two men on the back seat. He lifted his hands and stuck out his thumbs, jogging them up and down as his mother pointed the bright red nose of the Eurocopterin the direction of Nuuk.

There's no going back, Fenna realised. The aircraft picked up speed and Fenna settled in her seat.

Chapter 19

Sermitsiaq lies to the north of Nuuk. The mountain's flat angular crown listing to the west, piques the interest and captures the hearts of locals and visitors, not least with a pinched triangular peak focusing its granite energy into a single point. Its shadow does not reach Nuuk, and yet its reach is global, figuring prominently as it does on corporate and media logos and thousands of social media websites and galleries. Fenna studied the mountain, as Panninguaq called in her approach to the tiny provincial airport of Greenland's capital. Sermitsiaq, she noticed, resembled a wedge with the lower ridge curving around the mountain's base. *I've seen better mountains*, she decided, as the Eurocopter settled on the tarmac beside a Bombadier Dash 8 airplane. The bright red and white spotted liveries of both aircraft were a stark contrast to the large patches of brilliant snow covering the landscape surrounding Nuuk and crowning Sermitsiaq in gold, as the sun captured the higher of the two ridges. The rotors of the helicopter slowed from a thunderous chop to a slow protest, as the edges and tips bit at the cold, damp air until Panninguaq applied the rotor brake and the ground crew approached the aircraft.

"Welcome to Nuuk," she said and removed her flight helmet.

Fenna tugged the headset from her head and slipped it over a hook in front of her. She turned to watch Hong Wei and Lorentzen do the same. Anguteq bounced his calves on the seat, as he waited for the men to exit the cabin. He high-fived one of the ground crew before shouldering his backpack and racing across the tarmac to the airport building, launching into the legs of an elderly Greenlander that Fenna assumed was the boy's grandfather.

"He is pleased to be home, eh?" Lorentzen said, as he picked up his own pack and carry-on suitcase.

"Home?" said Panninguaq. "Home is further north. Nuuk is just where we live."

Fenna caught the look on Lorentzen's face, and, for a moment, his guard was down and she thought she recognised a longing for the north, something they each seemed to share. Hong Wei collected his luggage without comment, following the boy's path around the parked aircraft, head down and focused on placing each foot as securely on the slippery surface as possible.

"He's quiet," Fenna said and gripped her holdall.

"I think efficient is the word," Lorentzen said and gestured for Fenna to walk alongside him. "What little I know of Hong Wei suggests that he is a cautious man who appraises each situation economically, stripping away the flesh and cutting to the bone. He is a details man, with no interest in cosmetics." Lorentzen paused for a moment as he slipped, regained his footing and continued. "The Chinese chose their man carefully, and they trust him implicitly. If he signs off on the mine, then they will invest heavily, but ruthlessly. You can be sure they will maximise their profits with little or no thought extended to the Greenlanders. That's why I'm here."

"You?" said Fenna. "You're a negotiator?"

"No," he said and laughed. "That would be a mistake. My job is to do the field research and provide the details, including the cosmetic ones that Hong Wei will ignore. Isukasia is deep in Nuuk fjord, at the very end of it, in the mountains," Lorentzen said and pointed to the north east, his arm pointing straight between the airport building and the hangars. "But the traffic, tugs, barges and aircraft, will impact the wildlife and the environment between here and there in a way unprecedented in this part of Greenland."

"You're an environmentalist?" Fenna said and frowned. *Not what I imagined.*

"A tree-hugger? Me?" Lorentzen laughed again "God no, and," he said, "don't mention Greenpeace here in Nuuk. They are not welcome, not since their campaign against seal hunting. Those images of seals being clubbed in Canada in the 70s have haunted the Greenlanders for decades now. No, I'm not an environmentalist. I'm a pragmatist. It's about what the environment can cope with, before permanent damage results. The added challenge in Isukasia is the strain that a mine of that scale will place on Nuuk. Remember, there are only 15,000 people in Nuuk. The last figures for the mine suggested there might be as many as 7,000 workers, all of them Chinese, working in, around, or for the mine. They will need their own town, their own hospital." Lorentzen paused as they reached the airport building. "The politics of this project are splitting the country," he said and pushed the door open.

Panninguaq raised her eyebrow and said, "Like I said. Welcome to Nuuk."

Fenna followed Lorentzen inside, nodding at the policeman standing by the door to the waiting area and check-in desks. The sight of the policeman's dark blue jacket stalled Fenna for a second, her eyes drifting to the Heckler & Koch USP Compact pistol holstered at his hip. Fenna caught the policeman's eye; the thought of Maratse, and his boyish appreciation of a good gun battle, made her smile.

Hong Wei was waiting by the exit. He picked up his bag as they approached and waited as Lorentzen agreed to meet Panninguaq at the airport the following day.

"We'll be three, again," he said.

"No problem. You've chartered the chopper," she said. "I fly where you tell me to."

"Great," Lorentzen said and turned to Fenna. "Where are you staying? Hotel Hans Egede?"

"Yes," she said.

"So is Hong Wei. Let's get a taxi." Lorentzen shook hands with Panninguaq. "Until tomorrow."

Fenna went to follow him, but Panninguaq caught her arm.

"You seem familiar," she said. "Have we met?"

"No, I don't think so."

"Never been in Greenland before?"

"A long time ago," Fenna said and hiked her thumb toward Lorentzen. "I'd better be going."

"All right. I was just sure that…"

"Yes?"

"Last year there was…" Panninguaq paused and studied Fenna's face.

Come on, Fenna thought. *I don't need this.*

"No," she said. "I must be mistaken. I'll see you tomorrow."

"Okay," Fenna said and smiled. "Thanks for the flight." She walked out of the airport, her breath misting a cloud of smoke as passengers waited, cigarettes clamped between their lips and their eyes focused on the approaching snow clouds with the air of experienced travellers.

"We got in just in time," Lorentzen said, as he hurried Fenna to the taxi. The driver took her bag and tossed it into the boot. Fenna climbed into the back beside Hong Wei as Lorentzen got in the front. He turned in his seat as the driver pulled away from the airport, accelerating along the road running parallel to the runway. "It should clear up later," he said and pointed at the clouds. "But I have the feeling our pilot can cope with a little snow."

"A little, maybe," said Fenna. She caught the look on Lorentzen's face, his raised eyebrow, and realised, not for the first time, that she was struggling to find the balance between ignorance and showing an interest. *I'm not very good at this*, she thought. *Not yet.* "What?" she said as Lorentzen continued to look at her.

"There's something about you," he said. "I'm not sure what it is. Something familiar."

"You're mistaking me with another woman," she said and forced a laugh.

"No," he said. "I don't think so. Besides, I heard the pilot say as much. There's more to you, *Fenna*, than meets the eye."

Fenna wrestled with her thoughts and the façade she needed to maintain during the ten-minute drive into Nuuk. The lights of passing cars caught the twist of heavy flakes of snow as they tumbled to the ground. Ravens picked at the trash and fishing gear abandoned beneath the hulls of small boats and skiffs grounded for the winter. She spared a brief thought to the ravens teasing sledge dog puppies in Ittoqqortoormiit, only to be reminded at the first sight of Nuuk's housing blocks, that there was a world of difference between the settlements of Greenland and its capital. *And I need to remember that*, she mused. *I need to keep the two Greenlands separate – and the two Fennas.*

The bustle on the street outside the hotel snapped her attention back to the moment, as did the cold air entering the cab as Hong Wei opened the door to get out. Lorentzen paid the driver and Hong Wei collected his luggage. Fenna stepped out onto the street, orientated herself for a moment, taking in the activity around the entrance to the *Brugsen* supermarket, the buses, taxis and pedestrians, before grabbing her holdall and following the men inside.

"I'll see you in the morning," Lorentzen said, as he helped Hong Wei check in at the main desk. The Chinese man picked up his bags and made his way to the elevator. Fenna checked in, tapping her finger on the desk as she waited.

"You'll find the Internet is hellishly expensive," Lorentzen said, as the clerk handed Fenna her key card. "We got broadband a few years ago, but you get more gigabytes for less money with a mobile phone in Denmark than a cable connection here."

"I'll stay off the net," Fenna said. *He wants something*, she thought as Lorentzen glanced at his backpack leaning against the desk.

"We haven't established your role," he said. "And how Tunstall Mining just happens to have a Danish representative on their books."

"They are international," Fenna said. She felt her cheeks begin to flush and waved the key card in her hand. "I had better find my room."

"There's a bar. On the top floor."

"Okay." Fenna picked up her holdall and took a

step toward the elevator.

"Maybe later?" he said. "To get to know you, and find out more about your remit?"

"Sure," she said and glanced at her watch.

"It's four hours earlier than you think."

"Right," Fenna said, "I forgot."

"Easy mistake. How about I meet you in the bar at six?"

"Okay. I'll see you then." Fenna walked to the elevator, pressed the button and waited for the door to open. She walked in, conscious of the proximity of Lorentzen as he waited in the lobby, watching her as the door closed. When it did, Fenna leaned back against the side and breathed.

"Damn," she said. She closed her eyes for a moment and then opened them at a ping as the elevator stopped on her floor, the fourth. She found her room, entered and tossed her holdall on the bed. She closed and locked the door, changed her watch to the local time, and looked down on the snowy street. Snow clung to the light blue of the supermarket, the warm glow of its lights like a beacon in the grey gloom of the storm. Fenna took a moment by the window to get her bearings, picking out the Bank of Greenland building, the tallest building on the horizon. Then she pulled off her jacket and flopped on the bed.

Panninguaq's curiosity and Lorentzen's suspicions cantered through her mind and she wondered if the mission was compromised, if it was nothing less than a monumental mistake to return to Greenland.

"In a country with just over 50,000 people, everyone knows someone, and that someone..." she sighed and closed her eyes. "That someone knows me."

Fenna propped herself up on her elbows and looked around the room, stopping to focus on the small kettle and the complimentary coffee and tea. She swung her legs over the side of the bed and pulled off her boots and socks. She padded across the carpet, filled the kettle with water from the bathroom, and prepared a cup of coffee. She dug the LOMROG report out of her holdall and made space on the small desk beneath the flat screen television hanging on the wall. Fenna flicked to the profile of Lorentzen, tucked in at the back of the report.

"You're a lonely guy, Dr Lorentzen," she said, as she looked through the report. "Why? What did I miss?" Fenna paused and traced her fingers over a few lines of scribbled notes in the margin. They were feint – *a bad photocopy*, she thought. Fenna read the lines, and then again, aloud, she processed the new information. "Parents died in car crash. Lorentzen, aged seven, pulled out of the car by firemen..." Fenna stopped reading. "I wonder," she said, remembering information gleaned from the profile during her first reading. "A history of short-lasting relationships, problems with attachment. And no wonder. Christ, if..."

She looked up at the sound of knocking on her door.

"Just a minute," she said and closed the report. She stuffed it into her holdall and zipped the bag shut. Fenna glanced around the room and took a few slow breaths before walking to the door. "I thought you said six o'clock," she said as she opened it.

"Now when did we agree that, *love*?" Burwardsley

said and pushed her inside the room with the flat of his hand.

Chapter 20

Whether it was her training or the survival impulse she had been nurturing Fenna didn't know, but when Burwardsley's palm pushed against her chest, she let the momentum carry her into the room toward the desk. She grabbed the lamp and swung it at him. The two-pronged plug caught in the socket tightening the short electric cable with a soft snap and whipping the lamp out of her hand just as it connected with the side of his head.

"Fenna. Stop," said Burwardsley as he batted the lamp away from his face. She kicked at his right shin, and swung her left fist at his chin. She cried out as her knuckles connected with the Englishman's bone, her hand rasping against the stubble protruding through his skin. "Jesus. Fenna. You'll have hotel security her in a second."

Fenna leapt up onto the bed and swung her foot, aiming a kick at Burwardsley's head. He blocked her kick with his forearm, wrapped her leg within the crook of his arm and slapped his hand into her chest. Fenna crashed onto the bed and Burwardsley followed her down, his weight crushing her body as she struggled beneath him, stuttering short breaths as she spasmed for air.

"For fuck's sake," Burwardsley said. "Calm down and I'll let you go."

Fenna flicked her eyes at his and fought to increase the pause between each of her breaths until her chest stopped heaving and her heart adopted a rhythm that approximated that of strenuous exercise and not the feral beat of fight and flight. She trembled as she looked Burwardsley in the eye.

"Better?"

She nodded.

"I'm going to let go," he said and loosened his grip on her leg. Fenna flexed her fingers and Burwardsley paused, raising one eyebrow as he looked at her. "Konstabel?" She relaxed and he let go, shifting his weight as he pushed himself off Fenna and off the bed. She watched him as he walked to the door, closed and locked it, he picked the lamp up off the floor and put it on the desk. He fiddled for a moment with the lampshade, bending it back into shape between his fingers, turning the side with the dent in toward the wall. He pulled the chair out from beneath the desk, placed it in the space between the door and Fenna and sat down to face her.

Fenna lay flat on the bed. Her left leg hanging over the edge as if she had yet to reconnect with it. It was remote, detached, spent of energy, useless. A strand of hair was trapped within the lashes of Fenna's left eye, but she ignored it, peering through the hair, ignoring the irritation as she stared at Burwardsley. He stared back, dwarfing the chair beneath him, his hands resting on his knees, pale against the dark blue denim of his jeans. His arms were locked, elbows pointing to each side. Fenna flicked her eyes past him toward the door, her only escape route, blocked. She looked out of the window, listening to the faint buzz of the street below, the occasional shout and drunken slur, four floors below her. She turned her head back to Burwardsley as he coughed.

"You wouldn't make it," he said and nodded toward the window.

Fenna said nothing.

Burwardsley looked at Fenna's face and she felt his gaze blister her skin. "Black suits you," he said. "Although I liked it before." He paused and Fenna watched as his eyes softened and his cheeks relaxed. He wiped one large hand across his stubbled face. Fenna heard the tiny hairs scratch against his palm. "I never told you," he said. "How hard it was for me to hunt you."

Fenna closed a mental hand around her heart, willing it to stay within her chest, fearing her sternum plate, the cradle of her ribs, could not contain it. She had to get out, but her heart was the only part of her body not paralysed by Burwardsley's presence, his words. She wrestled her mind free of his grip, wrangled her thoughts into play and began to think.

What does he want? And why can I never beat him, this man, my Achilles?

"Of course," he said and placed his hand on his knee. "I thought it was all over, that you were gone and what happened on the island, onboard the ship ... I really thought it was all over. And yet..." He paused again and leaned forward. "Why are you back in Greenland, Konstabel?"

"Why are you?" she said, her eyes twitching, surprised at the sound of her own voice.

"That," he said, and sighed, "is a longer story."

"But you're not sightseeing, are you?"

"You never believed I was."

"No."

Burwardsley stood up and Fenna watched as he found the kettle and made coffee. As the water boiled she shifted position, pushing herself up against the headboard of the bed, drawing her knees into her chest. She wrapped her arms around her legs, and, for a brief moment, her wrists itched with the memory of rusted dog chain leashing her to the wooden wall of a distant cabin, the site of her first interrogation at the brutal hands of the man now serving her coffee in a paper cup on the opposite coast of the country. *That was the other Greenland*, she thought, *the other Fenna*. She took the coffee and waited until Burwardsley sat down before taking a sip. The chair creaked beneath his massive frame.

"I'm not sightseeing," he said and blew on the surface of his coffee. "This is personal."

"What is?"

"A good question." Burwardsley turned the cup in his hands. "I said I didn't like hunting you."

"You could have fooled me," she said and remembered the buzz of the skidoo and the exchange of lead as they shot at each other across the ice, the thunder of the helicopter changing pitch as it banked away from the clouds of snow obscuring Fenna, confusing the hunters, providing shelter and reprieve, only to deliver her into the hands of Humble and introduce her to the dark bowels of terror on the lower decks of *The Ice Star*.

"I'm a professional," he said and shrugged. "I happen to be very good at what I do, and people pay me well for it."

"A gun-thug for hire," Fenna said and sneered.

Burwardsley lifted the cup to his lips and stared at Fenna as he drank. He put the empty cup down on the desk. Fenna counted a full two minutes before he said anything.

"I heard about what you did to Humble," he said, a smile curled across his lips. "What I didn't hear was how you got away with it."

"I was lucky."

"No," he said and shook his head. "You had help."

"Yes."

"It's good to have friends like that, people who can get you out of a tight spot. Of course, that kind of help usually comes with a hefty price tag."

Fenna caught a scent of the desert, burnt sand, blood and sweat. *I know*, she thought. *And he knows too*.

"Piece of advice," he said. "There'll come a time when the price is too high, and you're forced to do things that don't sit well, things that keep you up at night."

He's talking about Dina, Fenna realised. She lowered her knees, tilted her head to one side. "You see her too," she said. "You see Dina."

Burwardsley scratched his face again. Fenna leaned forward, searching his eyes. Her breath caught in her throat as he looked at her and she saw it, a flash of white, a reflection, the tip of the iceberg. She knew that following it would lead to the frigid depths below, where the demons floated dark beneath the surface, where Dina was.

"Yeah," he said. "I see Dina. She's naked, her skin pale, smeared in all kinds of shit. She's shivering, but not from the cold." Burwardsley paused. He looked at Fenna. "I'm here on my own dollar," he said. "You started something and... Shit. Would you believe I'm actually ashamed that it was you who finished things? A skinny Danish girl, with tiny tits and tiny fists?" He laughed and, despite herself, Fenna laughed too.

"I've learned how to use them," she said. When

Burwardsley raised his eyebrow she added, "Really, I have." *Just not with you.*

"Well, that's good, I guess. But Dina," he said and they both stopped laughing. "Dina killed Lunk. You and your Danish friends got rid of Humble. Now there is only one guy left."

Fenna sat up. "You're going after Vestergaard? *The Magician?*"

"I have a lead," he said. "In my previous, more reputable life, I did a stint in the Arctic Cadre of the Royal Marines. I met a couple of Danes when on exercise in Norway. We used to sell whisky to the Norwegians, and, after a particularly good night, this Dane and I..." Burwardsley laughed. "Let's just say he owes me one."

"And he's here? In Nuuk?"

"Yep, he's at your Arctic Command Headquarters. But I wonder, are they even *yours* anymore, Konstabel? You went dark after Toronto," he said.

"And how do you know about that?"

"Perhaps we have a mutual friend?"

Fenna thought for a moment. *Nicklas,* she wondered. And then he was gone as she shifted gear, processing what Burwardsley had said, and wrestling with this new side, the new Burwardsley. *And yet, not so new after all.* She had seen the first signs when he had searched her outside the cabin at Ummannatsiaq. The cabin where Dina had died, taken her own life.

"Perhaps," she said. "But why do you think he is in Nuuk?"

"Vestergaard? Maybe. I don't know for sure. A man like that will be where you least expect it. Pulling strings, creating small pockets of chaos."

"So why are you here?"

"Because this is where the trail ends, and I intend to pick it up again."

Her stomach turned, as if someone had gripped it, squeezed it, tugging it in another direction, another course than the one she was already following. She pushed away images of Dina that threatened to overcome her. *Let him have them, for the moment at least.* But she couldn't stop the feelings of guilt and betrayal. And then the chair creaked and Burwardsley stood up.

"Where are you going?"

"To my hotel." Burwardsley paused by the desk to write something on the notepad. "My mobile number," he said.

"I want to help," she said and swung her legs off the bed and stood up.

"There's nothing you can do. Not yet," he said and shrugged. "Besides, you have your own mission."

"Yes."

"I'll be in touch when I know more. Who knows, perhaps you can help me in the end."

Burwardsley walked to the door, the tread of his boots pressing into the carpet. Fenna followed his tracks. She reached out and tugged at his fleece jacket, pulling back in an awkward recoil as he turned to look at her.

"Listen," she said.

"What?"

"I just want to say that..." Fenna ran her fingers through her hair, gripping two tiny fistfuls as she searched for the words. *Christ, my mind is a mess.*

"Fenna?"

"It's just that, well, I appreciate what you said.

I've been having those same dreams. Maybe not the same, exactly, *my* Dina, she twists at the end of that whip, and I'm trying to cut her down, but she's too heavy, and the room, the fucking room is splinters and bullets, and I'm there in the middle of it all..." Fenna loosened her fingers and let her hands fall to her sides. "I'm there," she said, softly, her eyes glistening. "And you're there, and she's dying, killing herself, and I didn't do anything to stop it. I let her die, and Dina, she's..." Fenna's last words caught on her lips.

"You did what you could." Burwardsley took a step toward the door and reached out for the handle. "I'll be in touch," he said and opened the door. Fenna waited as he turned in the corridor. He paused for a moment and then looked at her. "You did the right thing," he said. "You did all you could. It was me who chased her there. It was me who pulled that whip around her neck."

"No," Fenna said. "Humble did that. And that monster, Lunk."

"Sometimes, I tell myself that," he said. "But at the end of the day, love, no matter how small a part we played, you can always find a way to make yourself responsible. Whether you're responsible for doing something, or responsible for *not* doing something. It's all the same. Given your new career, you might want to remember that." Burwardsley nodded. "I'll be in touch."

Fenna listened to his footsteps as he walked along the corridor to the elevator. She heard the soft rumble as the doors opened, and again when they closed. His words caught in her mind as she closed and locked the door. She tried the lamp on the desk, blinking in the glare of the bulb before turning it off again. She tidied the top cover of the bed, rearranged the pillows, tossed the paper cups into the waste paper basket, until there were no more signs of the man she had hated until now. She looked at her watch and realised any thoughts about Burwardsley and Dina would have to wait.

She walked into the bathroom, stopped in front of the mirror and clicked the mental switch she had discovered since her experience in the desert. "And until then," she said, as she smoothed a wet finger over her eyebrow. "I have a job to do."

Fenna fetched her holdall from the room. She stripped, glancing at the bruises healing slowly on her body, as she picked out a black bra and panties from among her clothes. Fenna pulled on her jeans, and applied a little make-up to cover the stubborn traces of her panda eyes, before tugging a tight-fitting t-shirt over her head. She ruffled her hair with her fingers and leaned in toward the mirror.

"You, girl," she said, "are seriously messed up. But with a little luck, you might just get through this. And yet..." Fenna felt the words extinguish on her tongue. The life of an investigator, a PET agent, one of Jarnvig's pawns, she realised, was far from straight forward. "But I'm in the game now," she said, as she pulled her boots over her bare feet. "And it's time for the next round."

Chapter 21

The Skyline Bar on the top floor of Hotel Hans Egede was busier than Fenna expected it to be, so early in the evening. She found Lorentzen at a table furthest from the piano on the small stage opposite the bar. He stood up to greet her, but she didn't recognise the man sitting next to him.

"Fenna," Lorentzen said as he gave her a hug and kissed her cheek. Fenna twitched at the familiarity, and then leaned in to the kiss, playing her role as she imagined she should. She sat down and looked at the man opposite her. "This is Kaptajn Christian Bertelsen. He's with Arctic Command, here in Nuuk," Lorentzen said, as he sat down.

"Hello," said Fenna, as Lorentzen caught the eye of a waiter and ordered her a beer. *I'm not supposed to meet anyone from Arctic Command*, she thought, and prayed that her basic disguise held up to the Kaptajn's scrutiny.

"Christian hasn't been in Greenland long," Lorentzen said as the waiter arrived with Fenna's beer. "But new faces soon become old friends this far north," he said and Fenna wondered how many beers Lorentzen had had already.

"What is it you do, exactly?" Fenna said and took a sip of beer.

"Well, I…"

"He's got an interesting story to tell, actually," Lorentzen said and leaned forward in his chair. "You remember that man you didn't know at the airport?"

"What man?" Fenna said, glancing from Bertelsen to Lorentzen and back. *Careful, Fenna.*

"The one who thought you were a guide?"

"Yes," she said, and placed her glass on the table. The chill of the beer had made the glass slippery and, given the nature of Lorentzen's story, she didn't want it to slip out of her hand.

"It turns out he's not just another tourist after all." Lorentzen pointed at Bertelsen. "You tell her," he said as he leaned back in his chair and studied Fenna.

He's not as drunk as I thought.

"His name is Mike Burwardsley, I knew him back when I was on exercise in Norway."

"Yes?" Fenna said and glanced at Lorentzen. He was still watching her.

"Mike's name popped up on a watch list. I can't tell you too much, but I think you should keep an eye out, and let me know if you see him again."

"I don't know the man," Fenna said and frowned at Lorentzen. "Did you tell him that I did?"

Lorentzen shrugged. "It looked like you were talking…"

"He thought I was a guide."

"It looked like more than that," he said and stared at Fenna.

"Why do I suddenly feel that I'm the one you want to keep an eye on?" She looked at Bertelsen. "What do you know about me?" She waited for him to react and then said, "No. Don't look at him. What do you know about me, Kaptajn?" Fenna waited for five seconds before standing up and saying, "Fine. You've given me my answer." She turned to Lorentzen. "I'll see you at the airport in the morning. I think Panninguaq said we should be there at seven. I'll be early." She moved toward the entrance, stopped and said, "Thanks for the drink."

Fenna reached the elevator before she heard the sound of her name. She pressed the button to go down.

"Fenna, wait," Lorentzen said, as he walked past the leather sofa outside the bar and joined her in front of the elevator.

"So many questions," Fenna said and pushed the button again.

"Questions I had to ask."

"Is that why you asked me to join you for a drink? To ask questions? Is that why you brought your friend?"

"Hey, listen," he said, as the elevator doors opened. "These are interesting times. I vet everyone I meet."

"Good for you," Fenna said, as she brushed past the guest coming out. It wasn't difficult to play the role of the offended and affronted young woman, she realised, it was a good mask for the tumult of thoughts and apprehensions that were spinning through her mind. *Don't blow this*, she told herself. *Not now.*

"Fenna," Lorentzen said, as reached his arm inside the elevator to stop the doors from closing.

"Goodnight, Karl," Fenna said. She crossed her arms and waited for him to leave. The doors closed and she relaxed as the look on his face suggested he might have miscalculated. She spent the thirty second descent from the top floor to her own wondering at the turn of events, wondering about the watch list that Burwardsley had been put on, and if he knew that his so-called friend at Arctic Command had him under surveillance. *And if they saw him come into my hotel room?*

Fenna laid on the bed fully-dressed. She watched the flickering carpet of green Northern Lights swathing across the night sky as she tried to sleep, all the time anticipating a knock at the door. Would it be Burwardsley, the police, or a team of heavies from Arctic Command? The thought kept her awake and it wasn't just the bruises she needed to cover up around her eyes the next morning.

Two cups of coffee later, and Fenna ordered a taxi at the front desk. She thought she had seen Hong Wei at the breakfast bar, but chose to ignore him, deciding instead to travel alone to the airport. Nuuk airport was quiet, with just one member of Air Greenland's staff opening one of two check-in desks. The café was open, and Fenna bought a cinnamon pastry, found a chair facing the door and waited for Lorentzen and the Chinese man to arrive. Just as she finished her pastry Hong Wei walked through the door. He sat down next to her without a word, focusing instead on the Smartphone in his hand, his thumbs blurring in a flurry of texts. Lorentzen arrived a few minutes later, wearing a flat smile on his face as he approached Fenna's table.

"I'm sorry about last night," he said, as he pulled out a chair. He sat down opposite Fenna. She stared at him, took in the practical clothes he had chosen to wear, and realised that, apart from the duvet jacket she had put on, and the spare clothes in her daypack, she was wearing the exact same clothes as the night before.

"Don't mention it," she said, as Panninguaq opened the door to the baggage reclaim area and beckoned for them to follow her.

"Sorry," she said as she shook hands to greet

them. "But we need to get going if we are going to beat the weather. Spring in Greenland is changeable at best," she said, as she pointed through the window at the dark clouds forming in the distance. "It should clear up again this afternoon, but if we don't take off in the next ten minutes, we'll be grounded most of the day."

"Let's get going then," said Lorentzen. He gestured for Hong Wei to follow them out of the baggage area and onto the tarmac. He slipped and Panninguaq caught his arm, guiding him to the helicopter. She showed him to passenger seat next to her, but Hong Wei pointed instead at the back seat and she helped him buckle in.

"I'll sit in the back," Lorentzen said and walked around the aircraft. Fenna climbed in beside Panninguaq and listened as she talked the ground crew through her pre-flight checks. It might have been easy banter, but, in Greenlandic, it sounded guttural and exotic. *Almost feral*, Fenna thought. Fenna tuned-in to Panninguaq's chatter, starting at the sudden switch to Danish as the pilot lifted the Eurocopter into a hover and taxied to the runway, the helicopter's nose dipping slightly, as she feathered the control sticks and pedals.

When they were clear of the airport and Nuuk lay behind them, with Sermitsiaq to their left, Fenna asked Panninguaq what she thought of the mine.

"What do I think of it?"

"Yes, you know, in terms of Greenland," Fenna said, hoping that Lorentzen was listening, as she played her role of fact-gathering mining representative.

"It's ugly, environmentally unfriendly, and

expensive," Panninguaq said, her voice shushing in Fenna's ear through the headset.

"So you're against it?"

"I didn't say that."

"Then what do you mean?"

"It's complicated," Panninguaq said and gestured at the stark mountains, prominent in their coating of snow, spotted and patched with ice. The Greenland ice sheet shone white in the distance, and Panninguaq adjusted course toward it. "You see this," she said.

"The mountains?"

"The mountains, the sea, the ice, all of it. It's beautiful. It's my home, my country. But we have a lot of it. If the mine opens, and even with all the implications that has for the country, and the environment, it will still be just a small part of Greenland."

"So, you're saying you're for the mine?"

"No," Panninguaq said and paused. "And yes." The rotors whined above her and the airframe juddered as she lowered the nose to increase speed. Fenna felt the vibrations through her seat and the soles of her boots. "If Greenland is ever going to be truly independent, it needs money, and the only thing we have is our natural resources – in the sea and in the ground. We need to invest in tourism and we need to start mining or drilling if we want to be economically free of Denmark." She dipped her head toward the back seat. "Your Chinese friend knows this, and so do his politicians."

"Which makes it even more important to make the right decision," Lorentzen's voice chattered through the background hiss of Fenna's headset. *So, he* is *listening*, she thought.

185

"You're right," said Panninguaq. "But they should be decisions for Greenland to make. Even if they are environmentally wrong ones. It is still *our*environment."

Panninguaq stopped talking and concentrated on flying up the length of Nuuk fjord and into the mountains. The mine site popped out of the landscape with orange and red fuel barrels, white tents, two large timber-framed administration buildings with white pine sidings, and a larger mess hall painted red. Panninguaq slowed the aircraft into a slow, low orbit of the camp as Hong Wei took a rapid series of photographs with his Smartphone. Fenna spotted small digging machines, their yellow plates a stark contrast to the dark granite and dirt-speckled snow on the ground.

"Everything has to be flown in," Panninguaq said. "Although there is talk of a road."

"They fly it in from Nuuk?"

"No. They ship it up the fjord, and then charter a helicopter to lift it from the deck of the ship to the camp. It takes time."

At a nod from Hong Wei, Panninguaq flew the helicopter to the landing pad – a square of snow marked by white-striped fuel barrels, one in each corner. She landed, shut down the engine and slowed the rotors to a stop with the handbrake above her head. Lorentzen was the first to step out of the helicopter. He helped Hong Wei onto the skids and onto the ground. A tall, bearded Dane in a grimy wool sweater approached them, and Lorentzen introduced him as the leader of the camp. Hong Wei shook the man's hand, and then greeted three of his own countrymen as they approached. Fenna hid a smile when she noticed they were wearing alpine duvet suits. She was still smiling when Lorentzen tapped her on the shoulder.

"This is Bjørn Eskelsen," he said. "Veteran geologist and administrator for Isukasia."

"Such as it is," Eskelsen said. "And who are you?"

"I'm with Tunstall Mining. I'm here to have a look around."

Eskelsen glanced at Lorentzen. "The Chinese are backing the mine. What does Tunstall want?"

"A potential piece of the action or a buy-out. Who knows?" said Lorentzen. "But if the rest of the company are as pretty as she is, the more the merrier, I say."

That didn't take long, Fenna thought, *men treating women like playthings*, as she followed them toward the camp. She waved at Panninguaq as the pilot prepped the aircraft in case of strong winds and snow flurries. Panninguaq flashed the fingers of her right hand twice and continued working.

Ten minutes. Fenna waved again. She continued along the track, catching Eskelsen's comments as they drifted toward her on the wind blowing in from the southwest.

"… a skeleton crew. I've just sent most of the men into town for the weekend. There's nothing much more to be done here before people start making some decisions."

"So how many men are here?" Lorentzen asked.

"You, me, the Chinese, and the two ladies," he said and glanced over his shoulder.

"And there's a storm coming. Should be cosy."

"It might not come to anything," Eskelsen said.

"But…"

"This is Greenland," they said together and laughed.

This is *Greenland*, Fenna thought, as she followed the men. She watched as they ducked into the first of the two administration buildings. She could see the Chinese men were already inside and decided to check on the mess hall, figuring it would be less crowded.

The mess hall, the size of a large rectangular cabin, reminded Fenna of the hunting cabins the Sirius teams used when on patrol. The walls were bare but for a single geological map, and a nude pin-up. She spotted the ubiquitous bookshelf and traced her finger along the cracked spines and mildewed pages. The heat from the wood-burning stove radiated as far as the ring of chairs arranged around it. Fenna paused at the sight of a black jacket hanging from the back of one of the chairs. The dull yellow emblem caught her eye. The emblem depicted three lions beneath the Danish crown, embroidered on a dark green patch. She walked over to it and smoothed her hand over the material, glancing over her shoulder as if the owner – a Greenlandic policeman – might walk in any minute.

Fenna smiled at the feel of the fabric, remembering the one man in uniform that had shown her any sense of kindness or understanding since Mikael had been killed and she had been framed for his murder.

"Maratse," she whispered. "Where are you now?"

On impulse, Fenna knelt down and slipped her hands inside the pockets. She found a packet of cigarettes, almost empty but for two whole cigarettes and a foul-smelling half-smoked one. She frowned and pushed the packet back inside the pocket. In the opposite pocket she found a couple of rusted metal clasps and a swivel, the kind used to anchor sledge dogs on a chain to the rocks. *There are no sledge dogs in Nuuk.* Fenna slipped the piece of rusty metal back into the pocket and checked inside the jacket. Fenna's fingers caught the leather edge of a thin wallet. She pulled it out and opened a police identification card. Fenna smiled at the flood of emotion she felt on seeing the picture of David Maratse, his bushy black eyebrows and his walnut skin, bronzed in the sun and glare of the ice.

"Maratse," she said and then frowned. "What the hell are you doing here?" Then she recalled Eskelsen and the tally of men he had related to Lorentzen. "But you wouldn't leave your jacket behind," Fenna said and closed Maratse's ID card. "Why didn't he say you were here?"

There was a tramp of feet in the snow outside the mess hall. Fenna slipped Maratse's card inside his jacket and scanned the cabin for a way out. She saw the window, prayed it could be opened, and ran toward it, just as the person coming into the mess hall banged the snow from his boots on the step outside the door.

Chapter 22

The window creaked open a few centimetres and started to vibrate in the wind; the snowstorm had caught up with them. Fenna leaned into the frame, slipping one leg over the sill before dropping to the ground. The strap of her daypack caught on the window latch. Fenna twisted beneath it, trying to tug herself free as the tramp of boots on the planks of the mess hall floor suggested more than one person had entered. She heard the men's voices and then Panninguaq's soft laugh.

"Come on, Fenna," she said, the words chased from her lips in a flurry of snow. Fenna felt the flakes tickle her cheeks, catch in her hair, as she pressed her toes into the ground and pushed upward, freeing the strap from the latch. She bent her knees and ducked beneath the frame of the window. She heard a man grunt and close it, the latch fastening with a stubborn squeal of metal that had seen too many winters, or one very long one. Fenna looked beyond the row of tents, and spied a path; the snow trudged and flattened beneath a hundred boot prints. She ducked around the side of the mess hall and followed the path just to the left of a long, low granite ridge. The snow thickened, gusting in flurries like airborne steams of tiny fish, darting in large clouds one way, only to be spun in the other. In the absence of predators, the wind played the role of the hunter, chasing the snow at whim, swirling the flakes around Fenna's feet and plastering her hair with cold, wet clumps. It was heavier, denser, wetter snow than the dry, light crystals of the far north of Greenland. Fenna felt the cold faster too, much like Greenlanders complained at how cold winters in Copenhagen were, compared to the north. Fenna tucked her hands into her pockets and followed the path in anticipation of finding some kind of shelter. *Why else would there be a path?*

Her hunch was right. At the base of a large, smooth rock face, Fenna spied a shipping container, its doors dogged closed. She grasped the handle, flinching in anticipation of the freeze-burn of cold metal on warm skin. The air temperature was high enough that Fenna felt only the dull cold of the metal – its bark was worse than its bite, as the handle squealed all the way into the open position. Snow licked at the rubber lip insulating the edge of the door as Fenna opened it. The grey light of the snowstorm lit the first few metres of the interior, just enough to reveal the heel of a boot and to elicit a moan from someone inside the container. She opened the door wider and the light fell on the bloodied face of Sergent David Maratse of the Greenland police.

"Maratse," Fenna said, as she stepped inside the container, the hollow ring of her boots echoing around the space until she knelt beside the policeman, the cardboard packaging of the supplies between which he was bound absorbed the last echo of her steps.

She cleared his airway first, removing the dirty rag that filled his mouth. Maratse gasped for breath, as the snow settled on his tongue and dissolved. Fenna checked the pulse in his neck, untied his hands and began to search the policeman's body for wounds and bleeding. Maratse, his eyes closed, protested with soft moans and weak waves of his right hand. His left hand, Fenna noticed, was still, and lay flat on the

191

floor. A first glance revealed that it was dark with bruises. Two of the fingernails were split and bloody, the nail prised from the skin by several millimetres. Fenna didn't touch them. She cupped her hand to Maratse's cheek and waited for him to open his eyes.

"Maratse. It's Fenna. Look at me," she said, as she shuffled closer to him.

"Fenna?" he said and groaned. "You shouldn't be here."

"Neither should you." Fenna laughed and Maratse joined her, coughing as he tried to sit up. "Don't," she said. "Stay still."

"*Iji.*"

"What happened?"

"Chinese," he said and coughed.

"Why?"

"Ask them," he said and chuckled. "Cigarette?"

"No," Fenna said and smoothed Maratse's fringe from his forehead. She felt the sweat on his brow and wondered if he was bleeding internally. "I need to get you out of here."

"*Iji.*"

The snow was thickening. *We're not flying in that, even if I could get Panninguaq away from the Chinese. Must be another way,* she thought and then turned to look at Maratse. *Stabilise him first. Make him comfortable.* She smiled.

"What?" said Maratse. His eyes followed Fenna as she smoothed her hands down each of his legs, worrying her fingers inside the lip of his boots, checking the temperature of his skin with her finger, checking for blood.

"Nothing. I'm going to look after you."

"Good," he said. And then, "Cigarette?"

"Nope," Fenna said and knelt by his side. "Best if you don't anyway." She looked outside. "The snow is going to slow things down. I'm not sure when and how I'm going to get you out." She took his right hand in her own. "Where does it hurt?"

"Stomach," he said and flicked his eyes down his body. Fenna tugged at the black wool sweater, and then the light blue police shirt beneath it. Even in the low light of the snowstorm, Fenna could see that Maratse's stomach was black with bruises, swollen and – she pressed her fingers against his skin – hard to the touch. Maratse grimaced and pushed her hand away.

"Cross-fit? You've been working out," she said and laughed, her voice softened by the snow.

"*Iiji*," he said and fidgeted. Fenna helped him into a sitting position as he shuffled backwards to lean against the boxed supplies.

"So tell me again, why are you here, and why did they do this?"

"Ittoqqortoormiit."

"Yes?"

"A research ship came into port."

"*Odin*?"

"*Iiji*. The crew came ashore. They had a body with them. A scientist."

"Johansson," Fenna said and nodded. "He was murdered."

"Accident, they said. Not murdered," Maratse said. He squinted at Fenna in the gloom. "How did you know?"

"I'm here because of the same ship," she said. "I will tell you later. Keep going."

"There was another man. He wanted to tell me

193

something. But he was killed in a bar fight."

"By one of the crew?"

"*Naamik*," Maratse said and wrinkled his brow. "By Samuel, my brother-in-law."

"Why?"

"Paid to do it, he said. I came here to Nuuk to find out."

"Why here?"

"You met the man with the beard?"

"Bjørn Eskelsen? The camp leader? Yes, I met him."

"*Bjørn*," Maratse said and laughed. "The *bear*."

"Yes."

"Strong. He was also on the ship. He paid Samuel."

Fenna sat on the floor of the container and crossed her legs. "You know this for sure?"

"*Iiji*. Samuel is a drunk, but not a liar." Maratse looked at Fenna, his eyes glistened in the grey light. "Life can be difficult," he said. "Money, even a little bit, can make a difference. That's why he did it. That's why Samuel killed the man from the ship. I just need to make it right. Maybe keep him in jail, in Greenland."

Because killers are sent to Denmark, she remembered. *A double sentence.*

Maratse coughed and Fenna studied his face, remembering the smile that creased his cheeks when they had fled across the ice, windows shattering from Burwardsley's bullets. He looked different without the cigarette between his lips, parked in the gap between his teeth. Fenna wished she smoked, or that she had brought his jacket at least.

"Fenna," he said, "why are you here?"

"I'm here because of the ship, and the dead man you carried off it."

"And what are you doing?" Maratse paused to cough. He wiped his mouth with the back of his hand, and Fenna saw the blood smeared on his skin.

"Don't worry about that. I have to get you out of here."

"*Iijii,*" Maratse said and shrugged. "Maybe."

Fenna stood up. She tugged at the hem of her jacket and tightened the straps of her pack. "Wait here," she said and laughed and then added, "Don't move."

"I'll be here," Maratse said and smiled as Fenna stepped toward the door. "Konstabel," he said.

"Yes?"

"Cigarette," he said and pointed at his mouth.

"Sure," she said and slipped out of the container. Fenna pushed the door closed, leaving a gap the width of her hand for air and light. She squinted into the snow and scanned the path for tracks. There were none. *And why should there be? Everyone will be inside.* And she knew exactly where. *Huddled around the stove, in the mess hall.* Fenna leaned into the wind and jogged down the path to the camp.

She almost ran into the row of tents, the white fabric lost in the snow. A loose guy snapped in the wind and she followed the sound as the snow thickened. The mess hall loomed to her left, but Fenna jogged around it and back on the path toward the makeshift helicopter pad. Panninguaq had plugged the air intakes with bulky baffles. The rotors were weighted, the shrouds securing them taut when Fenna tested them. *We're going nowhere,* she realised.

On the far side of the helicopter Fenna spotted a

wooden stake, flashed at the top with fluorescent orange paint. She followed it, ignoring the snow as the ground sloped beneath her feet, shuffling her way across hidden patches of ice, from one marker to the next. The wind dropped as Fenna entered a narrow gulley. She peered through the snow and tried to remember the terrain they had flown over, how far the fjord was from the camp, and how on earth she was ever going to get Maratse down the path.

"And even if I do," she said, licking at the snow settling on her lip. "All the boats have left for Nuuk." *A skeleton crew*, Eskelsen had said.

A tap of rock behind her, to her left, caught Fenna's attention and she froze, resisting the urge to duck and move into cover. She called out instead.

"I guess it's too late to hide?" she said, looking back up the path in the direction of the helicopter.

"That depends," said a man's voice. Fenna's breath caught in her throat as the man stepped into view, a rifle held in his mittened hands, the barrel levelled at Fenna's chest. His beard, heavy with snow, reminded Fenna of Mikael. *The Yeti*, she thought and smiled. "You're amused?" Bjørn Eskelsen said as he took a step toward her. "I didn't expect that."

Fenna turned her hands at her sides, palms outward. "Not amused. Just at a disadvantage," she said and shrugged. "What's a girl to do?"

"Ordinarily, I wouldn't know. But then you're not quite an ordinary girl, are you?"

"No," she said. "I guess not."

Eskelsen slung the rifle over his shoulder. He lifted his leg and set his foot on a boulder. "You found the policeman," he said and jerked a mittened thumb over his shoulder. "Didn't you?"

"Yes."

"You know him?"

Fenna nodded. "Yes."

"You know why he's here?"

Fenna lowered her hands and waited for Eskelsen to speak. She watched as he lifted his foot and took another step toward her. She studied him as he moved, listing to one side, like a stricken ship. He paused mid-step as he noticed her watching him.

"What's wrong with your leg?"

"Mining accident," he said and shrugged. "Why? What's your interest?"

Fenna said nothing. She pressed the tips of her fingers into her legs, felt the beginnings of the familiar surge of adrenalin. *Control it, Fenna*, she thought. *Use it.*

"How is he?" Eskelsen said. "Your friend. The policeman."

"My friend?"

"Yes, Konstabel," said a second voice. Fenna flicked her head to her right as Lorentzen manoeuvred around a boulder above her. "It's Konstabel Brongaard, isn't it?" he said, as he joined Eskelsen on the path in front of her.

"How long have you known?"

"About an hour. Bjørn told me," he said, looking at Eskelsen. "Your friend mentioned you in an earlier chat."

"The Chinese have a way of making people talk," Eskelsen said. "It's not my thing, but they are useful when suitably invested."

"Apparently," said Lorentzen, "the Chinese, are more interested in you than they are in the mine. Your friend followed Bjørn to Nuuk, and, Greenland being the small country that it is…" Lorentzen paused to chuckle. "Well, when Bjørn told the Chinese about his little problem, they became quite animated at the prospect of chatting with officer Maratse. Isn't that right, Bjørn?"

"It is," he said. "And now they are even more excited to talk to you, Konstabel."

"Which presents us with a bit of a dilemma," said Lorentzen.

"Such as?" Fenna said, as she tasted the adrenalin pulsing through her veins.

"Whether we should let them."

Chapter 23

The fjord, Fenna remembered, was to the southwest. She could just see the black water if she squinted through the snow flurries thickening around her and the two men. A glance at Lorentzen suggested that he was getting cold, in spite of his experience in the field. Eskelsen, Fenna noted, was hardened to the elements, a sign that, despite the limp, he was comfortable with the environment and used to long periods in camp. *Leading the camp*, she remembered. *He is here because he understands the terrain.* The thought lingered as her gaze shifted to the rifle in his grasp.

Lorentzen clapped his hands and Fenna looked up. "Our friends will be wondering where we got to," he said and took another step closer to Fenna. "Hong Wei might be a quiet fellow, but I can assure you he is quite the chatterbox when you get to know him. And I have decided that you *should* get to know him," Lorentzen said with a quick nod at Eskelsen. "Intimately," he added. He wiped a swathe of snow from his forehead and brushed the thick flakes from his fingers. Fenna watched him and took a step along the path as Eskelsen levelled the barrel of the rifle at her chest. "It's a shame, really," he said.

"What is?" said Fenna as she passed Eskelsen, navigating between the snow-frosted boulders in the path leading toward the landing pad.

"I'm curious to get to know you, I think we might have had fun together."

"You don't think this is fun?" she said and cast a glance over her shoulder. Eskelsen was close behind her, the end of the barrel within a metre of her back. *And he has a gammy leg*, she thought.

"As much as I love Greenland," Lorentzen said, peering through the snow as he picked his way around the boulders. "I have grown accustomed to certain luxuries."

"It's your age then," Fenna said and smiled at the pause her words gave the geologist. "Or is it just one too many society functions?" Fenna ignored the scowl on Eskelsen's face and stared at Lorentzen. "You've grown soft, in here," she said and tapped the side of her head with a finger. "It'll be your belly next, and what pretty young thing will have you then? When the grey hair on your temple isn't rakish, just retired." She turned her back as Lorentzen opened his mouth to retort. Eskelsen, she saw, was smiling. Fenna slid her heels along the patches of old ice as Lorentzen stumbled to catch up.

"You think I fell for you, Konstabel? Is that it?"

"Your profile says you like black hair."

"My profile? Hah," he said and snorted. Fenna heard the tumble of loose granite beneath his boots. "My profile is phoney."

"So's my hair," she said. *Let him come*, she thought at the sound of more grit being ground into the path.

"I admit, I'm intrigued, Konstabel," he said as he stumbled into step alongside Eskelsen. "What else do I like?"

"Let it go," Eskelsen said as Lorentzen brushed past him.

"My tits," Fenna said as she reeled him in, step by step. "You don't like more than a handful. All the breasts of all the women you have ever been with," she said, "could fit in the palm of your hand." Lorentzen stopped in front of Fenna. "Am I wrong?" she said and gestured at her chest. As his gaze dropped she kicked his right knee and scraped the thick tread of her boot down his shin.

"Move," Eskelsen said as he limped to one side of his colleague.

"Fuck," Lorentzen said, as he twisted and reached for his knee. Fenna moved with him, using his body as a shield between her and the barrel of Eskelsen's rifle. Eskelsen pressed the barrel over Lorentzen's shoulder as Fenna leaned into the geologist and slammed her elbow up to catch his chin, whipping his head back toward Eskelsen. She curled her left fist into Lorentzen's sternum as he cried out, and then silenced him with her right in his stomach. The wind from his lungs brushed her fringe as Fenna shoved his body into Eskelsen, closed her left hand around the barrel of the rifle and yanked it free as Eskelsen caught Lorentzen before they tumbled onto the path. Fenna changed her grip and slammed the butt into Eskelsen's forehead. She held the rifle in the ready position, poised like a hunter waiting with a harpoon above a seal's breathing hole in the ice, until Eskelsen's head lolled to one side. Fenna slung the rifle on her back and then jammed two fingers inside Lorentzen's nostrils.

"Up."

"Fuck. Stop," he said, as he pushed himself onto his feet only to have Fenna fell him again with a kick. Lorentzen crumpled beneath her and Fenna let his head crack against a boulder. He groaned and cupped the back of his head in his hands. Fenna ignored the blood staining the snow clinging to his skin.

"Your profile," she said, "suggested you were bored in Nuuk. So how's this for excitement?" Fenna took a handful of Lorentzen's hair and forced him to crawl away from the path and down the side of the mountain toward the fjord. Lorentzen cried out as he scrabbled across the rocks to keep up with her. Fenna noticed he was favouring his left knee, protecting his right.

She stopped on a small plateau about twenty metres from the path. Eskelsen's body was just visible when she squinted through the snow. Fenna let Lorentzen catch his breath as she slipped the rifle from her shoulder and chambered a round.

"I have a dilemma," she said, as Lorentzen looked up at her. "The mission or the man?"

"What man?" Lorentzen said, his words absorbed by the snow as the air thickened around them.

"The policeman, my friend. He needs a hospital." Fenna glanced toward the path, relaxing her shoulders as she identified the outline of Eskelsen's knee. "But the mission..." she said and paused. Eskelsen was still there. *But, did he move?*

"What mission?"

Fenna blinked in the snow and focused on Lorentzen. "The Pole," she said. "Why did you sell out?"

"I don't know what you mean," he said and pressed his hands around his knee. Fenna kicked it and he wailed.

"You fiddled with the instruments, and changed the results. Now some politician is about to present the findings to UNCLOS and Greenland loses the Pole."

"Denmark," he said through gritted teeth. "Denmark loses the Pole, or did you forget who you are working for, Konstabel?"

Fenna shrugged and took a step back. She lifted

the rifle and aimed it at Lorentzen's chest. "My friend chased Eskelsen all the way here to this camp. Eskelsen had a man killed in a bar in Ittoqqortoormiit – probably the only bar – and I'm guessing that was to cover for you. Am I right?" she said with a glance toward the path. She frowned and took a step to the right, squinting through the snow.

"You think Eskelsen is covering for me?" Lorentzen started to laugh. "That's rich. I can't wait to tell him."

"Tell him what?" Fenna said and shifted her attention back to Lorentzen. *He's still lying there, Eskelsen. Isn't he?*

"Tell him your little theory. Really, girl," Lorentzen said and sneered. "You are just a very *little* girl in a very big game." Fenna paused and took another small step away from Lorentzen. She flicked her eyes from him to the path and back again. *I can still see his knee…*

"Keep talking."

"If I must, but really, *girl*, you haven't been sent here to find out the truth."

"No?" she said and gripped the rifle in one hand as she brushed the snow from her eyes.

"No," Lorentzen said and laughed. "You've been sent to cover it up."

"What?" Fenna said and frowned at Lorentzen. He spoke but she didn't hear his words as she realised it wasn't Ekselsen's knee she had been staring at. *It was a fucking rock.*

Fenna ducked into a squatting position and scanned the terrain to either side of Lorentzen. He turned his head as Fenna stood and followed a shadow of movement, as it lumbered through the snow. She lifted the rifle and tugged the butt of the stock into her shoulder, but the shadow was gone. *And too far away*, she thought. *Damn, Fenna. Stupid.*

"And now you have a problem," said Lorentzen.

"What's that?"

"The policeman just got upgraded from friend to bargaining chip. At least he will live for a little while longer, until you get him to a hospital, or Eskelsen puts you both in the morgue."

"Not today," Fenna said, her voice low as she considered her options. She bit her lip and looked down at Lorentzen. "You said I was sent to cover up the truth?"

"You were listening?"

"I was, and now you better start talking."

"And yet," he said. "Every minute you spend with me is another minute Eskelsen has to reach the camp, and your friend."

"You're right," Fenna said. She took three quick steps backward, raised the rifle, and pulled the trigger. Lorentzen screamed as the bullet tore through the flesh, ligament, and bone of his left knee.

Fenna ignored Lorentzen's screams as she ran, chambering another round into the rifle, skirting around large boulders, leaping over flat ones, as she charged up the path toward the camp. She tried to focus, but could not ignore Lorentzen's words. *I'm covering up the truth? But for whom, and to what purpose?*

She slowed as she reached the helicopter, the sight of the snow layering the rotor blades twisting at her stomach as she realised they were not flying out of camp. *Not anytime soon.* The crack of a small calibre saloon rifle forced her into cover as she ducked behind an empty oil drum marking one of the four corners of the makeshift landing pad. Fenna pressed her body into the rusted metal surface as two more rounds snapped through the air above her head.

"Stop shooting," Eskelsen said, his English scarred at the edges with a blend of barroom accents. Fenna imagined he had picked up the varied inflections on his travels in the north. "You'll hit the bloody helicopter."

Fenna nodded a quick *thank you* at the bright red Eurocopter. "At least they want to get home," she said and took a breath. "Let's see how much." She stood up and raised her rifle, searching for targets as she took slow steps toward the helicopter. Eskelsen's Chinese associates were almost comical in their puffy down suits. Fenna spotted one of them through the rifle sights as he ran from one side of the path to the other. She tracked him, leading the rifle in front of his body, firing before he reached a large boulder. The man's suit deflated, expelling a puff of bloody feathers as Fenna chambered another round. "Two men down," she said and searched for another target. "Just four more to go."

Snow drifted around the tubular skids of Fenna's protecting angel. She squinted around the flurry of flakes, searching for her next target. *Another puffed-up Chinese man or...* Fenna swore and lowered her rifle as Panninguaq stumbled onto the path with Eskelsen's hand around her throat and Maratse's service pistol pressed to the side of her head. She heard Panninguaq whimper as Eskelsen shoved her down the path, toward the helicopter.

"No," Fenna breathed. "Not again."

"Drop your rifle, Konstabel," Eskelsen said, as he manoeuvred Panninguaq to the perimeter of the landing pad. "It all ends here."

"For you, maybe," she said and let the rifle slip from her grasp and into the snow at her feet. *For me*, she thought as she fought the urge to retch, *it is just beginning.*

Eskelsen shoved Panninguaq to the side and lumbered across the snow, the USP pistol aimed at Fenna's chest, as he bent down to pick up the rifle. Fenna noted the bloody gash on his forehead with a smile. He nodded for her to walk past him. Panninguaq was shivering, her eyes flickering from Eskelsen to the helicopter.

"Prep it," he said. "I want to be able to fly as soon as the storm lifts." Fenna looked up at the sky, her gaze resting on a whiter patch of grey before Eskelsen pushed her forward with the barrel of the rifle. As they passed the dead Chinese man Eskelsen spoke in English, ordering the dead man's colleagues to go down the path to find Lorentzen.

"I didn't kill Lorentzen," Fenna said.

"Perhaps you should have," he said and pointed. "First tent, on the left."

The last few metres were the longest Fenna had ever known. She rubbed her wrists and thought of Burwardsley and Bahadur – the Gurkha with the wicked blade – and the last time she had been interrogated. *But I've changed since then,* she thought as Burwardsley's image was replaced with that of the Gunney. Her first kill. The Chinese man, her second. *Number two was easier,* she realised before her stomach contradicted her and she doubled up and retched onto the snow.

"Not so tough now," Eskelsen said. He slung the rifle over his shoulder, gripped Fenna by the hair and pressed the pistol into her neck. He pushed her through the door of the canvas walled tent, grunting that she should go inside. "I wouldn't worry though," he said as they entered and Fenna sniffed at the warm air and the coppery stench of blood – a lot of blood. "We're not going to hurt you. Not to begin with anyway."

Fenna blinked in the glare and heat of halogen worklights as the judder of a diesel generator changed pitch as Hong Wei pressed metal paddles onto Maratse's bare and bloody skin. The lights flickered, Maratse screamed, and Fenna retched.

Chapter 24

Hong Wei let go of the paddles when the wooden handles began to smoke. The lights went out and the tent descended into a grey pallor as Maratse's scream receded in a long, slow, wail. Fenna wiped spots of bile from her lips with the back of her hand and took a step toward the policeman.

"Don't," said Eskelsen and motioned with the pistol that she should sit in a folding chair to her left. Fenna looked at Maratse as she sat down, holding his gaze for as long as she could before looking away.

"The generator," said Hong Wei as he pulled off a pair of thick rubber gloves. "Has stopped."

"I'll fix it," Eskelsen said, his English less accented than the Chinese man's. He pressed the pistol into Hong Wei's hand as he walked past him to open a flap in the corner of the tent. The floorboards creaked as he limped across them. Fenna watched him leave and then faced the Chinese man as Hong Wei leaned against the desk to the right of Maratse. They watched each other as Eskelsen fiddled with the generator.

"This is unfortunate," Hong Wei said.

"The generator?" Fenna said, stumbling over the words as she glanced at Maratse.

"No," he said. "This." Hong Wei waved his hands around the tent. "You and me, here. This man. His pain. All most unfortunate."

"You're the one hurting him."

"Me? No," he said and shook his head. Hong Wei pointed his finger at Fenna. "You. You are the one hurting him."

Fenna swallowed as Hong Wei stood up and

walked the two steps to the chair in which Maratse was sprawled and bound, the thin copper wire cutting into the skin of his wrists and ankles. She stood up when Hong Wei pressed his finger into Maratse's bruised and swollen stomach.

"Hey," she said and took a step forward.

"Sit down, Konstabel," Hong Wei said and pointed the pistol at her face. "This man is unwell. He does not have time for us to discuss things. So, you must tell me what I want to know, and quickly. Maybe then, there will be time for your friend."

With another glance at Maratse, Fenna sat down as the generator lurched into life with a shudder and a belch of blue smoke. It settled into a steady rhythm as Eskelsen released the choke and entered the tent. The barrel of the rifle caught on the flap. Fenna watched as he fiddled it loose, unslung the rifle, and placed it on the desk. Eskelsen took the pistol from Hong Wei as the Chinese man reached for the rubber gloves he had thrown onto the floor.

"Wait," said Fenna. "You don't need to do that."

"Do what?" Hong Wei said, as he pulled on the gloves. Eskelsen stood behind Maratse.

"That," she said and nodded at the paddles on the floor, the insulation tape wrapped around the base of the handles was melted, the cables snaked with sticky streams of Maratse's blood.

"You will tell me everything?"

"Yes," she said. "I'll tell you anything," she added as she slumped into the chair.

"No, Konstabel, not just *anything*," Hong Wei said and pressed his finger into Maratse's blistered skin." Fenna held her breath as the policeman moaned. "You will be specific. Do you understand?"

"Yes," she said, her eyes fixed on Maratse.

"Good," Hong Wei said and picked up the paddles. Fenna watched as he hung them from the back of Maratse's chair. He kept the gloves on, she noticed. "First," he said. "Tell me what you know about Lorentzen? Why are you so interested in him?"

Fenna thought for a moment. *The mission or the man? What would Nicklas do? What would Jarnvig want me to do?* Then she thought of Greenland and Lorentzen's words about securing the Pole for Denmark, not Greenland. *When did I become such a Greenlandophile?* She wondered and then looked at Maratse. *When he saved me, and when Dina died. That's when.* Fenna made her decision.

"We think Lorentzen fiddled with the instruments on the LOMROG expedition," she said and glanced at Eskelsen. "But maybe we were wrong."

"Maybe you were," said Hong Wei. "But what does it matter?"

"If the results are wrong they cannot prove that the continental shelf of Greenland is attached to the geographical North Pole."

"Yes. And?"

Fenna shrugged and said, "Denmark wants the Pole."

"So do a lot of countries. Russia," said Hong Wei, "has already claimed it."

"They claim a lot of things. Usually by force," she said, as she flicked her eyes toward the paddles on the desk.

Hong Wei smiled as he considered Fenna's response. "How do you know the results are false?" he said and paused to scratch at his ear, frowning at the stubby tips of the gloves. "How do you know?"

"There was a log, kept by one of the scientists on the expedition. It says as much, before he was killed," she said and turned her attention back to Eskelsen.

"Strange things happen at sea," he said and shrugged. "Lorentzen asked me to meet him in Ittoqqortoormiit."

"Where you tried to cover up Johansson's death with another one," she said and looked over at Maratse. "That's why he is here."

"Some policeman follows me all the way from the east coast of Greenland, that's his problem," said Eskelsen.

"But," Hong Wei said and held up his hand. "No matter. The results are interesting," he said and pointed at Fenna. "What she knows is not important. *Who* sent her – *that* is important. She must tell us now." Hong Wei picked up the paddles. "Tell us," he said, as he flicked the switch for current and pressed the paddles into Maratse's chest.

"Stop," Fenna shouted as Maratse screamed. A bloody mist steamed from the policeman's chest, dissipating as the generator stopped and the camp was quiet. "I can tell you," Fenna said in the hush.

"I know you will," Hong Wei said. He grimaced as the paddles came free of Maratse's skin with a sucking sound. Maratse fainted, his head lolling back on the seat, hanging over the edge toward Eskelsen. Hong Wei tossed the sticky paddles onto the desk beside the rifle and removed his gloves for the second time; Fenna hoped it would be the last.

And I just have to give him a name. That's all.

The smell of charred flesh and fresh blood pricked at her nostrils and her conscience. Fenna thought for a moment as she considered what she knew, what it might mean, and, ultimately, the consequences of doing so. *We're never getting out of here*, she thought. *Not without something to whet their interest, something to suggest that this game is bigger than even they thought.* She pressed her hands to her cheeks, feeling the rough skin of her fingers on her lips. "*The Magician* sent me," she said and looked at Hong Wei.

"A magician?" said Hong Wei. "Like a wizard? Hah," he said and picked up his gloves.

"Wait," said Fenna and waved her hands for him to stop.

"Sit down," Eskelsen said and pointed the pistol in her direction. "And tell him what he wants to know."

"I *am* telling him."

"No, Konstabel," said Hong Wei. "You are wasting my time, and his," he said and nodded at Maratse. "There is no proof of anything. We can kill you both without a trace. There are many accidents in Greenland, and a fire at a remote mining camp is very difficult to stop."

"You kill us," Fenna said and stood up, "then you will never find out who is working against you." Fenna faced Eskelsen as he lowered the pistol, the wrinkles on his brow tugging a fresh stream of blood from the open wound she had given him.

"Talk," he said.

Okay, she thought. *Make it good.* Fenna sat down and rested her arms on the chair. She curled her fingers around the ends. "Do you know who I am?" she said and waited.

"An agent with the Danish government," said Hong Wei.

"PET," said Eskelsen.

"And before that?" she said and watched as Hong Wei glanced at Eskelsen. The Dane shook his head.

"No," Hong Wei said.

"Then you've never heard of *The Ice Star*?"

"Should we?"

"It's a ship," she said. "A luxury adventure cruise ship with an ice class that makes it relatively independent."

"Why is this important?" Hong Wei said. He paused at the distant sound of rotors beginning to turn.

"That'll be the pilot," said Eskelsen. "I told her to be ready to fly as soon as the weather lifted."

Hong Wei turned back to Fenna. "Talk faster."

Fenna thought of the two remaining Chinese men that were likely with Panninguaq, making sure she didn't leave. She took a breath and started, "I was onboard that ship, together with men working for *The Magician*."

"What men?" said Hong Wei. Fenna enjoyed the tic of irritation pulsing in his right cheek.

He's used to knowing everything. He takes pride in it, she thought as she considered what to tell him next, and what to leave out. "There are other countries playing this game," she said. "China is only an observer, the *real* players," Fenna said with a nod toward Eskelsen, "control men like him, women like me, and others…" she paused. "Like you."

"You are saying this *Magician* is a player?"

"Yes," Fenna said, "with a seat at the main table." She waited as Hong Wei seemed to process her words. Maratse groaned, his head lolling to one side as he opened one eye. Fenna's heart skipped a beat. *He's alive.*

"You have access to this man?"

"You want to meet him? I can…"

"That is not what I asked," he said and shook his head. He turned to Eskelsen. "Give the gun to me." Hong Wei looked at Fenna as he held out his hand for the gun. "Do you know who I am?"

"An advisor to the Chinese. High up in government. Probably something to do with intelligence," Fenna said and shrugged as Hong Wei took the gun from Eskelsen. She watched as he tested the weight in his grasp. "You weren't mentioned in my file."

"No? Interesting," he said. "Perhaps, later, I can tell you why, Konstabel. But, first, tell me more of this *Magician*."

"He orchestrated a plot to humiliate the Danish sovereignty mission. I was on that mission."

"And you put a stop to it? The humiliation?"

"In a way," Fenna said and snapped her head toward Eskelsen as he snorted.

"You're the one? The woman who killed her partner? Jesus."

"I didn't kill Mikael," Fenna said. *How many times am I going to have to repeat that?*

"This is public knowledge?" Hong Wei said.

"Only if you know the right people," Eskelsen said and shrugged. "I have met a few guys from the Sirius Patrol. She," he said with a nod at Fenna, "is the first *girl* to get selected."

Girl, Fenna thought. *Like it is a bad thing, a plaything.* She took a long breath. She noticed the light inside the tent was less grey, brighter, and the snow no longer scratched on the canvas. Even Maratse's blood seemed to have stopped pooling on the floor. *Optimism will be the death of me*, she thought and gauged the distance between her and Hong Wei. *Too far.*

"And *The Magician*? How was he involved?" said Hong Wei, as he turned his attention back to Fenna.

"Behind the scenes, pulling strings, but he was there in the beginning. I met him. I just didn't know who he was. But I found out that he was working for the Canadians."

Hong Wei said nothing. The floorboards creaked as Eskelsen shuffled on his feet, searching for a more comfortable position for his leg. Maratse lifted his head until Fenna cautioned him to let it fall again with a flash of her hand. The policeman winked at her and mouthed the word cigarette, and if Fenna had had one, she would have taken a bullet just to put it in his mouth and light it, to give him that one last smoke. Instead, she hid her smile and waited.

"Do you know how important the Pole is?" Hong Wei said.

"I have an idea."

"The money from shipping alone will make control of the sea routes around Greenland and across the Arctic very expensive, and very lucrative." Hong Wei paused to walk across the tent to stand at the wall to the right of Maratse and Eskelsen. He held the pistol in his left hand, smoothing his right on the canvas wall. "If there is oil in Greenland, it will take years before it can be extracted. If Greenland is to make money, it needs to make it now. If Greenland owns the Pole, it can make that money, but not without Denmark."

"No," said Fenna. "Greenland could never patrol

the sea. It has no navy."

"No military forces whatsoever," said Hong Wei. "China needs that sea route, and it needs it to be cheap." Fenna waited as Hong Wei took a step away from the wall of the tent. "This mine," he said and gestured with his right hand, "will never earn enough money to pay for itself. It would be cheaper to buy the country…"

And finance its independence, Fenna thought. *Patrol the coast. The Arctic sea lanes.*

"…which is what we are doing," he said. "One harbour and one airport at a time. You have seen the plans, Konstabel?"

"Yes," Fenna said and remembered the artist's impression of a new Nuuk, a capital city the Greenlanders could be proud of, one that would catapult them onto the world's scene.

"And you approve?"

"They are ambitious."

"Futures are built on ambition," Hong Wei said. "Which is why the results of the LOMROG expedition were never falsified, just hidden."

"Hidden?" said Fenna as she leaned forward.

"What?" said Eskelsen.

"Yes," Hong Wei said. "The results were hidden. Not falsified. Lorentzen did not tamper with the machine, he used another machine."

"You can't hide that kind of equipment on a ship," Eskelsen said and tugged at his beard with his hand.

"There was another ship."

"The *Xue Long*," said Fenna.

"Yes. On a parallel course, but a week later."

"I had a man killed for him," Eskelsen said, his

voice low as he looked at the back of the tent in the direction of the landing pad.

And I was sent to cover the truth, Fenna thought, as she remembered Lorentzen's words. "*The Magician?*" she said.

"I need to meet him," Hong Wei said. "I will need an introduction. Can you arrange that?"

"I know a man who can," Fenna said and nodded at Maratse. "If you will help him."

"Yes, of course. We will put him on the helicopter."

"The helicopter?" Eskelsen said and took a step forward. "No-one is getting on that bird before I say so. I'm the camp administrator."

"You were," said Hong Wei as he raised the pistol and fired.

Maratse started at the crack of the gunshot as Eskelsen crumpled to the ground, and then Fenna was at his side, untwisting the wires around his wrists and ankles, releasing him from the chair and buttoning the tatters of cloth that used to be his shirt.

"Cigarette," he said and coughed.

"I don't have one."

"My jacket. Over there," he said and pointed a bloody finger at a wooden chest on the far side of the tent. "They collected my things," he said as Fenna picked up Maratse's jacket and fished the crumpled packet of smokes from the inside pocket. She slipped half a cigarette between the policeman's bloody lips and lit it with the lighter stuffed inside the packet. Maratse rolled the cigarette into the gap in his teeth and coughed a cloud of smoke into the air above his face.

"You're going to be all right," Fenna said and

covered his chest with the jacket.

"*Iiji*," he said and grinned.

"Still better than picking up drunks?"

Maratse smiled and closed his eyes. "*Iiji*. Much better."

Fenna stood up and watched the blood pool beneath Eskelsen's head as Hong Wei rifled the dead man's pockets, throwing his wallet and identification badge onto the wooden floor. Fenna glanced at the rifle on the desk and took a step toward it.

"Konstabel," said Hong Wei, as he pointed the pistol at her. "Don't."

"Okay," said Fenna and stepped closer to Maratse. "What do we do now?"

"Now," Hong Wei said and stood up. "We start a fire that is very difficult to put out."

Chapter 25

The fire licked at the walls of the tent as Fenna dragged Maratse along the path to the helicopter. Blood dripped from his wrists into the cuffs of his jacket as he smoked the last cigarette from the packet. Fenna tugged the policeman closer to her body, curling her arm around his waist to grab his belt. She pulled his left arm around her shoulder as she encouraged him to take one slow step after another until they reached the helicopter. The two Chinese men wearing puffer jackets lapped them several times with crates and gear that Hong Wei wanted to be flown out. Then they dowsed the other tents and equipment with aviation fuel and lit them. Fenna wrinkled her nose at the acrid stink and blinked through the thick smoke as the wind curled it down the path and enveloped them. She stopped at the first barrel that marked the corner of the landing pad and let Maratse rest as she walked toward the helicopter. Panninguaq sat in the pilot's seat, her face hidden behind large aviator glasses and her hair. Fenna took a step toward the cockpit window only to stop when she noticed Lorentzen finishing the knot on a fresh bandage around his knee.

"You didn't believe me, did you?" he said, as Fenna stopped to face him.

"About what?" she said.

"Cleaning up. Eskelsen is dead, isn't he?"

"Yes."

"As I said, you're here to clean up."

"I came here to find out the truth. To see if you had falsified the LOMROG data."

"I didn't. Not in so many words."

"No. But you still withheld it," Fenna said and paused. "How much did they pay you?"

"The Chinese? Enough," he said and tossed the empty bandage packet onto the ground. "How much are they paying *you*?"

"I don't take bribes to shit on my own country."

"Ah, and which country is that, Konstabel? Because it seems to me that you are becoming less and less Danish in your actions. You might want to watch that. Your boss, Jarnvig, doesn't appreciate disloyalty," Lorentzen reached for the flask of water by his side and waved at the smoke drifting down from the camp. "We're not so different," he said and took a swig of water. "We could even have been friends."

"You don't have friends," Fenna said. "You sold Eskelsen out in a heartbeat."

"Bjørn? He knew the risks. The minute the Chinese got involved, well… it was only a matter of time before this happened."

"This?"

"The cleaning up. You think the Chinese want the world to know how deeply they are grubbing in the Arctic? They have observer status on the Arctic Council, Konstabel. They are courting Finland, and the Alaskans. Do you think they want anyone to discover the other activities they are engaged in?"

"No," Fenna said and waited.

"Then you might want to consider how long you've got before it's your body burning in some conveniently remote location."

Fenna opened her mouth to speak and then stopped at the sound of rotors thudding through the air from the south, from Nuuk.

"Not so remote," she said and ran back to Maratse. "Come on. Let's get you out of here." Fenna heaved Maratse onto his feet and pulled him across the landing pad. "Panninguaq," she yelled, waving with her left arm. "Get out of the chopper."

Panninguaq opened the door a fraction and pulled the headset to one side, strands of her hair twisting in the wind as she freed her left ear. "What?"

"Get out," Fenna said. "There's another helicopter coming. We need to move. To get away from Hong Wei."

The crack of Maratse's pistol and the snap of the bullet in the air above the helicopter confirmed what Fenna already knew. It was too late. The Chinese intelligence operative had finished overseeing the destruction of the camp and was ready to leave.

"Start the helicopter," Hong Wei shouted as he marched toward them, the snow sticking to his heels and the toes of his boots. "Get in," he said to Fenna. "Bring your friend."

Fenna opened the passenger door as Panninguaq checked the instruments. She helped Maratse onto the backseat and then looked at Lorentzen as he held up his hand.

"I could do with a lift," he said, as Fenna reached down to help him.

"No," said Hong Wei. "I will help him. Get inside, Konstabel."

Fenna nodded and closed the door. She walked around the nose of the aircraft and opened the rear passenger door as the rotors began to turn. She stepped onto the skids and paused at the sound of one shot being fired from the pistol, and then a second. She turned as Hong Wei followed her path in the snow and gestured for her to get inside with a wave of the gun. Fenna climbed in and closed the door. She leaned over Maratse and looked down at the entry wound in Lorentzen's head and the stain of blood on the front of his jacket. She leaned back on the seat and watched as Hong Wei got in beside Panninguaq. He put on a spare headset and motioned for Fenna to do the same.

"I have some friends on the way," he said and pointed to the south. "They will pick up my associates and clean up the rest of the mess. Now," Hong Wei said, as he fastened his seatbelt, "keep quiet and enjoy the ride." Fenna noticed he kept the pistol trained on Panninguaq.

As Panninguaq twisted the collective and pulled back on the stick, the Eurocopter lifted off the pad in a tornado of snow, a whiteout that reminded Fenna of the documentaries she had seen of troops being lifted out of the dustbowl of Afghanistan. She thought of her father, bit her lip, and buckled Maratse's belt before fastening her own.

Dad, she thought, *you were Special Forces. You pushed me in this direction.* Fenna thought of the conversation she had had with Solomon on the flight across the Atlantic, how he stressed the importance of family. *And yet*, she thought and looked at Maratse as he gritted his teeth beside her. *Sometimes sharing the same blood isn't enough, you have to spill it together too.*

As they flew down the fjord Fenna considered her next move and wondered if Burwardsley had made any progress in finding *The Magician*. The irony was not lost on her, that the very man she and Maratse had fled from across the sea ice in a bullet-ridden police Toyota was now the only man who might be able to save her and the policeman she had become so fond of and now felt responsible for. *I have a tendency to do that*, she thought, *to feel responsible for people*. Now she needed to plan as best she could, with the limited resources she had, and the dubious allies she could muster.

She put her thoughts on pause as Panninguaq flew past Sermitsiaq, and the shadow of the mountain seemed to reach out and pluck at Fenna's arms. She wished it could, that the mountain might swallow her and end this – *all of it*. But they were soon beyond the mountain's reach and Fenna suddenly realised why Hong Wei had remained so calm – there were friends waiting for him in the harbour. He tapped Panninguaq's leg as she vectored in towards the airport.

"Land there," he said and pointed toward the helicopter pad at the stern of a massive red-hulled and white-decked icebreaker, dwarfing the cruise ships and naval patrol boats as it loitered in the sheltered bay to the east of the commercial dock. Fenna tried not to be impressed, but when Maratse fidgeted by her side for a better look, she exchanged a smile and raised her eyebrows as Panninguaq circled the Chinese icebreaker, the *MV Xue Long*, and hovered above the deck to land. "You are impressed," Hong Wei said, as he turned in his seat to look at Fenna. "Just wait until you get on board."

I am impressed, she thought. *We have nothing like this. And yet…* Fenna pushed thoughts of the impressive ship and the equally impressive commitment China, a non-Arctic nation, was making to polar research. *They are building a second*, she remembered, as the helicopter touched down on the landing pad. And then her thoughts were racing as the efficiency of the Chinese Arctic Research Mission took over. Fenna watched as Maratse was lifted onto a stretcher and wheeled across the deck and into a lift. She walked after him only to have Hong Wei catch her by the arm and point her in the direction of a door leading inside the main structure.

"What about Panninguaq?"

"She stays," he said and nodded at the deckhands securing the aircraft.

"As a hostage?"

"As a guest."

"And what am I?

"An asset, for the moment. Come with me."

A tall man with a jagged scar on his chin met them at the door. Hong Wei handed him Maratse's pistol and gave a few short commands in Chinese before leading Fenna inside.

"The northeast passage," he said, "cuts 4,000 miles off the shipping distance from Shanghai to Hamburg." Hong Wei paused to let a group of crewmen scurry past. "Even ice-free, the waters in the Arctic are still dangerous. We will need ships like the *Xue Long* to escort our container ships. Expensive, but time is money, and if we save time, we save money."

"She looks like a container ship," Fenna said, as she followed Hong Wei down a stairwell to the next deck and into a cabin.

"She used to be," he said as he shut the door. "But then my country bought it and refitted it. A bit like what we are going to do with you."

"I'm not going to work for the Chinese," she said and clenched her fists at her sides.

"But your mission is over. Cleaned up. I cleaned it up for you, and now you work for me."

"I work for the Danish government."

"Of course." Hong Wei poured two mugs of coffee from a pot at the end of the small cabin. He gestured at the table and placed Fenna's coffee in front of her as she sat down. "It has been a long day," he said and sipped at his coffee. "It can be difficult to keep track of the time when the sun does not go down."

"Or when it doesn't come up."

"I would not know. I have never experienced an Arctic winter." Hong Wei took another sip and studied Fenna. "You did not react when I shot Eskelsen. He was your countryman."

"He was going to kill me."

"And Lorentzen? He was not going to kill you, but still, no reaction when I shot him."

"I've seen a lot of death recently," Fenna said and sighed. "I'm getting better at dealing with it." A brief image of Dina challenged her words as the Greenlander twisted beneath the dog whip in her mind's eye, but Fenna ignored it, pushed her away. *Save the living*, she thought. *There's nothing I can do for the dead.*

Hong Wei put his mug down and leaned on the counter. "I have never heard of you, and this troubles me. I'm the head of intelligence for all things pertaining to the Arctic. I should have heard of you."

"Are you trying to impress me?" Fenna said. "Because I'm just too tired."

"I'm merely paying you a professional compliment, or should I just pass it on to your boss, Per Jarnvig?" Fenna looked up and Hong Wei smiled.

"Some things I *do* know, but this *Magician*. Perhaps he has another name, because that one I have never heard. Tell me more about him, and then we will approach your contact."

"He is Danish," said Fenna, "as far as I know. His accent and mannerisms were perfect when he interrogated me."

"When?"

"Actually," Fenna said and paused as she realised it was true, "just a few months ago. It was in March, this year."

"You have been busy."

You have no idea, Fenna thought and scanned the room with a quick twist of her head from right to left. It was spartan, efficient. She had the feeling that *efficient* was the official motto of the *Xue Long*. Something she was not, she realised, as she considered the wake of bodies and destruction she left in her path, on her quest for the truth. *The truth*, she wondered. *What truth? What am I searching for?* And then she remembered. She recalled how she could cope with being in close proximity to Burwardsley, the one man who scared her, because they shared a common goal, to finish things, not for themselves, but for Dina.

"You seem lost in your thoughts, Konstabel," Hong Wei said. His words jogged Fenna out of her mind and into the present.

Just lost, she thought and stood up. "We need to find a Royal Marine Lieutenant called Burwardsley. He has been tracking *The Magician* since March."

"And where is this Marine?"

"He is here, in Nuuk."

"Because the man we seek is here?"

"Perhaps. I don't know. But this is where the trail led Burwardsley."

Hong Wei shook his head. "Perhaps our little chat over coffee has confused you, Konstabel. Perhaps you have forgotten just what I will do to discover the things I need to know, to find the people I need to talk to. Your story about a wizard intrigues me as I have heard similar stories of a man, perhaps even an organisation that is manipulating events in the Arctic faster than the Arctic states can react. But, be smart, Konstabel, because I will not hesitate to visit our friend in the ship's medical bay if you need the slightest help in remembering why you are here, still alive, and not blistering in a flaming tent in the mountains. Do you understand?"

"I do," Fenna said and stuck out her chin. "More than you think."

"Then are you ready to make contact with Burwardsley?" Hong Wei said and Fenna almost smiled at the difficulty he had in pronouncing the Lieutenant's name.

"I need a phone," she said and held out her hand as Hong Wei fished a mobile from his pocket. Fenna pulled a crumpled note from her pocket and dialled the number Burwardsley had given her. She looked at Hong Wei, choosing to focus on him and what he might do to Maratse, instead of thinking about what Burwardsley had done to her. The dial tone stopped and Burwardsley answered. "It's Fenna," she said. Hong Wei took the mobile from her hand and turned on the speaker. He put it on the table between them.

"Nice timing, *love*," Burwardsley said. "Where are you?"

"In the bay. On a ship. We need to meet."

"That could be difficult."

"Why?"

"I have some new friends, and they seem keen for me to stay put."

"Then I'll come to you."

"Hah," Burwardsley laughed. "You'll need a small army."

"Mr Burwardsley," Hong Wei said, as he leaned over the mobile.

"Fenna? What the fuck. Who's this?"

"Who I am is not important. What is important is that I happen to have a small army. You said that you needed one. Can I be of assistance?"

Burwardsley was quiet for a moment and Fenna pictured him thinking it through.

"Yeah, all right," he said. "Bring your army."

"Very well. We will see you very soon."

"Wait," said Burwardsley. "Fenna, can we trust this guy?"

"No," she said and finished the call.

The Sea

NORTH ATLANTIC OCEAN, GREENLAND

Chapter 26

Fenna followed Hong Wei out of the cabin and along the deck toward the mudroom where the scientists don their survival suits and gear ready for the field. He stopped at the doorway and gestured for Fenna to wait as he spoke to the same tall Chinese crewman who met them on arrival. Hong Wei beckoned for her to join him as the man left.

"The Air Greenland pilot…"

"Panninguaq."

"Yes. She will fly you to the airport from where you will take a taxi to your contact's location," Hong Wei said and paused for a moment to study Fenna's face. "You work for me now. Do you understand?"

"You think you've turned me?"

"I don't need to. You'll work for me of your own accord because I have something of yours."

The mission or the man, thought Fenna. *Now the mission is the man.* "I will need proof. Constant updates, and," she said. "I'll need a phone. They took mine in the desert. I haven't had one since."

"I will provide you with a phone, and I will send reports…"

"Video."

"… of the policeman's progress. Believe me, he is receiving the very best care."

"Because of what you did to him," Fenna said through gritted teeth.

"And I can do it again," he said and waited for Fenna to relax. "Now, do you understand what is required of you?"

"You mentioned something about an army?"

"Yes," Hong Wei said and laughed. It was the

first time Fenna could recall she had heard him laugh. She shivered at the harsh tones, as unfamiliar to him as they were to her. "In my official capacity as a representative of the People's Republic of China, I visited one of the schools in Nuuk. The new one, in the new part of town. As a gesture, the school has taken a Chinese teacher on exchange. Chen is one of mine. The small army I mentioned is her class. I think you will find that children are the best means of diffusing a tense situation, especially *en masse*. You are in luck. They are cooking seal meat at the school tonight – a fundraiser. Chen has her class. She will bring them to the location of your contact on the pretence of collecting something. You will accompany them."

"You've thought this through," Fenna said.

"It is my job."

"And after that? You will get Burwardsley and me back on the ship?"

"Yes, of course." Fenna studied Hong Wei's face as he reached inside his jacket for a mobile, thinner and smaller than the one she had used earlier. "This," he said, "is what the American's call a *burner*."

But who is burning whom? Fenna wondered as she took the mobile. She slipped it inside her pocket. Her thin fingers trembled, catching on the hem of the pocket. *Treason*, she thought, *makes me nervous*. And then she thought of Maratse in the medical wing, and Hong Wei's personal interest in his well-being.

"I'll need a weapon," she said.

"I don't think so," Hong Wei said and gestured toward the door at the far end of the mudroom. "Up the stairs and onto the deck. Your helicopter is waiting."

Fenna walked past Hong Wei. She paused at the door and looked back. "Just to be clear. I give you information about *The Magician*, and you let Maratse go."

"We are agreed."

"And what about me?"

"We'll see how useful you are this evening. Perhaps I will have need of further information."

"But you will let Maratse go for this one piece of information?"

"Yes," Hong Wei said and Fenna really wanted to believe him. "Are we clear?"

"Yes," she said and opened the door. Fenna heard the rotors of the Eurocopter whine as she jogged up the stairs, through a second door, and onto the open deck. She felt the mobile vibrate in her pocket and took it out. Hong Wei's text gave her the time and location of her meet with Chen. She had twenty minutes.

Panninguaq was quiet as Fenna slid into the passenger seat. Fenna slipped the spare headset over her head and heard her talk to the tower at Nuuk airport, confirming her approach and landing permission. Panninguaq lifted the Eurocopter off the deck and into the air, hovering into a slow turn before dipping the nose to gain speed and then climbing above and around the city. Fenna could see the high rises of Qinngorput, the new part of the town, and the long, straight road sloping down to the school. She imagined Burwardsley watching the helicopter from the balcony of one of the apartments and her stomach twisted at the thought. The old cliché, the enemy of my enemy is my friend, distracted her from the view and Panninguaq's voice coming through the headset.

"This for my son," she said and Fenna looked at her.

"What?"

"Anguteq. He is the only reason I'm doing this."

"Doing what?" said Fenna. She recognised the tremor in Panninguaq's voice, the roar of the rotors couldn't hide it.

"Keeping my mouth shut."

"About what happened at the mine?"

"Yes, *what happened at the mine*," Panninguaq said and whipped her head to one side, staring at Fenna, her hair caught in the seatbelt and in a strip of old Velcro on the headset. She yanked it free and glared at Fenna. "That man, he…"

"Killed someone," said Fenna. "Yes."

"He sent someone to talk to me."

"Who?"

"I don't know his name. A man. Tall…"

"With a scar on his chin? Yes, I've seen him."

"He said that if I wanted to see my son again, that I had better keep my mouth shut. That there were people everywhere," she said and took a ragged breath. Fenna listened as Panninguaq fought with the next sentence. "They even have someone at the school, he said."

"I know," said Fenna.

"You know? How do you *know*?"

"Panninguaq…"

"No. Don't tell me. I'm leaving. Tonight. I will fly to Kangerlussuaq. I'll take Anguteq to Denmark tomorrow morning."

"They will have people in Denmark too," Fenna said, but Panninguaq ignored her and the airport loomed in the near distance. Panninguaq said nothing more to Fenna, sparing words for the tower only as she talked through her approach and set the aircraft down on a square trolley close to the two main hangers. Panninguaq shut down the engine, applied the rotor brake and then glanced at Fenna.

"I don't want to see you again," she said and waited for Fenna to leave.

Fenna took off her headset and stepped out of the helicopter. She took a last look at Panninguaq and then walked across the tarmac to the gate, slipping outside and around the arrivals, enjoying the anonymity of an internal charter flight.

It was Hong Wei's men at the mine, she thought as she caught the last available taxi. *So Lorentzen won't be missed yet. I have a little time at least. Before the shit hits the fan.* Fenna gave the address to the driver of the taxi and settled into the back seat. The road looped around the runway and Fenna wasted a few seconds looking at Sermitsiaq, its summit lit by the evening sun, as bright as midday in Denmark. *It's growing on me*, she thought. *That's something.* But the sight of the mountain, the fjord, the small patches of cotton growing along the road, the brightly painted houses – bigger than those in the settlements, but just as colourful – couldn't distract her from Burwardsley. Someone she had hated yet now, *I need him*, she thought, *if I am going to save Maratse.*

The driver turned left at the T-junction and Fenna could see the *Xue Long* – Chinese for *Snow Dragon*, sitting in the bay and the arrival of the navy's *Knud Rasmussen*, grey and insignificant beside the red hull and white decks of the Chinese icebreaker. Fenna stared at the vessel until it disappeared behind the new high rises of Qinngorput.

"The school," said the driver and slowed at a roundabout, the wheels slushing through the puddles of melting snow, as they drained into the ditches either side of the road.

"Yes," said Fenna. "Wait," she said, as she looked to the right and saw a small army of children striding up the long road leading up to the row of five towers looking out to the bay. "Up there. Take me all the way to the top."

"*Aap*," said the driver as he drove past the school and past the group of children. The children's clothes were tidier and cleaner than those of the children Fenna had seen in Ittoqqortoormiit, but the faces were the same, only some were paler. *No glare from the ice*, she realised as the taxi slowed to a stop at the top of the hill. Fenna paid the driver and got out.

"Wait for me," she said and gave him an extra one hundred Danish kroner.

"Where do you want to go?"

"Back to the airport," she said and closed the door.

She spotted the first surveillance team within a few seconds of getting out of the car. A discreet black SUV, but with two men wearing light blue shirts sitting in the front. Fenna kept an eye on them as she took out her mobile and the scrap of paper with Burwardsley's number on it. The policeman looked at her as she dialled.

"Yes?" Burwardsley said after two rings.

"I'm outside," said Fenna. "Which building?"

"Number three," he said. "You're coming up?"

"I have friends." Fenna waved at the Chinese exchange teacher and her Greenlandic colleague. She flashed three fingers and waited for the class to pass her before tagging along behind them.

"Christ. You have kids with you."

"You can see me?" Fenna said and looked up.

"I'm on the balcony, fifth floor, facing the bay. Can you see the men below me?"

"Yes. Third floor."

"Exactly. They are the ones we need to get past. Get the kids to stop outside their door."

"Fine," Fenna said and jogged to catch up with the teachers at the head of the class. "Hi," she said in English as she slowed to walk beside them. "You're here to pick something up?"

"Yes," said Chen before her colleague could answer.

"Great. It's the second flat on the third floor. They might not be expecting you, but just go right in."

"Okay," she said and ushered the class inside the building. Fenna got into the lift and watched the children as they climbed the stairs, pleased that Anguteq was not among them. She hoped they would provide the necessary distraction.

The lift stopped at the fifth floor. Fenna jumped as the doors opened and Burwardsley slid between them. He pushed the button for the ground floor. She pressed herself against the glass wall of the lift and stared at him.

Burwardsley glanced at her as the lift started to move and said, "You're going to have to get over that if we're going to work together, love."

"I know," she said. "It's just…"

"I get it. I do. You just can't dwell on it. Dina's gone. Humble's dead. Move on."

"I can't."

"Why not?" he said, pausing as the lift neared the third floor and the excited chatter of children and deep male voices filtered through the thin doors of the elevator.

"They have Maratse."

"The policeman? Fuck. What the hell is he doing here?"

"It's a long story and…" Fenna froze as Burwardsley towered over her, grabbed her arms and twisted her to one side. Fenna held her breath as he leaned in close to kiss her.

"Just pretend. I don't want them to see you."

"They already have," she said, as two men, wearing the classic black uniforms and tactical vests of a counter terrorist unit, disappeared inside the apartment, shoving the children to one side, only to reappear with helmets and Heckler & Koch MP5s. Fenna slipped out from beneath Burwardsley and nodded at the door of the elevator. "There will be two cops in a car at the far end of the parking area."

"And beyond that?"

"A taxi. He's waiting for me."

"Well, this is going to spook the shit out of him."

"Yeah," Fenna said and felt her cheeks crease for a second.

"Having fun all of a sudden, Konstabel?"

"Maybe," she said and grinned. "It's the adrenalin."

"Just keep telling yourself that." Burwardsley took a breath as the lift stopped and the door started to open. "We go fast and hard," he said. "I want you on my right. Driver's side."

"Okay," Fenna said, noticing the sound of boots

tramping down the stairwell.

"Forget them," Burwardsley said. "Take out the driver. Take his weapon if you can. Get in the taxi."

Fenna started to nod only to feel her head whip back as Burwardsley yanked her out of the lift and propelled her at the glass doors at the building's entrance. She lifted her arms as Burwardsley shoved her toward the right-hand door, battering through it – one hand slamming into the glass pane, the other into Fenna's back. As they cleared the steps and the door recoiled with a snap of hinges, he pushed Fenna to the right as the policemen in the car opened the doors of the vehicle.

He's fast, Fenna noted as Burwardsley outstripped her, his legs pounding the surface of the car park, she could almost feel the vibrations, and then he was at the car and kicking the door into the policeman, grabbing the man's pistol with his left hand as he backhanded him in the face with his right.

"Move it, Konstabel," Burwardsley shouted, as Fenna reached the driver's door. The policeman was already outside of the car and drawing his weapon. Fenna barrelled into his chest and butted him in the head. The policeman staggered and Fenna followed him down onto the ground, straddling his chest and punching him once in the face, and a second time in the breastbone.

"Stop fucking about, Fenna." Burwardsley wrenched the passenger door open and pulled the policeman toward him, locking the man's neck within the crook of his left arm. Burwardsley fired two shots in the air and then placed the pistol to the policeman's head.

"What are you doing?" Fenna yelled at

Burwardsley, as she pulled the driver's pistol from his holster. She swore as the pistol jerked to a stop at the end of the safety wire. It took another few seconds to find the policeman's multitool on his utility belt and cut the pistol free, and then she was up, on her feet and running for the taxi.

Fenna glanced over her shoulder and saw the two Danish soldiers – *Frømandskorpset*, she guessed – as they sought cover behind two vehicles, one man talking on the radio clipped to his vest as the other aimed at Burwardsley. *They'll block the road*, Fenna thought, slowing as she realised they were never going to get to the airport.

"Just keep going," Burwardsley said, the policeman's heels dragging across the tarmac as he jogged to the taxi.

"No," the taxi driver said as he got out of the car.

"Get in," Fenna yelled. "Get in the fucking car."

"*Naamik*," he said, as he stumbled and ran down the road.

"Drive," Burwardsley said, as he opened the back door and stuffed the policeman onto the backseat. Fenna climbed behind the wheel, tossed her pistol onto the dashboard and slammed the door. "Just go," Burwardsley said, as he knelt on the edge of the backseat and fumbled with the cuffs on the policeman's belt. "Fuck," he said, as Fenna spun the car in reverse and the tips of his boots scraped the surface of the road.

"Are you getting in?" she said and crunched into first gear.

"Drive for fuck's sake," he said and grabbed the headrest behind Fenna's head, catching a handful of Fenna's hair beneath his fingers. Fenna tugged her head free and accelerated around the top of the road, threw the car into second and stomped on the accelerator. The car jerked as she caught third gear halfway down the hill.

"Are they behind us?" she shouted as she accelerated into fourth.

"Stop shouting, Konstabel," Burwardsley said, as he snapped the cuffs around the policeman's wrists, forced his massive body through several contortions Houdini would have been proud of, and closed the passenger door. "We're all right. Relax. Drive."

"Relax?" Fenna said. "How the fuck can I relax?" She caught herself for a moment, her heart hammering in her chest, pulsing at her throat, thudding in her ears. She glanced in the rear-view mirror. "We just kidnapped a policeman."

"And the night is still so young," Burwardsley said and laughed as he checked the pistol in his grip.

Chapter 27

The taxi squealed around the roundabout as Fenna braked into third gear and accelerated past the school, the smell of fresh seal smoked across the road and through the window Burwardsley had opened. Fenna swallowed the saliva that seemed to ignore the adrenalin flooding her body to remind her that, at some point soon, she really should eat.

"I'm starving," she said, as she threw the taxi into a tight right turn and pressed her foot down on the accelerator pedal.

"Then you're in luck," Burwardsley said. "Gotta love police utility belts," he said and held up two magazines. "Extra ammo, cuffs, and…" He paused. "A Mars bar."

"Share it?" Fenna said and blasted the horn at a gaggle of kids on bikes.

"It's yours," he said and peeled the chocolate out of its wrapper. Burwardsley broke it in half, reached around the driver's seat, and pushed it into Fenna's open mouth. "Now that your stomach is satisfied. Let's talk."

"All right," Fenna said, her words chunky and rich with chocolate.

"What the fuck are you doing with the Chinese?"

"They've got Maratse?"

"Who's *they*?"

"Hong Wei. Chinese intelligence. On the ship in the bay."

"Okay," Burwardsley said and looked at his watch. "You're going to hit a roadblock after the pass, before the turn for the airport, in about forty seconds."

"You know this?"

"It's what I would do."

"Fair enough," Fenna said and accelerated into fifth gear.

"Keep it in fourth," Burwardsley said and shoved the second half of the Mars bar into Fenna's mouth. The engine protested as Fenna dropped down a gear.

"What about you? Why were you being watched?"

Burwardsley looked through the back window before answering. "Seems my mate at Arctic Command doesn't remember the old days as fondly as I do."

"Not when he puts a Counter Terrorist unit on you."

"That's who they were? I thought they were a bit more pro than the usual goons."

"Why didn't they pick you up?"

"Waiting for you, I guess." Burwardsley grabbed the back of the passenger seat with his left hand and said, "Keep driving, Konstabel."

"Why? What are you going to..." And then she saw it, the roadblock, just as Burwardsley fired three shots through the windscreen. "Fuck," Fenna shouted as the glass shattered and the crack of the pistol cuffed her ears.

"They won't shoot back because of our guest," Burwardsley said with another glance behind him. "The two behind us are gaining," he said and turned around. "Look to the right of the roadblock, there's a patch of gravel. Bump the car over the curb and gun it."

"Okay," Fenna said and tugged at the seatbelt.

"Forget the fucking belt, Fenna. Just drive."

Fenna ignored the spinning blue lights of the police Toyotas blocking the road. She dropped the taxi into third and accelerated, pushing the needle of the rev counter into the red. Fenna yelled louder than the engine and floored the accelerator as she swung the taxi at the curb.

"To the right," Burwardsley shouted and slapped at Fenna's arm. "Gravel – piled up like a ramp. Use it, Konstabel."

With both hands on the wheel, Fenna slurred the car to the right, up the gravel, and bumped the car up the curb and onto the rough open surface in front of a small supermarket. She swerved to avoid a child running after a dog, swerved again to avoid the dog and then slammed into the side of a Volkswagen. The engine stalled as the taxi continued rolling toward the smooth surface of the road, the tyres slick with melting snow.

"What the fuck?"

"I know, I know," Fenna yelled and prayed the car would start as she turned the key in the ignition. Burwardsley leaned out of the passenger window and fired at the counter terrorist team speeding toward them in a black SUV. The engine stuttered into life and she shifted into first gear and accelerated onto the road.

"Go."

Fenna shifted from first through third, flicking her gaze from the road to the police roadblock as it unfurled into a column of vehicles flashing after them.

"Just fucking drive, Konstabel," Burwardsley shouted between taking pot shots at the pursuing vehicles. He stopped to change magazines. Fenna breathed in the lull, her stomach cramped and her mouth dry.

"Fuck," she said and laughed.

"What's the plan, Konstabel?" Burwardsley said, as he slapped a new magazine into the butt of the pistol. "How are we getting out?"

"Hong Wei said he would pick us up."

"He lied."

"Yeah, I know," Fenna said and smoothed the car into fourth gear. She looked to the right at the runway, craning her neck to better see the bright red Bell Huey helicopter sitting on the tarmac. It looked like it was being prepped for launch.

"So? New plan?"

"Working on it."

"All right," Burwardsley said, as the taxi lurched forward. The policeman lifted his head and groaned. Burwardsley pressed the man's face into the seat and changed position to sit on his back. "Our friend is getting restless."

"Okay," Fenna said, as she braked into the corner. A quick glance in the mirror stung her eyes with the flash of blue lights. She blinked and accelerated. As the taxi approached the airport she pointed through the shattered windscreen and said, "See the helicopter?"

"The Huey?" Burwardsley said, as he looked between the seats. "Yeah, I see it, *love*. You can't fly, can you?"

"No, but it's being prepped. The rotors are spinning."

"Then we're out of time."

"Not yet," Fenna said and floored the accelerator. The image of another high-speed chase in another part of the country flashed across Fenna's mind. She grinned at the memory, of emptying the magazine of Maratse's M1 rifle through the back of the police Toyota, the exact replica of the ones chasing them to the airport. *Except this time*, she thought, *I'm driving*.

"Hold on to something," Fenna yelled, as she accelerated toward the gate between the runway and the airport building.

"Do it," Burwardsley shouted as he lay flat on the policeman. Fenna crashed the taxi through the airport gate. The vehicle spun to the left, the wheels chewing on the gate in a shower of sparks, as they careened toward a Dash 8 aircraft, parked in front of the arrivals lounge. Fenna shouted again as the taxi slammed into the landing gear beneath the starboard wing of the aircraft. The taxi stopped and Burwardsley pushed himself off the policeman, opened the passenger door on the driver's side and crawled out. Fenna joined him on the tarmac, pausing to reach inside and grab her pistol from where it had fallen into the passenger foot well.

"We've got one chance," Burwardsley said, as he grabbed Fenna by the shoulder and ran across the tarmac. He lifted the pistol and pointed it at the pilot in the helicopter, ignoring the wail of sirens and the bark of commands through loudspeakers behind them. Burwardsley thrust Fenna toward the rear sliding door and yanked open the door to the co-pilot's seat. He climbed in and thrust the pistol at the pilot. "Fly," he said, with a quick glance at Fenna as she scrambled into the aircraft and slammed the door shut.

Fenna pushed her hand against the floor to lift

herself up, frowning as she pressed against something soft, a backpack, with Spiderman sprawled across it. She looked up into the wide brown eyes of a young boy, buckled into the backseat as his mother lifted the helicopter into the air and away from the crash and chaos of men and equipment below them.

"Anguteq?" Fenna said and tried to smile. The boy said nothing. Fenna crawled onto the seat beside him and sat down. She buckled the seatbelt across her lap and looked at the pilot. She wasn't surprised to see the long black hair beneath the helmet, nor the patient rage of a mother waiting for the moment to fight for her son. Fenna grabbed a headset from the hook on the bulkhead and slipped it on. "Panninguaq," she said, "listen to me."

Panninguaq flew out toward the bay, her lips tight, her knuckles the colour of snow. Burwardsley pointed at the *Xue Long* as it made its way out of the bay and Panninguaq followed his directions, her eyes flicking from the pistol in his lap to the horizon and back again.

"Panninguaq, it's going to be all right. I'm going to fix this," Fenna said. She tried another smile with Anguteq, but the boy just stared at her.

"How?" Panninguaq said, her voice low but defiant.

"Your friend is leaving, love" Burwardsley said. "What's the plan?"

Fenna ignored him and continued speaking in Danish. "I've been set up," she said. "But if you get me on that ship, me and my friend, we will fix this, and then you won't have to worry about Anguteq, you can stay in Greenland, in Nuuk…"

"If I get you on that ship?"

"Yes."

"You'll fix this?"

"Yes," Fenna said.

"I don't believe you."

Burwardsley coughed and cut through the silence as Fenna thought about what to say next. He turned in his seat, flicked his eyes at the boy and then waved his pistol at Fenna. "We're not going to achieve much with these," he said. "Your friends are going to be all tooled-up."

"We'll make do."

"Sure, and we're just going to land on the deck?"

"No," she said. "We'll jump onto it."

"Great," he said and faced forward as Panninguaq flew the Bell Huey 212 past the harbour and over the sea in the wake of the Chinese icebreaker. Burwardsley looked down at the bay beneath them. "It looks like your old friends are joining the party," he said and pointed at the grey hull of the *Knud Rasmussen*, and the sea frothing at the stern of the naval patrol vessel.

"Then we'll have to be quick," Fenna said and slumped back in the seat. Anguteq shifted his wide eyes from the gun in her hand to her face. Fenna wiped a strand of hair from her eye and tried for the third time to elicit a smile from him. She stuck out her tongue and, after a moment, Anguteq did the same. *Small steps*, she told herself. *Get on the ship. Get to Maratse. Wait for the navy. We're going to be all right.*

She looked up as Anguteq curled his tiny brown hand around her little finger. He tugged at it, and she smiled. A moment of reprieve. The quiet before the storm. Fenna tugged her finger free and held Anguteq's hand as Burwardsley directed Panninguaq toward the stern of the ship. She listened as he gave the commands in English, his northern accent punching through the chop of the rotor blades with practised authority. Anguteq's hand was warm, hot almost, and Fenna felt the sweat bead between their skin. She sighed and expelled all the breath from her lungs, wanting the next lungful to capture at least some of the calm the boy provided, in the still of the moment, the one that always preceded action of the most violent sort. She felt the vibration of the helicopter change in pitch, noticed the attitude was more angled, more aggressive, and then the helicopter was flaring, nose up, above the landing deck, and the rush of Arctic sea air goosebumped her skin and whipped at her hair, as Burwardsley crawled into the back, slid the passenger door open, and stepped out onto the skids.

Fenna let go of Anguteq, tugged the headset off her head, and unbuckled her belt. She played the canvas belt through her fingers as she joined Burwardsley on the skids. The tips of her hair stung her eyes as she leapt after the big Marine Lieutenant to land hard on the deck of the *Xue Long*. And then Anguteq's soft brown eyes were gone, lost in the flash of gunfire.

"Suppressing fire," Burwardsley yelled, as he tossed Fenna his spare magazine and rushed the first of the Chinese guards to step onto the deck, starboard side. With a slap to the man's chest, Burwardsley ripped the Changfeng 9mm submachine gun out of the man's hands and sprayed the port side with a long burst of lead.

Fenna gripped her pistol in two hands, aiming up at the gantry running along the deck above the landing pad. She fired two rounds, moved forward, firing another two rounds until the magazine was empty and she was crouching beside Burwardsley as he prepared to enter the mudroom.

"You ready?" he said, as Fenna slapped a fresh magazine into the grip of her pistol.

"Yes," she said and remembered to breathe. It was automatic now. Burwardsley was the lead. She was his second. Fenna had his back. One room after the other. One stairwell at a time. Until they had Maratse, or they were dead. *But I am not ready to die*, she thought and allowed herself a last glimpse of Anguteq's eyes, of Dina's playful smile, peach juice dribbling from her chin, of Mikael's ice-beard, of dancing lessons with Nicklas', of…

"Fenna?" Burwardsley said.

"I'm ready," she said and shook her head. "Let's go."

"Because, if you're not…"

"Hong Wei sold us out. I'm ready. Let's do this."

And the memories were gone, and it was one volley of lead after another as Burwardsley cleared the way with short controlled bursts. Fenna followed behind him, covering the corners, the shadows, suppressing her demons, looking for dragons – *snow dragons*, the Chinese kind.

Burwardsley scavenged magazines from the crewmen bleeding at his feet, tugging them from their belts as he stepped over their bodies. After the initial resistance, the crew of the *Xue Long* withered into a retreat before the hail of bullets from the Royal Marine Lieutenant with one last goal in sight and little to lose. Fenna tapped his shoulder and pointed at the stairwell.

"Down one deck," she said. "Second room on the port side of the ship."

They smelled the medical bay before they saw it, a wave of antiseptic splashing down the corridor. Burwardsley stopped at the door and nodded for Fenna to stack up – positioning herself ready for a dynamic entry.

"Ready?" he whispered.

"Yes."

"And when we're in?"

"We wait for the navy."

"And a prison cell," Burwardsley said and snorted.

"Yes."

"So long as we're together, *love*," he said and winked.

Fenna almost laughed, but then he nodded, a single dip of his stubbled chin, before he peeled into the medical bay, and Fenna followed him.

Chapter 28

Fenna pressed her left palm against Burwardsley's shoulder, her pistol steady in her right hand. As Burwardsley moved she moved with him, only to stop when he stopped, and to lower the pistol when he lowered the submachine gun. Maratse was bleeding, and the ship's doctor had his hands inside the policeman's stomach as his assistant passed him swabs and forceps to save the Greenlander's life. *We're too late*, Fenna thought, and then she saw Hong Wei. He nodded toward Maratse and flicked his head toward the crewman in the corner – the one with the jagged scar on his chin.

"Impressive," Hong Wei said, looking at Burwardsley. "I ordered six men to stop you, and now I have six bodies, two more than the ship's morgue can accommodate." He gestured with his hand at Maratse. "This man, at least, can be repatriated before his body begins to rot."

"He's not dead," said Fenna.

"Not yet."

Fenna let the pistol hang by her side, her fingers loosely wrapped around the handle as she took a step closer to the operating table around which the *Xue Long's* medical staff exchanged brief commands and updates.

"Careful," Burwardsley said and Fenna heard the metallic clack of the sling bevel screwed into the stock as he shifted his grip on the weapon.

"As you can see," said Hong Wei. "The doctor and his team are doing their very best to save your friend's life." Fenna could indeed see – more than she wanted to. The skin of Maratse's stomach peeled

251

away from his gut like the petals of a viscous flower. Gone was the bruised blue skin, to be replaced by swollen organs peeping through a steady stream of dark red blood pooling around coagulated lumps of black blood, old and stubborn. "Of course," Hong Wei continued, "they will stop whenever I order them to do so."

Fenna looked up to meet the Chinese man's eyes. "I thought you were going to pick us up," she said, "as agreed."

"Ah," he said and straightened his back – Burwardsley and Hong Wei's bodyguard tensed, and, for a moment, the smell of antiseptic and blood was lost in a tense flood of adrenalin. Fenna recognised it, caught a whiff of her own sweat as the same chemicals surged through her body. She swallowed and whispered to Burwardsley to stand down.

"The navy will be here soon," she said.

"Then I suggest we get down to business," Hong Wei said with a glance at Burwardsley. "This is your associate? The one with the information about the mysterious *Magician*?"

"Yes."

"And what do you have for me?" Hong Wei said.

"How about your *associate* lower his weapon and then we can talk," said Burwardsley, with a look toward the scarred man holding his machine pistol tight to his body, the folding stock creasing the shoulder of the thermal top he wore beneath the contours of his slim-fitting body armour. At a nod from Hong Wei, the man lowered the pistol. Fenna noticed the doctor's shoulders sag for a moment as the man sighed behind the mask covering his mouth and nose. Burwardsley lowered his weapon, and the only sounds were the doctor's hushed commands and the soft, wet, sucking noises of soft tissue being squeezed between bent forceps and gloved fingers.

Hong Wei spoke as the first distant whops of the navy's Lynxhelicopter reverberated through the open doors and down the corridors of the *Xue Long*. "I was promised information," he said.

"I have the number of a man trusted by *The Magician*," Burwardsley said.

"A Greenlandic number?"

"No," he said and shook his head. "International. Area code forty-five."

"Denmark," said Fenna.

"And the rest of the number?" said Hong Wei. "What is it?"

"Listen, mate," Burwardsley said, looking over at Maratse, unconscious on the table. "I need some assurances, because…" he paused to glance at Fenna. "He is not going to make it."

"It is doubtful," said Hong Wei. "I agree."

"Assurances then…"

Fenna turned her head at the sound of soft footfalls in the corridor outside. *Just a few men*, she thought, *or several moving very quietly*. If Burwardsley or the Chinese had heard the arrival of the Danish Counter Terrorism Unit they did not show it. Fenna took a breath as she imagined them stacking-up on either side of the door. She opened her mouth and closed her eyes in anticipation of the flash-bang grenades they would use. *Maratse would probably enjoy the excitement*, she thought as her lips creased into a thin smile. *He'll be pissed to hear he missed it*. She breathed out as the first of two stun grenades was tossed into the room, grateful for a second that the wet sounds from within the policeman's stomach were lost in a brilliant flash of white and two explosions that made her ears ring and her head spin. Fenna dropped to the floor as rough-gloved fingers shoved her head toward the deck and kicked the pistol from her grip. She imagined Burwardsley dropping to the deck beside her, the heavy thud and English expletives suggested as much, and then the hood was pulled over her head and cinched tight at her throat. She was cuffed, punched, and dragged by her elbows out of the medical bay and along the corridor, her heels bumping on the steps, her shins scraping the lip of the Lynx' door as she was stuffed inside it, her nose bleeding as her head was pressed onto the metal floor. Fenna caught a stale breath of air, the hood billowing into her mouth as she breathed in, and heard the grunt of the men stuffing Burwardsley inside the helicopter alongside her.

"Fucking outrageous," he said and Fenna almost smiled, and then the doors were closed and the rotor noise increased in pitch. She closed her eyes and tried to think as the helicopter lifted off the deck of the *Xue Long* and made the short flight back to the *Knud Rasmussen*. Thoughts of the grey navy patrol ship lingered in her mind, and the prick of a needle in the left cheek of her bottom was almost too quick to notice. Fenna lifted her head only to lose control of her muscles and then it was black, and all trace of the world beyond the hood was gone.

Few twenty-four year old women have seen as many prison cells, or variations of the same, in such a short space of time as Konstabel Fenna Brongaard. The grey walls, smooth but for the chunky angular bolts and button-head rivets, staggered around her as she opened her eyes. The weight around her wrists and ankles suggested it was useless to try to move, but the cold metal chair goose-bumping her flesh surprised her, and, when she blinked the rheumy pus from her eyes, she realised she was naked, and so was the man chained to the chair opposite her. He grinned and blew at his blond hair tickling his eyes. Fenna started at the sudden noise and at his voice.

"Hello, *love*," Burwardsley said. "Sleep well?"

"Fuck off," she said.

"I'd love to, but…" Burwardsley said and rattled the chains at his wrists.

Fenna shook her head and laughed. She turned away from the scars on Burwardsley's chest and the muscles ribbing his stomach. She scanned the room and tried to sense the movement of the ship through the soles of her bare feet.

"We're not on a ship."

"No," she said and frowned.

Burwardsley made a show of nodding at the cameras in the four corners of the square room. "Black site," he said and shrugged.

"But the Danes don't…"

"Who says it's the Danes?" Burwardsley raised his eyebrow and said, "We could be anywhere."

Fenna thought for a moment as the antiseptic and blood smells of earlier were replaced with a scent of Sonoran wind. *No*, she thought. "We're not in the desert."

"The desert?" said Burwardsley. "Shit, they must have given you more than me. We haven't been out long enough for them to get us out of the country. We're just not anywhere official."

"How would you know?" Fenna said and caught herself staring at the scars on Burwardsley's chest. "Is that why?" she said.

He followed her gaze and looked down at his body, nodded once and looked up. "Wait 'til you see my back."

"What happened?"

"Afghanistan," he said and shrugged.

Fenna swallowed and said, "Is that where you met Bahadur? Was he with you?"

"The little runt saved me," he said and was quiet for a moment. "Yes. Afghanistan is where I met Bad." Burwardsley's eyes misted for a second, and Fenna was suddenly impressed with the sense of loyalty, perhaps love, that fighting men might share with one another. But it was a feeling she could not know. *Not yet at least. It might be the same world*, she mused, *but the sex, my sex, always gets in the way.*

She turned away from Burwardsley's scars and looked for the door. It took a long minute before she found it, a feint shadow of dark grey grooved into the wall, outlining a square door. She scanned the room again, noted the corrugated effect of the far wall, the rectangular shape of the room, the sturdy metal beams in each corner. "This isn't a room in a building," she said. "We're inside a shipping container."

Burwardsley studied the room. "Like I said. A black site."

"You've been in one before?"

"Not as nice as this," he said and then, "It's different when you're working."

"For the British?"

"The British, the Yanks, the French,"

Burwardsley said and shrugged. "Hell, even the Aussies sent some people our way."

Fenna thought back to the wooden house in Ittoqqortoormiit where Burwardsley and Bahadur had stretched her, the thin puppy chain around her wrists pressing rusted teeth into her flesh, and the sharp nick of the Gurkha's kukri blade as Burwardsley had pierced her skin as he stripped the sweater from her back. *And now I am naked*, she thought and shivered, her arms flinching in an attempt to cover her breasts. Her movement caught Burwardsley's eye and he stared at her body and then looked Fenna in the eye.

"You won't understand," he said. "But I've seen too much skin to be aroused at just another pretty young thing."

"What does that mean?" Fenna said, as the cuffs rattled with another bout of shivering. She noticed Burwardsley's skin was paling and looked around the room for some kind of vent. Burwardsley talked as she twisted her head back and forth, scanning the room.

"It means I had a wife, I have a daughter, I'm not the thug you think I am, I'm just damn good at what I do."

"And Dina?" Fenna said, the words chattering from her lips, the Greenlander's name heavy, laden with cold, all comfort frozen out of it. Her breath misted before her face.

"Dina..." Burwardsley said. He licked at his blue lips. Fenna watched as he trembled, pressed the soles of his feet together, tried to rub them. "I couldn't help Dina."

"Couldn't?"

"There were other things at stake," he said.

"Greater things."

"Greater than her life?"

"Not fair, Konstabel," Burwardsley said, his words slurring as he spoke. "You know that's why I'm here." He stared at a point directly above her head. "There. Right above you."

Fenna tipped her head back, caught a glimpse of the white-frosted tips of her hair, and saw the vent. "Shit," she said. "It's colder than…"

"The Arctic?" Burwardsley said and laughed. "We're trained for this, love. Remember that."

"But why are they…" Fenna's lips trembled over the words as her body began to shake. The metal chair sapped her heat and she felt her skin begin to stick to it. She lifted her bottom, tried to reposition herself on the chair. A fan began to blow. Fenna listened to the blades chopping through the frigid air as her hair tickled her face, her nipples budded upon her breasts, and her skin tightened, the tiny hairs on her arms and legs standing on end.

"Listen," said Burwardsley as Fenna lowered her head and tucked her chin to her chest. "Konstabel," he said, louder this time.

"What?"

"This is just the beginning. You have to be strong."

"But I don't know anything."

"You'd be surprised," he said. "It's not always what you think they want to know. It could be something else entirely."

Fenna didn't hear Burwardsley stumble over the *t* in *entirely*. She stopped listening to his words, could only hear her teeth chattering between frosted images of her treading water in the dark Greenland sea, the fingers of her hands stiffening around the collars of two sledge dogs. *Pyro*, she remembered, *and... and Hidalgo*. The lead dog's name had taken longer to remember, but she could see Mikael's face, the ice on his beard, his breath misting in the lamplight as he tossed the braided loop of rope at her and barked at her to, "Forget the fucking dogs and grab the line." She let go of the dogs. Fenna let go. Mikael's voice was lost in the black polar night as it folded upon her.

It was dark.

It was cold.

She supposed she was drowning, and then a warm wave washed across her shoulders.

A blanket? Fenna didn't know.

A mug was thrust between her thin frigid fingers. Fenna's nose tickled at the steam of cocoa, or something sweet at least. She heard a voice encouraging her to sip the drink, helping her with smooth firm hands, lifting the mug to her lips and telling her to do it again, to take another sip. The blanket scratched at her skin and Fenna felt the prickles of heat throb into warm waves of pain in her extremities. She felt her chest relax, her nipples soften, and her hair fall wet upon her cheeks. She looked up into the eyes of Per Jarnvig as he smiled at her.

"Welcome back, Konstabel," he said and walked around the desk between them and sat down. "You've had quite the adventure."

"Where am I?" Fenna said, as she lowered the mug from her lips and pressed her fingers around it. "What did you do? Why?"

"Lots of questions," Jarnvig said. "But I have one for you."

Fenna held the mug with one hand and tugged at the blanket. It slipped from her shoulder and revealed her left breast. Jarnvig stared as she put down the mug and gripped the blanket in both hands, pulled it around her shoulders and looked up at him. "What do you want to know?"

"Tell me about the girl," he said.

"What girl?"

Jarnvig opened a drawer and removed a remote control. He turned around and pointed it at a modest flat screen television mounted on the wall behind him. The screen brightened and Jarnvig muted the noise with a quick stab of a button on the remote. Fenna watched as the anchor of MSNBC cycled through a news story under the banner of *President Assassinated,* and a rapid ticker of information at the bottom of the screen moving too fast for Fenna to process. Jarnvig stood up. He walked the few steps to the screen and stood to one side of it. Fenna saw the familiar bulge of the 9mm pistol holstered in the shoulder rig beneath his jacket, she flicked her eyes back to the screen when Jarnvig clicked his fingers and pointed at a closed-circuit television screen capture of a blonde-haired young woman moving through a crowd at a bus station. Fenna caught her breath for a moment and looked from Jarnvig to Alice and back again.

"That one, Konstabel," said Jarnvig. "Who is she?"

Chapter 29

The fibres of the blanket scratched at Fenna's skin as Jarnvig turned off the television and returned to his chair. He tumbled the remote into the drawer, placed his elbows on the desk and laced his fingers together. Fenna waited as he took a long breath and then opened his mouth to speak.

"Just a minute," she said.

"What?"

"Lorentzen," Fenna said and shrugged. "Don't you want to know about him?"

"He's dead. Isn't he?"

"Yes," she said and frowned. "You've talked to Hong Wei?"

"And avoided an international incident. Yes, I've talked to him."

"And that's it? What about UNCLOS? The hearing?"

Jarnvig gestured at the screen behind him. "The Americans are preoccupied at the moment and the UNCLOS hearing has been postponed."

"But the Pole?"

"Will be there tomorrow. It can wait."

Fenna leaned back in her chair. It creaked beneath her. She tugged again at the blanket and wondered where they could have found one so small. "You tortured me," she said.

"I cooled you down. God knows you needed it. Since you were given this mission, I have had to clean up one incident after another." Jarnvig lifted his left hand and began counting the fingers, pressing each one with the tip of his right index finger. He started with the smallest. "The fire at the camp," he said and moved onto the next finger. "Assisting in the escape of a person of interest…"

"Burwardsley," Fenna said.

"… and the attack on two Greenlandic policemen – something you have a history of."

"When necessary," Fenna said.

"Don't be cute," Jarnvig said. He continued, "A shootout and a car chase, the hijacking of a helicopter…" He switched hands. "Attacking a foreign ship, resulting in the deaths of six Chinese nationals…"

"To save a Greenlandic policeman…"

"Now in an artificial coma at Queen Ingrid's Hospital in Nuuk."

So he's alive, Fenna thought and felt a brief flood of warmth through her body.

Jarnvig checked Fenna's relief with a warning, "The doctors say it is touch and go. There is some concern that he had been tortured."

"*Concern*? He *was* tortured. I was there. I saw it. He was electrocuted by Hong Wei, the same guy now crying International Incident because Burwardsley and I busted onto his ship."

"And killed six of his men."

Fenna threw up her hands. "God, you are impossible," she said and then bent down to pick up the blanket.

Jarnvig smiled and then said, quietly, "I'm not, God, Konstabel, but with the right cooperation, I can work miracles. You do remember Toronto?"

"Yes," Fenna said and sighed. "I don't believe you will ever let me forget."

"No. Probably not, but I also got you out of the desert."

Out of one shit storm and into the next, she thought. "Yes, you got me out of the desert, but I thought I was going after the Pole, at least to secure it."

"And you are, but..." he paused to nod once more at the television. "Things change. This is a dynamic world we live in, Konstabel. And," he added, "it comes with a price. Are you listening?"

"Yes. I'm listening."

Jarnvig opened the drawer to his left and pulled out a folder. Fenna saw the screen-capture of Alice clipped to the first of a thin sheath of papers. "The Americans want to know who she is," Jarnvig said and stared at Fenna. "I told them you could tell them."

"Then you lied," she said. "I was warned away from her. Nicklas warned me away from her." Fenna frowned. "They were your orders," she said. "You know who she is."

"Perhaps," Jarnvig said and turned the folder around to face Fenna. He lifted the photo of Alice and tapped the first line of a heavily redacted email, the broad black lines obscured almost everything but the date; it was the same day Fenna had arrived at the Desert Training Center. Jarnvig leaned back in his chair and folded his hands in his lap. "There is talk of a deep state in America. A group of powerful, strategically placed individuals..."

"Men," Fenna said and scoffed.

"And not a few women," Jarnvig said and continued. "There have been growing concerns that started in first term of the President's administration, and again during the recent campaign for re-election. These concerns accelerated last November, and a plan was put into action, one that played on the President's weakness for attractive young women."

Fenna shivered at the thought of her own actions when approaching Lorentzen, to gain his trust, in order to elicit information from him. *For what?* she thought. *Nothing. That particular mess has been cleaned up. I helped do it, and now...* Jarnvig's next words slapped her out of her thoughts as sharply as if he had back-handed her across the table.

"You might be surprised to know this, Konstabel, but you were under consideration, as a potential agent provocateur, a honey trap, a gartered assassin."

"What?" she said and clutched at the blanket.

"But," Jarnvig said and waved a hand in the air. "They soon discovered you were too impulsive, too tenacious, too tough, believe it or not."

"They were watching me?"

"Yes," he said and returned his hands to his lap.

"But you sent me there."

"I did."

"For training."

"Yes."

"And..." Fenna paused and collected her thoughts. She looked up at Jarnvig. "Did Nicklas know?"

"Yes," he said. "It was Nicklas who suggested you were not suitable. And so they brought in the girl."

"Alice."

Jarnvig nodded. "Yes. Alice."

"For fuck's sake, Jarnvig, she's just nineteen."

"I didn't recruit her, Konstabel."

"No? You just sent me instead."

"Not to recruit her. You're confusing things. I was approached by the Americans. They were looking for a young female who could be trained for a difficult and sensitive mission." He laughed. "Sensitive. I think we both know that subtlety is not your speciality. Anyway," he said, "as it turns out, they went with a naïve young girl, who could be moulded to their needs."

"So you knew who they were? This *deep state*."

"Far from it," Jarnvig said and shifted in his seat. "However, it is not unusual for intelligence agencies to reach out to one another, on occasion, when a job requires a specific profile or set of skills."

Fenna listened with half an ear as Jarnvig mentioned something about past understandings and periods of co-operation with different agencies under different administrations. She looked at the picture of Alice, recognised the fear in the young woman's eyes. *A girl, really*, she thought. *Alone in the world. Pursued by men*. Fenna nodded at the thought, and Jarnvig interpreted it as a sign to continue. She let his words wash over her and considered where Alice might be, and then recalled one of their conversations in the canteen. Alice had said she had a special place she had visited once. One that no-one knew about – not even her minders, the men shadowing her every move. *Men like the Gunney*, Fenna remembered and trembled again at the memory of his blood spilling across her fingers. *Did I clean up in Arizona, too?* she wondered. She almost laughed. *I'm a cleaner. That is my role in this game, to clean things up. Well*, she thought and nodded again, *I'm not done cleaning*. She looked up into the barrel of Jarnvig's 9mm and realised that neither was he.

"What are you doing?" she said.

"This is when it gets interesting," he said and tightened his grip on the trigger. "Do you remember the woman you met in the Major's office?"

"Yes?" Fenna said and swallowed as he nodded at the folder.

"Next page, the next sheet of paper."

Fenna turned the page and found a paper clipping from a local newspaper in Arizona. It was a short piece about the disappearance of an exotic dancer.

"Page three," he said.

The next page was another redacted email with details and names rendered unreadable, but for the number of Special Forces soldiers, the Gunney's men, killed in a helicopter crash overseas. Fenna didn't remember hearing about the crash, but... She tested the thickness of the stack of pages with a broken and blunt fingernail. There was one left.

"Go on," said Jarnvig.

"I don't need to," she said, her voice faltering. Fenna cleared her throat and stared at Jarnvig. "It's Nicklas, isn't it?"

"Page four," Jarnvig said.

Fenna placed her hands flat on the table, one on each side of the folder. "Where's Burwardsley?"

"Turn the page, Konstabel."

"Is he still being *cooled down*?"

Jarnvig said nothing. He shifted his grip on the pistol.

Fenna continued, "Did he tell you he had a mobile number? It belongs to a man trusted by *The Magician*. Do you remember him?"

"I remember telling you that he was no concern of yours," Jarnvig said. "Read the next page, Konstabel."

"I have an idea, that if I called that number..."

"If you had a mobile…"

"If I called it," Fenna said and straightened her back. She let the blanket fall from her shoulders. "I think I know who might answer it."

"Just," Jarnvig said and shook his head. He glanced away from her breasts and then back again, flicking his eyes from her lightly-weathered skin, the slim bulge of muscle in her arms, the fine hairs standing on end on her forearms, to her eyes, to her hair… "You would have been perfect for the job," he said.

"Alice's job?" Fenna said and lifted her chin. "Do you think I am pretty, Jarnvig? Do you?"

"Yes," he said, his words whispering out of his mouth. His cheeks flushing beneath the finely manicured stubble.

"You like my hair, don't you?"

"Yes."

"My face," she said and smoothed her hand along her jaw. Jarnvig nodded. She reached out and took his free hand. Fenna leaned toward him, her small breasts hanging above the desk like tiny pyramids, firm, pointed. She lifted his hand, turned it palm upwards, and cupped her breast in the curve of his hand. "You want me?"

"Yes," Jarnvig breathed. "I have wanted you since…"

"Since we met first met at the airport? Before Toronto," she said and pressed his hand hard against her breast.

"Yes," he said.

Fenna nodded and climbed onto the desk. She repositioned his hand on her right thigh, arching her back to brush the hair from her forehead. She smiled at him, glanced at the pistol and pressed it with a delicate touch to the surface of the desk. Jarnvig put his hand flat on the table, his fingers still wrapped around the pistol grip. When he looked up at Fenna she lifted her left knee and pressed it down upon Jarnvig's gun hand. He frowned for a second and then tugged at the pistol as Fenna slammed the heel of her left hand into his forehead and curled her right fist into his throat. Jarnvig choked, gasping for air as he released his grip on the pistol and slumped into the chair. Fenna moved into a crouch and used the lip of the desk to press down on Jarnvig as the chair tipped beneath him and they crashed to the floor. Fenna gripped Jarnvig's forehead and punched him twice more in the throat before spinning around to grab the pistol. The door had barely opened before Fenna had fired the first two shots through the wooden door and into the chest of the PET man guarding the entrance. She leapt over the desk and put another bullet through the opening and into the man's head.

Fenna burst through the door and into the carpeted corridor of what looked and smelled like the administration floor of an office complex. The shared reception at the end of the corridor was framed in an open plan room surrounded by rented office spaces, each with its own window and door. All the doors were closed, Fenna noted, and, apart from the dead man at her feet, the place was empty. Fenna ran down the corridor and stared out of the windows and into the sunlight lingering over Nuuk, enticing the capital of Greenland into a new day. She paused at the familiar sight of Nuuk's main street, the blue façade of the supermarket and the ubiquitous containers littering the building site beneath her.

I'm in the bank, she realised as she recalled the cityscape she had seen from the hotel. She moved to the window and looked down at the containers, pressing her fists against the glass as she scanned them, looking for one in particular – the refrigerated kind, the one with the police car parked by the side of it.

"Think, Fenna," she said.

She ran back to Jarnvig's office, her feet padding along the carpet, the fibres soft on her hard soles. She stopped by the side of the man and tugged the boots from his feet, discarding them after measuring them against her own. She unbuckled his belt and tugged his jeans off.

"Thank God for short men," she said and pulled on the man's jeans. She cinched the belt tight and worked a new hole into the leather with the buckle. The man's shirt was bloody. Fenna ignored it and went back inside the office. She walked around the table and stared down at Jarnvig's blue cheeks and his collapsed windpipe. She nodded once and then bent down to remove his suit jacket. Fenna buttoned both buttons and slipped the 9mm pistol into the waistband of the jeans; the weight of it tugged the belt towards her slim bottom and the grip pressed into her back. "Time to move," she said and grabbed the pages from the folder, stuffing them into the inside pocket of the jacket as she ran out of the office. The clock on the wall encouraged Fenna with a time uncivilised for most people. *And yet*, she remembered, *it's spring in Greenland. It's light. Everyone will be up.* When she stepped out onto the street after a short ride in the elevator, she was disappointed to know she was right.

Fenna skirted around the couples, kids and drunks as they stared at her bare feet, and climbed over the metal fence sealing the entry to the building site. She pulled the pistol from her waistband and crouched behind a cement mixer; the cold container was two car-lengths away.

I hope you're in there, Burwardsley, Fenna thought. *Because I seem to be all out of friends.* She bit her lip at the thought of Nicklas.

Fenna ducked at the sight of a policeman, a tall Dane, as he opened the door to the Toyota and lit a cigarette. Fenna scanned the car, allowing herself a brief smile when she realised he was alone. The man walked as he smoked, stopping to pick up a broken shovel handle. He banged the side of the container and laughed, and Fenna laughed with him.

You're alive, you British bastard, she thought and smiled. *He wouldn't do that if you weren't.* Fenna waited until the policeman tossed the shovel handle to one side and turned his back on her. She raced across the fractured earth and rubble, twisting the pistol in her grip as she closed on the policeman. If he hadn't turned, Fenna might have hit him in the back of the head. As it was, he caught the full brunt of her assault in the face, the blood spattering from his nose across her cheeks as he slumped to the ground. Fenna took the policeman's keys from his belt and moved on, running around the container to the door. She rushed inside and coughed at the chill air as she peered through the mist of her breath to see Burwardsley cuffed to the same metal chair in the middle of the refrigerated space. Fenna unlocked the cuffs with the keys as he cracked the ice beading his eyes and looked at her.

"Thought you left me," he said, his voice rasping over his blue lips.

"Thought about it," Fenna said and pulled the Marine Lieutenant to his feet. "Can you walk?"

"Yeah, I can walk," he said. "Daft buggers thawed me out every forty minutes. But..." Burwardsley paused to hold up his fingers. "I might lose these."

Fenna inspected the tips of Burwardsley's fingers and recognised the frostbitten flesh. "You might," she said and pulled him toward the door. "Let's get you some clothes."

She dragged Burwardsley to the car and jogged back to the policeman. He was, she realised, only slightly shorter than Burwardsley. *It's me that will need a change of clothes*, she thought as she stripped the policeman and bundled his jacket, shirt and trousers beneath her arm. She carried the boots in her hand, dumping the clothes at Burwardsley's feet. She waited until he was dressed, helping him with buttons, buckles and zips as his own fingers failed him.

"We need a new plan," he said, as Fenna zipped the fly of his trousers and buckled the belt. She knelt down to tie his laces.

"Then it's lucky I have one," she said and stood up.

"Care to tell me?"

"After we have been to the hospital." Fenna opened the passenger door and pushed Burwardsley onto the seat.

"Hospital?"

"I want to see Maratse," she said, as she climbed in behind the wheel. And I need some different clothes."

CHRISTOFFER PETERSEN

"Whose are those?" Burwardsley said and frowned.

"The jacket belonged to my boss."

"Belonged?"

"Yep. He's dead," Fenna said and turned the key in the ignition. "Any more questions?"

"I guess not," Burwardsley said. He switched on the heating as Fenna bumped the Toyota through the gate and onto the street. "You might want to wipe that blood off your face before you go inside," he said.

"It's not mine."

"I didn't say it was."

Fenna reached up to angle the rear-view mirror toward her head, wiping away the blood with the back of her hand as she studied her face. She looked beyond the blood, beyond the dirt of the mining camp and the grease and grime of ships and helicopters. Fenna looked into her own eyes and saw the eyes of a killer. She stopped the car.

"What are you doing?" Burwardsley said and opened his eyes as Fenna opened the driver's door.

"Throwing up," she said and retched. The small puddle of bile on the road reminded her once again that she needed something to eat. She slammed the door shut and drove in the direction of the hospital.

"Are you going to do that a lot?"

"That depends," she said, as she parked behind the hospital.

"On what?"

"How many people I kill before this is over."

"Hah," Burwardsley said and laughed.

"You think it's funny I throw up every time I kill someone?"

272

"No," Burwardsley said, as Fenna turned off the engine. "I think it is funny you think one day this might be over."

One day it might be, she thought as she stared at Burwardsley. *One way or another.* Fenna took a breath, opened the door, and stepped out of the car. She looked up at the red and yellow beams of wood decorating the floors of the building, just a few stories high.

"Maratse," she whispered and shut the door. The mission had become the man, Fenna realised, but with each step she took toward the hospital entrance, she realised that the mission had always been about a man, and, perhaps, a girl.

The New Frontier

NUUK, GREENLAND

Chapter 30

Fenna ducked her head as she walked past the reception desk, conscious of her ill-fitting and unusual choice of clothes. With a quick glance at the building plan screwed into the corridor wall, Fenna located the stairwell and went down to the basement and the laundry room. She picked her way through the folded piles of trousers and smocks until she found the best fit for her small, wiry frame. *It's a long time since I worried about underwear*, she mused, smiling as she tied the draw cord at the waist of the trousers. Fenna found socks and clogs on a rack beneath the clean clothes. She pulled them on and dumped her clothes in the trash, folding a towel around the 9mm she returned to the stairs and made her way to the first floor.

She followed the signs for Intensive Care, pausing at the door to the small ward before walking inside. The Greenlandic nurse sitting at a small desk by the door frowned as she walked in.

"Can I help you?"

"Yes," said Fenna. "I'm just getting my bearings. I'm the new temp. Came in yesterday."

"Yesterday?" the nurse said and shook her head. "We're not expecting anyone."

Fenna pulled out the gun and let the towel drop to the floor. The nurse, to Fenna's surprise, took a gulp of air and thrust her hands above her head.

"Okay," said Fenna. She fought the smile creasing her lips and said, "You have a policeman here. Where is he?" The nurse nodded and dipped her head toward the end of the ward. Fenna laughed and lowered the gun. "You need to breathe." The nurse nodded again, her cheeks blossoming as her eyes bulged. "Really. Breathe. Now," Fenna said and let the gun fall to her side. The nurse exhaled with a rush of air and collapsed into the chair, lowering her arms like a clockwork drummer unwinding.

"Sorry," she gasped as she recovered.

"You did fine," Fenna said and nodded toward the last bed. She spied the familiar black of Maratse's jacket hanging on the back of a chair beside his bed. "How is he?"

"He's not well," the nurse said. "He's in a coma. The doctors…"

"Will he recover?"

"*Aap*. But he might have problems."

"What kind?"

"Motor control," the nurse said. She studied Fenna's wrinkled brow and added, "He will have difficulty walking."

Fenna took a step toward Maratse. "Can I see him?"

"*Aap*. Come." The nurse stood up and Fenna realised she was tiny. She followed her to Maratse's bed and stopped at his feet. Fenna reached out and smoothed her hand over the policeman's foot, the blanket rough beneath her fingers.

"I'm sorry," she said, sensing a tear well up and run down her cheek. The nurse reached out and took her hand.

"He's going to be all right," she said and squeezed Fenna's fingers. "I will look after him."

"Thank you," Fenna said.

"What about you?" she said. "Are you all right?"

"I'm fine. Maybe a little hungry."

"I have food," the nurse said. "Come." She led

Fenna away from Maratse and into a small kitchen area. She gestured for Fenna to sit at the round table, opposite the door. Fenna could see Maratse, could hear the rise and fall of his chest and the lungs of the machine helping him breathe. She placed the gun on the table and looked up as the nurse placed a plastic food container between them, the smell of fish wrinkled Fenna's nose as the nurse removed the lid. "*Ammassat*," she said and snapped a small dried fish from a clump and handed it to Fenna.

"Capelin," Fenna said, as she recognised the fish. "Thank you." The nurse studied Fenna's face as she ate. Fenna nodded and took another fish as the nurse smiled and poured her a glass of water. "They're good."

The nurse raised her thick black eyebrows and said, "My father dried them on a rock, in the sea, away from the dogs. Then my sister brought them on the plane last month. Ten kilos." She nodded at the box. "These are the last."

"They're good."

"*Aap*." The nurse pulled her mobile from her pocket and swiped her hand across the screen. She turned the mobile toward Fenna. "The dayshift starts soon," she said.

"Okay," Fenna said and stood up. She tucked the pistol into the waistband of the trousers, pulling it out again as the weight of it strained the draw cord. She held it in her hand and smiled. "Thank you for the fish."

"You're welcome."

"And thank you for looking after my friend." The nurse raised her eyebrows again – a Greenlandic *yes*. "When he wakes up, will you tell him Fenna was here?"

"*Aap.*"

"And tell him that I'm sorry."

"I will tell him."

"*Qujanaq,*" Fenna said, her tongue tripping over the unfamiliar assembly of Inuit syllables. The nurse's eyes widened and she reached out to pat Fenna's hand. Fenna turned to leave. She paused for one last look at Maratse, his puffy eyes and swollen cheeks, the small tube inside his nose taped in place, a larger one secured with a mask to his mouth. The machine pressed air in and out of his lungs with a soft clap and hiss. Fenna lost herself for a moment in the serenity of Maratse's recovery, then forced herself to walk away, to turn her back on the one man she knew she could trust.

But he can't help me now, she thought as she picked up the towel by the desk and hid the gun on her way out of the ward. She stopped at the sound of a cart being pushed by an orderly making his way to the ward with breakfast.

"Do you need anything?" he asked, as he stopped in front of the door to Intensive Care.

Fenna glanced at the breakfast rolls and cartons of juice. She tucked the towel beneath her arm and took two rolls and a couple of drinks. "It's been a long night," she said and thanked him.

"It's going to be a beautiful day," he said, as she walked away.

For you, maybe, Fenna thought as she walked toward the main entrance. *For me... well, I'm not so sure.* Fenna waved at Burwardsley as he watched her approach the police car. He opened the driver door and Fenna climbed in behind the wheel.

"You're a nurse now?" he said as she gave him the rolls and juice.

"I'm full of surprises," Fenna said and turned the key in the ignition. The Toyota's engine rumbled into life and Fenna placed her hand on the gearstick. She turned to Burwardsley and sighed. "So," she said. "We need a plan."

"We do."

"And we should move."

"Where are we going to go? There's maybe twenty kilometres of road in Nuuk, and that includes the runway."

"Then we should park somewhere."

"We are parked."

"Somewhere discreet."

"Konstabel," Burwardsley said and sighed. "You don't *do* discreet," he said and laughed.

"No," Fenna said and grinned. "I really don't."

"You really don't, love."

Fenna switched off the engine and leaned back in the driver's seat. "But we still need a plan."

Burwardsley licked crumbs of bread from his lips and wiped the rest off the front of the police jacket he was wearing. Fenna watched as he fumbled with the straw of the orange juice carton. He swore and passed it her.

"I can't bloody open it."

"But can you still shoot?" she asked, as she pressed the sharp tip of the straw through the plastic sleeve and jabbed it through the circle of foil in the top of the carton. She handed it to Burwardsley.

"Too bloody right I can," he said.

Fenna studied the white tips of his fingers and remembered the cold bite of the north that threatened her own fingers when patrolling with Sirius. She thought of Mikael, how he chided her to remember her gloves, before the man sucking orange juice through a straw beside her killed him.

"Why did Mikael have to die?"

Burwardsley tossed the empty carton onto the floor. He took a breath and looked at Fenna. "Don't," he said. "The future is going to be difficult enough without worrying about the past, love. You're going to have to move on."

"Like you have," she said and thought of Dina.

"Hey, killing your pal was one thing, but what Humble did to that girl. Well, it's just not right. It didn't sit well with me. Not with Bad either."

"You can't worry about the past," Fenna said and snorted. She wiped a thin stream of snot from her nose with the back of her hand.

"You can't bring it back either."

Fenna looked up as a raven landed on the roof of the police car and clawed its way down the windshield. She watched as it stalked back and forth in front of them, the scratch of its claws on the bonnet the only sound as Burwardsley watched with her. She remembered the ravens teasing the sledge dogs in the north. They knew the length of the dogs' chains. When the dogs were fed, one raven would tease the dog, hopping just out of reach as it thundered toward it, while another would steal in beneath the taught chain and carry the fish head to safety. The ravens heckled the dogs with throaty caws between tearing at the dried fish with black beaks. *A simple distraction,* she mused. *To get what we want, what we need, to change our future.*

"I know what we need to do," she said and

pointed at the raven.

"I'm listening."

"We need an ally."

"We do."

"My government wants the Pole, and I can give it to them. All I need is proof that the data from the machine used in the LOMROG expedition is false."

"So you need the machine?"

"It's not that simple," Fenna said. She paused for a moment as the raven squirted a stream of white shit onto the bonnet and took off. "Data collected by the Chinese contradicts Lorentzen's data. If we can get that from Hong Wei…"

"Never gonna happen, love," Burwardsley said and shook his head. "Forget about it."

"He'll give it to me."

"Because?"

"I have something he wants. Something bigger than the Pole, at least for the moment."

"And that is?" Burwardsley said and turned in his seat.

Fenna pressed the palms of her hands against her eyes and rubbed. "Shit," she said. "It's all so fucked up."

"Fenna?"

Fenna took a long breath and stretched her hands, curling her fingers around the steering wheel, squeezing until her knuckles turned white. She exhaled and said, "I know who killed the President of the United States."

"What?"

"I know who did it," she said and turned to Burwardsley.

"How the fuck can you know that?"

281

"I was in the desert. Jarnvig sent me to some secret training facility in Arizona."

"You were at Fort Huachuca?"

"Like I said…" Fenna laughed. "Secret." She went quiet as an image of Nicklas threatened her resolve. She bit back on her tears.

"You're going to have to learn to trust me," Burwardsley said.

"I know." Fenna let go of the steering wheel and folded her hands in her lap. She picked at the cotton trousers and said, "There was a girl. Nineteen years old. She had no reason to be there. It was weird. I was getting messed around, hounded by Special Forces thugs…"

"I know the type."

"Yeah," Fenna said and looked at him. "I'm sure you do. But while these guys had no problem beating the fuck out me, she was untouchable. Under twenty-four hour guard, apart from about fifteen minutes in the canteen every night."

"Where you were?"

"Once I knew she was there, yes. We met a couple of times before we were discovered." Fenna paused as thoughts of the Gunney and his crew – all of them dead, all traces of their existence covered, deleted, just like Nicklas. *And Jarnvig*, she thought. *Don't forget him.*

"And you know she did it? Assassinated the President?"

"She was being groomed. The whole thing orchestrated by some *deep state*." Fenna looked at Burwardsley, expecting to see a smile on his face, surprised when she didn't. "You believe me?"

"Why shouldn't I?" he said and shrugged. "Look

at us, love. We're sitting in a stolen police car, wearing borrowed clothes, outside a hospital where a man was nearly tortured to death, after *we* were tortured… I mean, come on. Tell me the rest."

"Okay," Fenna said and lifted her hand. She pushed her fingers through her hair and said, "Jarnvig said the Americans were looking for a female agent, that I was a candidate, but I was too tough."

"Hah," Burwardsley sad and laughed. "I could have told them that."

"Well, they found Alice instead."

"That's her real name?"

"As far as I know."

"And how do you know she did it?"

"Because they have her picture plastered over the news."

"Then she doesn't have long to live."

"Nope," said Fenna. "They are cleaning up."

Burwardsley shifted in his seat as a police car drove past the car park. He watched as it drove out of sight. "Start the car," he said.

Fenna pulled her seatbelt on and started the engine. She peered around Burwardsley as the police car nosed around the corner and stopped, the driver and his partner staring at them through the driver's window.

"Just supposing Hong Wei gives you the data," Burwardsley said, as he stared at the policemen. "Are you going to give him the girl's name?"

"Yes," Fenna said and shifted the Toyota into first gear. She kept her foot on the clutch.

"It won't be enough."

"I know," she said and released the handbrake. "That's why I'm going to tell him where to find her."

"You know where she is?"

"Yes," Fenna said. The word caught on her lips as the driver of the police car turned on the blue emergency lights.

"And you're going to give her up?" Burwardsley said. He ignored the police car as it pulled into the car park and turned to look at Fenna. "That's not like you."

"No," she said. "It's not. But…" Fenna gripped the steering wheel with her left hand and the gearstick with her right. "You and me…"

"What about us?" Burwardsley said and frowned.

"We're going to be the ones to go and get her."

"Christ. You've got it all figured out."

"Not all of it. But we needed a plan. Now we have one." Fenna held her breath as the police car rolled towards them. She could almost hear the gravel tickling beneath the wheels. "The Pole," she said, "is all about leverage. The Chinese need leverage to force their agenda in the Arctic, and I can give it to them."

"That's great, Konstabel. Really, it is. But," he said with a nod toward the police car, "*they* don't know the plan."

"No," she said and lifted the clutch, "they really don't." Burwardsley's head thumped into the headrest as Fenna floored the accelerator and rammed police car. She yelled as the driver's door buckled under the impact. Fenna kept her foot on the accelerator, pushing the police car in a slow circle as Burwardsley braced against the dashboard and the policemen in the harried Toyota fumbled for the pistols in their belts.

"They're going for their guns," Burwardsley said, cringing at the screech of metal and the scream of the fan belt, as Fenna gripped the steering wheel and pressed her foot to the floor.

Chapter 31

Burwardsley pressed the blunt white tips of his fingers against the plastic dash as Fenna shoved the police car into a large American pickup – an import almost twice the size of the Toyota. As Burwardsley jolted forward in his seat, she shifted into reverse, backed up two metres, and then accelerated into the police car a second time. The policemen raised their hands and Fenna gritted her teeth and suppressed a smile as she reversed once more. The bumper of the Toyota peeled off with one end jammed inside the wing panel of the police car, the other wobbling on the gravel car park as Fenna continued backing away until she stopped, threw the Toyota into first and accelerated past the police car and onto the road.

"You're enjoying this?" Burwardsley said, as he tugged the seatbelt around his chest and fumbled with the buckle.

"Yes," said Fenna as she pulled the latch plate from Burwardsley's fingers and secured it. "Can't a girl have a little fun?" Burwardsley stared at her as Fenna weaved her way between two cars, drifted onto the wrong side of the road and accelerated toward a bus. "What?"

"Discretion, love, is the better part of valour."

"Really?" Fenna said, as she swung the Toyota out of the path of the bus and roared down the main street, barely glancing at the Hotel Hans Egede.

"Henry IV," he said. "The result of a private education. But no amount of Shakespeare rammed down my throat was ever going to clean my gullet of a real Manc accent."

"What?"

"Like right now," Burwardsley said and grinned at Fenna. "I'm buzzin' for this."

"So you're getting a kick out of it?" she said and slowed for the T-junction at the end of the road.

"It means I'm happy. Extremely happy."

"Well, all right then," Fenna said and braked into the corner. "We're going back to the airport. Are you happy about that?"

"Extremely," Burwardsley said and leaned around the seat to look through the rear windscreen.

"How many?"

"Two police Toyotas and a…" Burwardsley paused. "A black SUV," he said and faced forward. "Your pals from the navy are back again."

"Then we can't disappoint them, can we?" Fenna smiled and accelerated up the street. At the base of a low rise she dropped into third and powered up the incline as the road dissected the rock, throwing up a sheer wall on both sides. "If we make enough noise," she said, "if we attract enough attention, then Hong Wei will hear of it."

"And you think he will just waltz in and pick us up? He's out of his jurisdiction. I think your plan is flawed."

"We'll see," Fenna said and shifted into fourth at the crest of the hill. She powered down the road, braking at a small roundabout before roaring up the hill leading toward the airport. The SUV, she noticed, had pulled away from the police and was gaining on them.

Burwardsley pressed his blunt fingers into a series of buttons on the dash between them, grinning as the siren wailed and the flash of the emergency lights reflected in the windows of the apartments on each side of the road.

"Should've done that earlier," he said and leaned back. "Where's the gun?"

"At my feet," Fenna said and shook her head. "Leave it. We don't want to get shot."

"Fair enough." Burwardsley dipped his head and pointed at a crossing ahead. "Watch the kid on her bike."

"Fuck." Fenna hit the brakes, slewing the Toyota to the left and then correcting it to stop just before the roundabout, as a Greenlandic girl crossed the road. Fenna gripped the wheel and took a series of deep breaths, her heart pounding as the girl, her black hair twisting beneath her helmet in the wind, stopped on the pavement and waved.

"Close one," Burwardsley said.

"Yes," Fenna said. She nodded at the girl and lifted her foot off the brake just as the SUV slammed into the rear of the car and punted the Toyota into the middle of the roundabout. Fenna swore as she fought to wrestle the car back onto the road. Burwardsley turned in his seat and called out as the SUV careered toward them. Fenna threw the car into first and accelerated.

"Go left," Burwardsley shouted.

"No," she said and continued straight. "It's a residential area. I'm taking us out to the airport."

"Then this ride will be over real soon."

"It wasn't meant to last forever. Just long enough to…

"Make some noise. Sure, I get it. But that was before you killed a PET officer," Burwardsley said and shrugged as Fenna swung the car to the left and onto the road to the airport. The Toyota's tyres crunched through the glass leftovers of the roadblock that had been set up in the same position the day before.

I know what I'm doing, Fenna thought and accelerated. When the rear window disintegrated under the first burst of 9mm bullets, she questioned herself, and then willed the car to go faster.

"We're reaching the end game, love. We might need the gun."

"No," Fenna said and shook her head. "We need to stay alive. For Alice."

"For Alice? Come on. That's a long shot. I'm doing this for Dina."

"She's dead, and we can't save the dead," Fenna said and spat blood from her mouth.

"Are you hit?" Burwardsley said. He pressed his hand around the back of her head. Pushed his fingers through her hair, checking for blood.

"Get your hands off me," Fenna said. "I bit my tongue. That's all." She jerked her head to one side as another burst of lead raked the driver's side of the Toyota.

"Calm down."

"It's okay," she said, staring straight ahead. She could see the curve in the road at the end of the runway. "There's a gravel road straight ahead. I don't know how far it goes. That's where this ends."

"Sure. Okay."

"I just need to know you are with me on this," Fenna said and slowed to drop down a gear.

"All the way."

"Really? Because a moment ago you said…"

"I take it back. You're right. Dina's gone. I can't redeem myself, can't make amends. If I'm going to hell," he said and grinned at Fenna, "I'd rather go with a pretty girl…"

"Fuck off, Burwardsley."

"Sure, all right," he said and laughed. "Now don't hit me. I'm going for the gun."

Fenna bounced the Toyota over the lip of the road and onto a track. Stones raked the chassis as Burwardsley reached down between Fenna's legs and pulled the gun out from behind her feet. He sat up and smoothed his hands over the weapon as Fenna slipped the Toyota into four-wheel drive and accelerated off the track and onto a wide path leading down to the fjord. She looked up and smiled at the sight of the mountain as the sun reflected on the last stubborn patch of winter snow and Sermitsiaq cast her shadow on the slopes below the summit. She switched off the siren.

"It's funny," she said and nodded toward the mountain. "It's one of the most boring peaks, but it's growing on me."

"What? That mountain?"

"Yes," Fenna said, as she wrestled the Toyota up and over a flat granite slab. She grimaced at the wrenching sound coming from the axles as she dropped the Toyota over the lip of the boulder and bumped onto the path. "During all this time, through all this drama, it's just been sitting there."

"It's a mountain. That's what they do."

"I know," Fenna said and sighed. "I *do* know." She looked up at the sound of a helicopter approaching and slowed the Toyota to a stop.

"Here?" Burwardsley said.

Fenna nodded. "Here," she said and looked out of the window. "In the shadow of the mountain."

Burwardsley watched as the police leapt out of their vehicles and set up a perimeter. The Counter Terrorism unit exited the SUV, checking their MP5s with a casual professionalism that brought a grim smile to Burwardsley's face.

"I'm sorry about your partner," he said without turning around. "I'm sure he was a good bloke."

"He was," Fenna said and turned in her seat. She released their belts. "Everyone I know is dead or about to die," she said.

"Speak for yourself, love," Burwardsley said, facing her. He rested his head against the headrest and studied Fenna's face. "You think we are going to die?"

"You said we were going to hell. If we step out of the car…" Fenna's words shrank beneath the *whop whop* of the helicopter as the Navy Lynx settled on a patch of rough grass fifty metres in front of the Toyota.

"I said we were going to hell. I didn't say we were going to die."

"There's a difference?"

"With all that you have been through?" Burwardsley laughed. "I thought you'd know."

Fenna raised her eyebrows and shrugged as the roar of the helicopter receded and she imagined the pilot powering down. A quiet wind rolled all sound into a bundle and spun it out of the valley toward the town of Nuuk. Fenna could hear the scratch of the stubble on Burwardsley's cheek against the fabric of the chair as he breathed, his chest swelling and falling in a steady rhythm. Fenna smiled and reached out to take his hand.

"You didn't kill Mikael," she said.

"Thanks, love. But you know I did. I gave the order."

"You didn't pull the trigger."

"I may as well have. But," he said and smiled, "thanks."

Fenna flicked her eyes away from Burwardsley as five men exited the helicopter. Her body stiffened and Burwardsley looked in the direction she was staring.

"Bloody hell," he said and shifted his grip on the pistol.

"No, Mike," Fenna said and squeezed his hand.

"But you know who that is? Right?"

"Yes," Fenna said and took a breath. "It's Vestergaard."

The five men, four of them carrying MP5s trained on the Toyota, walked across the grass, sidestepping boulders, and stopping within ten metres of Fenna and Burwardsley. The unarmed man at the head of the group took a step forwards, and the four men shifted position, as if they were one, covering him from all angles, fingers on the triggers, the submachine guns an extension of their bodies. Vestergaard made a show of removing his glasses, wiping them with a handkerchief and peering into the car.

"Lieutenant Burwardsley?" he said, "Mike, is that you?"

"Yeah," he said. "It's me."

"And who have you got beside you?" he said and took a step to the right. His men moved with him. "Konstabel Brongaard? What a surprise." Vestergaard looked at his men and smiled. "I know them," he said, "I know them very well indeed." The men kept their eyes on the Toyota, their weapons on Fenna and

Burwardsley.

"Put the gun away," Fenna whispered.

"I could take him," Burwardsley said, "right now. Redemption."

"No, Mike. You couldn't." Fenna smoothed her hand out of Burwardsley's and reached forward for the pistol. "Give it to me."

"Fuck off, Konstabel. I'm going to end it."

"No," she said. "Not like this. I won't watch you die."

"You won't have to," he said. "I'm pretty sure that, after I drop that bastard, they'll kill us both."

"And they will have won. Again."

"We're never going to win, love. So long as he is alive…"

"That's quite the discussion you're having in there," said Vestergaard. "Why don't you both come out and we can talk. Together. Just like old times, eh?"

"You're a traitor, Vestergaard, and I don't talk with traitors," Fenna shouted.

"Traitor?" he said and laughed. "Tell me, Konstabel, how many Danes did you kill this time?"

"Just the one," she said. "Your pal, Jarnvig."

"That's right. Per Jarnvig. We found his body about an hour ago. But," he said and took another step toward them. "I'm willing to let that go."

Fenna pressed her hand to her chest as if the pressure alone might slow her heart to a normal rhythm. *How does he do it?* she wondered and looked at Burwardsley. *How does he stay so calm?*

"Will you come out?"

"If we get out," Burwardsley said, "we're dead."

"No," Fenna said and opened the door. "I don't

believe that."

"Fuck. Fenna, wait." Burwardsley twisted to grab her but she was already out of the door. Two of Vestergaard's men covered Fenna while the other two took an aggressive step toward the Toyota, closing the distance between them and Burwardsley to five metres. Fenna turned her palms at her sides, waited for Vestergaard to nod, and then walked around the Toyota to within two metres of the man who had interrogated her only half a year earlier – the man who had accused her of killing her partner.

"Konstabel," he said and smiled.

"Premierløjtnant," she said and nodded. "But I could perhaps call you *The Magician*?"

"*Magician*? Yes, I like that. But there are no magicians in Greenland, Konstabel. Although if you know where to look, I'm sure you can still find a shaman or two," Vestergaard said, "I happen to know where to look."

"Of course you do," Fenna said and took a step closer. "What about the Chinese? Do you know where to find them too?"

"Ah, you were expecting Hong Wei. That surprises me," he said and frowned. "After what he did to your friend, the policeman."

"There was no-one else left," she said and shrugged. "At least he was consistent. I knew he was evil. He wasn't pretending to be nice, to be on my side."

"And now that you know who I am. Are you willing to talk to me?"

"Yes," Fenna said. The wind tickled the hair from her brow and she looked over her shoulder at the mountain. She turned back to Vestergaard, lifted her chin and stared at him. "I have something you can use."

"The name of the girl who killed the President?"

"Better than that. I know where she is."

"Now that," Vestergaard said and lifted his finger, "that *is* interesting." He paused for a moment to study Fenna. "What do you want?"

"There is some data…"

"Forget the Pole, Konstabel," Vestergaard said and sighed.

"I won't. Not if there is a chance to do something, for Greenland."

"For Greenland? Jesus wept, you are a very confused patriot."

"Yes, I am. But that was my mission," she said. "I want to complete it."

Vestergaard turned his head as the Counter Terrorist team closed on the rear of the vehicle. Burwardsley made a show of lifting the pistol by the barrel and tossing it out of the passenger window. Vestergaard nodded and the men moved in to drag Burwardsley out of the Toyota. He absorbed the first blow to his back with barely a stumble. It took two more before the men had the Royal Marine on his knees and his hands cinched within a plastic strip behind his back. Burwardsley grinned at Fenna.

"I guess it was my turn," he said and twisted to show her the strips pinching his wrists.

"Leave him," Vestergaard said, as one of the navy men raised the butt of his MP5. "We were partners once. Weren't we, Mike."

"You could say that," Burwardsley said with a nod, "but I'm with the Konstabel now."

"Really? I must say," Vestergaard said and turned

to Fenna. "This is all very interesting."

"I'm glad you're amused," she said. "Now, here's what I want."

"I'm listening."

"The real data from the LOMROG expedition, the Chinese research, and the proof to back it all up."

"To complete your mission?"

"Yes."

"Done," Vestergaard said, "and you'll give me the location of the girl?"

"No," Fenna said and shook her head.

"No?"

"You get us into America and we'll get the girl."

"We?" he said and frowned. "Oh, you mean the two of you?" Vestergaard laughed. "If you don't mind me saying – and it's more of an observation, really – but it seems that the two of you have some unfinished business."

"We do."

"Dina," Vestergaard said and paused to look at both of them in turn, "is dead. Humble is also dead. Even the swine that raped her is dead. She – the Greenlander – killed him. You need to understand, there are no more loose ends. Apart from the two of you," he said and shrugged.

"Three," Fenna said.

She watched as the frown on Vestergaard's brow deepened for a moment, and then the creases in his cheeks replaced the frown with a laugh. His eyes brightened as he looked at Fenna.

"Yes," he said, "of course. I'm still alive. I'm a loose end."

"You are."

"And you want to kill me?" Vestergaard said and

motioned with his hands for his men to stand down as they pressed into a tight defensive ring around him.

"I do," Fenna said. "Just to clean things up."

"Very well," Vestergaard said, "I understand." He took a moment to regain his composure and said, "You'll bring the girl to me?"

"Yes."

"And I'll give you the data."

"No," she said. "You need to sort that out first. The UNCLOS hearing has been postponed, not cancelled. The Americans will be back on their feet soon enough, and the Chinese have lost their leverage. I want to read about it in the papers, because if I give you the girl…"

"Then the Americans owe me, and I have leverage. Yes, I understand, Konstabel." Vestergaard took off his glasses and wiped the dust from the lenses. "What I don't understand is what you will do once you have given the girl to me." He put his glasses on and tucked the handkerchief in his pocket.

"That's simple," Fenna said. "I'm going to kill you."

Vestergaard paused for a moment. He looked at his men. He looked at Burwardsley. "What do you think, Mike? Will she do it?"

Burwardsley looked at Fenna. "Yeah, she'll do it."

"Very well," Vestergaard said and signalled for his men to move in. "I will arrange for you both to enter the United States, and I'll clear up this mess in Greenland."

Fenna stared at Vestergaard as his men surrounded her. She tilted her head. "Just one more thing," she said.

Vestergaard raised his hand and the men paused,

the barrels of their MP5s just inches from Fenna's chest and head. "Go on," he said.

"Lorentzen."

"Yes?"

"Did he work for you?"

"A lot of people work for me."

"But I was sent to look for a traitor," Fenna said and looked at Vestergaard.

"No, Konstabel, you were sent to tidy things up," he said, "and now that you killed Jarnvig, it's left to me to clean up after you, again."

"But if Lorentzen worked for you…"

"Go on," Vestergaard said and waited for Fenna. The man closest to her pulled a black cloth hood from his belt.

"If everyone works for you…"

"I can see you are struggling to comprehend all this," he said and smiled. "Let me help you to understand." Vestergaard took a step closer to Fenna and gestured for his men to cuff her around the wrists. "There are times when governments lack the political will to get things done for the greater good. Public opinion can be so trying, and it is during those times that governments and other organisations, turn to men like me. Men who can get the job done."

"Men," said Fenna, "like you."

"That's right."

Fenna grunted as the man holding her kicked her legs and dropped her onto her knees. She caught her breath and looked at Vestergaard.

"I tend to have a problem with men."

"Something I am very aware of, Konstabel," Vestergaard said and laughed. "Of course, if controlled or manipulated correctly, a problem like that can be useful."

"You think you can control me?" Fenna said through gritted teeth.

"Yes," Vestergaard said, "I do."

"We'll see," Fenna said, as she was pinned to the ground and the man pulled the rough hood over her head. She closed her eyes and took a breath of fetid air. *We'll see.*

THE END

A GREENLANDIC GLOSSARY

Constable David Maratse is from the east coast of Greenland. East Greenlandic is a dialect of Greenlandic. There is, to date, no real written record of the language and children in East Greenland are required to learn West Greenlandic. For Maratse to learn English, he would have had to learn West Greenlandic, then Danish and English as his fourth language. There are no foreign language dictionaries translating East Greenlandic words to English. English is predominantly taught through Danish, with all explanations and points of grammar written in Danish. Many East Greenlanders learn English, but it is far from easy.

Here is a very brief glossary of the few East Greenlandic words used in *The Ice Star*, and the English equivalents.

<u>East Greenlandic/English</u>
iiji / yes
eeqqi / no*
qujanaq/ qujanaraali / thank you
iserniaa / come in
*Naamik (West Greenlandic) / no

ACKNOWLEDGEMENTS

I would like to thank Isabel Dennis-Muir for her invaluable editing skills and feedback on the manuscript, and Jes Lynning Harfeld and Sarah Acton for their assistance in translating *Isblink*.

Once again, while several people have contributed to *In the Shadow of the Mountain*, the mistakes and inaccuracies are all my own.

Chris

July 2017
Denmark

ABOUT THE AUTHOR

Christoffer Petersen is the pen name for an author living in Denmark. Chris started writing *The Greenland Trilogy* while teaching in Qaanaaq, the largest village in the very north of Greenland - the population peaked at 600 during the two years he lived there. He spent a total of seven years in Greenland. Chris continues to be inspired by the vast icy wilderness of Arctic and his books have a common setting in the region, with a Scandinavian influence. He has also watched enough Bourne movies to no longer be surprised by the plot, but not enough to get bored.

You can find Chris in Denmark or online here:

www.christoffer-petersen.com

By the same author:

THE GREENLAND TRILOGY
featuring Konstabel Fenna Brongaard

Book 1
THE ICE STAR

Book 2
IN THE SHADOW OF THE MOUNTAIN

Book 3
THE SHAMAN'S HOUSE

and

THE GREENLAND CRIME SERIES
featuring Constable David Maratse

Book 1
SEVEN GRAVES, ONE WINTER

Short stories from the same series
KATABATIC
CONTAINER
TUPILAQ
THE LAST FLIGHT